Author's Preface/Content Warning

Hello! My name is Kyle Viray, I wrote this book! Hopefully the cover caught your eye. As the content warning on the front cover suggests, this book contains extreme content. However, my aim with this novel is not for "shock value" (though, I know by including such things people are bound to view it as such and nothing more) but rather to show all aspects of humanity. But if you are curious (or perhaps squeamish) when it comes to the content here, I'll list it:

-Gore/graphic violence

-Sex

-Rape

-Incest

If you are turned off by these subjects, then that's okay. Not reading this book is a totally fair judgment call. This content is

rather taboo and grotesque. However, I have my own reasons for writing. Things like these happen regardless of what someone may think or like. Uncomfortable and revolting, yes. But in a cruel way, that's the way of life.

There's obscene, abhorrent acts people are capable of. You've seen it all around, maybe on the news, maybe on the internet, maybe somewhere else. Yes, I know a lot of the subjects mentioned prior are taboo. However, it is also true that things of this nature just happen. It's not a good thing, but to shy away from things like these is not something I wanted to do. To deny these things and pretend like it's not a part of life would feel like a disservice. People are composed of their worst traits, but also their best. Despite the horrible things people do, there's this inherent goodness in others. People are capable of so many things. Particularly, good and evil. It's a rather extreme juxtaposition. There are also morally gray people where you will have no idea who to root for. Or maybe, they keep swapping between who's right and

wrong. I had wanted to capture all of that here. Oh, and some of the content here is based on things I've witnessed myself, sometimes it's almost verbatim (enjoy guessing what those are as the book goes on).

There are things in this world that will disgust you to no end. These things can make you hateful, bitter, and deranged. However, there are also things that make you want to live and give you joy. Both of those exist at the same time. Life is a complex, fascinating game, isn't it?

I hope you find this novel to be more than "being edgy" or "for shock value". Those are not my intentions, despite the content here. Give it a fair shot you know? If you can stomach what I wrote, I hope you enjoy what I've created.

Table of Contents

Section 1:

Apolysis

Chapter 1

I feel the ground crack beneath my boots.

My fingers touch ash.

My feet step over the bones of the dead.

My eyes see the destruction laid before me.

Buildings crumbled and reduced to rubble.

The corpses of the innocent and guilty.

Red and gray.

It's those same two colors, day in and day out.

Blood from the corpses.

The ash of buildings toppled from explosives.

The only different color I see is green.

My uniform.

This world is hell swallowed whole. Once fearful aberrations are but a daily aspect of life. They are second nature for humanity. All out in the open, for everyone to see. For years and years, much of this has been the same. At first it was repulsive to the utmost degree. However, as time goes on, the more and more tolerable it becomes. It's awful, but one learns to live with it.

All around, the bodies of men, women, and children layer the street in various poses. A mother holding her newborn child, a father grasping the hand of his son, a young brother and sister lying next to each other, a couple holding hands as they accept their fate. All of them appear to have perished in various ways. Their cadavers remain frozen in time.

People have cracked under these conditions. Some lose themselves completely, to bring their extreme carnal desires to life. No consequences, no rules, no fickle laws or government to keep the people in check. Anyone can do as they please.

Suicide is a common means of escape. A loaded gun, a rope, or a knife. I pass by corpses of people hanging from ceilings, with bullet

wounds exiting the top of their head as a pistol remains near their hand, or even a knife lodged in someone's throat. At first, I thought those were murders. But that same pattern kept repeating. Ropes and guns are hard to come by. Knives? Not so much.

I think about it sometimes. The thought of ending it all. To put a permanent end to my existence. I'd be spared from seeing things I don't want to anymore. Some of it sounds peaceful. But I doubt I'll ever follow through. Perhaps I'm just scared.

After a while, I got used to it. When the world is at its last legs, it is both astonishing and repulsive how extreme people become. Whenever someone crosses the line-

I have a tendency to intervene.

I distinctly recall a moment where I had acted impulsively. During one of my scavenges, I had stumbled across something whilst walking around. A deserted city composed of seemingly empty buildings stood before me. As I walked, I heard a faint scream coming from one of them. I moved silently towards the screams and ended up near an abandoned warehouse, finding the source of it. Through one of the cracked windows I saw what was happening.

Five men were taking turns on a girl.

These men had weapons, not guns, but still somewhat threatening. I had a rifle with me and held the range advantage. All they had were simple melee weapons. Knives, pipes, and bats lay on the floor. None of these men appeared to be armed when I scouted them out. With this in mind, I walked in front of them with my rifle at the ready.

By this time, the girl's screams had slowly dissipated into a whimper. Three of them were in the act when I approached. The other two appeared to have finished. All five stood close and blocked my view of the woman. I could hear gagging sounds coming from her. I stepped forward and made myself visible. Two of them appeared to be finished and tried to put up a fight.

These two had their pants up.

They quickly grabbed nearby knives and charged towards me. I shot both of them in the chest. Their bodies hit the concrete. I watched as they writhed on the floor, attempting to breathe. The other three men stood still.

These three had their pants down.

A look of shock hit their faces and slowly, they dissolved into panic. The three men had begun to cry and begged for me not to shoot

them. Tears rolled down their faces as they all spoke to me in a language I did not understand, but the language of fear is universal. Behind them, I saw the woman they had raped, lying on the ground in a fetal position. She seemed rather young, but I could not tell what her age was as her hair heavily obscured her face. I shot two of the crying men straight through the chest and watched as both fell onto the floor instantly.

The last one dropped on his knees.

I approached him slowly.

He didn't move or run.

Didn't even bother to defend himself.

Upon closer look, this man looked familiar.

His skin was full of wrinkles.

His eyes reflected my face.

I grabbed him by the throat and drove a knife into his chest.

He gasped, and his eyes went wide.

I aimed higher this time and stabbed him again.

Then lower.

Then higher.

Then lower.

At some point, I stopped trying to decide where to aim my blade. At first, I could feel his body attempt to resist my attacks. But I could feel him getting more limp as I kept going. At some point, the foreign words he mumbled turned into unintelligible gurgles, then silence. I stepped back. The floor sounded wet. A puddle of crimson lay before me. My clothes had been stained with the same color. The other four had bled out.

Near the table was a door left slightly ajar, so I remained alert. Slowly, with my left hand and pistol in the other, I approached the door. I leaned close and tried to listen to any sort of sound—breathing, something moving, anything at all. As I listened, I carefully opened the door but couldn't discern any noise. I fully opened the door and a pitch black room stood before me. I removed the flashlight from my pocket and began to shine the light around with my gun still drawn. As I walked further into the room, my boots let out an echo. I had accidentally stepped on something. It felt soft and rubbery. I turned the flashlight down to see what I had stepped on. As I pointed it

downwards, I was able to make out a phallic shape. I shined the flashlight across the room.

On the floor there were various objects:

Dildos of various sizes (one was abnormally large).

Butt plugs.

Whips.

Collars.

A cattle rod.

Handcuffs.

And pliers.

There was still something here. An object of larger size. At first, it appeared to be a torture device. The shape of it resembled a rectangle with holes cut in. It is laid flat against the left hand side of the wall. To the right, was something else. This object resembled a wooden horse with two cylinders in close proximity near the back of it. Clear

fluids dripped down from both of the cylinders. Some dried, some still fresh. A couple spots on it were red. Next to this was a rope that stood upright on a pole, an open hole remained at the end of it. The space was open enough to stick someone's head through.

I don't need to stay in this room for much longer.

I stepped outside from there and tended to the woman lying before me. Daylight had crept through the awning. It illuminated her just enough for me to see the damage.

Blood ran down her legs.

Her clothes had been ripped.

Her right eye was swollen shut.

Strands of her hair were ripped from her scalp.

A few of her teeth were missing.

Her body was shaking as she held her knees against her chest. She didn't talk when I tried to speak with her. In response, I took my jacket off and wrapped her nude body with it. I slung the rifle to my

back, picked her up, and carried her. My boots stepped over the pools of crimson. Squishing sounds reverberated as I moved. Their bodies lay flat on the floor, lifeless and still.

I opened the door to the outside.

A loud creak came from it.

Sunlight had shone on both of us.

My eyes needed to adjust.

Loose pieces of debris crumbled beneath my boot.

Small pieces of rubble fall from the building next to me.

I tell her I'm taking her somewhere safe.

The woman holds her arms tighter around me.

She weeps quietly behind my shoulder.

I begin to walk.

Chapter 2

Before any of this had occurred, the UN set up camps in various areas for the cities reduced to ruin. America was the first to go. After that, the stories got worse. Canada, then South America, and eventually Europe. Nobody could tell what was truly happening.

The respective governments of those countries tried to gain control of the riots and destruction when it all happened, but it was simply too severe to be stopped. The body count had risen exponentially and by then, any attempt to supervise the chaos was inconsequential. Eventually, the chaos spread all around the world. Africa, Asia, Europe, and Australia all fell. The government had collapsed, and so had their respective citizens. During this time, the UN became more than just some joint peace group for multiple countries. They became the ultimate group to control the havoc that ensued, and they were now the only thing to prevent the world from imploding. Petty politics and resource wars were set aside to combat the greater threat at hand. All the countries came together and tried to unify their military power.

What once was a "military force" composed mostly of volunteers eventually became a worldwide unit of existing militaries from nearly every country. They had all banded together to control the situation. Soldiers were shipped to countries left and right. British troops sent to Asia, Koreans sent to Poland, and Australians in Russia. They obviously did not share a common language with the civilians there. A breakdown in global communication occurred because of it. Factor in the widespread panic, and it created more of a disorganized mess. Eventually, this giant clusterfuck spread the military forces so thin, most of those troops ended up dead and there were simply no more resources at the UN's end to keep it all going.

They had a plan at first. The UN would strategize which country would go where and eventually send troops/military weaponry/supplies based on manpower, resources, and severity in that area. But it became so hectic that the plan fell apart in a matter of months. Military powers from around the world just kept going around in random areas to try and contain the nationwide conflict, all to no avail.

For once, the countries that were at war tried to unify and create a sense of peace. Hell, it had gotten so bad that even North Korea dipped their hand into the fray. It only took a total societal collapse for it to happen. Though, I'll give them credit for the effort.

I'm not entirely sure how the world ended up this way. A nuclear holocaust would probably be an easy answer, but there were no nukes. There was political conflict, sure, but no bombs. Countries fought for the same reasons they always do. Power. Resources. Money. Soldiers are disposable anyway. Take people who either have nothing to live for or fight for their idealized version of their country (by this, I mean the government takes advantage of their innate desire for heroism). My best guess is that people just got strained thin. By the system, by the government, by everything. All simply went unchecked. Everyone has their own breaking point and I suppose, after years of continual abuse, the world has finally broken. It's not like it's better now though. I just miss the old days sometimes.

It was peaceful. I remember at points where I would lay back and observe the habits of other people:

A small girl begging her mother for ice cream.

A man sitting alone in a coffee shop with his laptop out.

A couple holding hands while strolling on the sidewalk.

A man with a dog, watching his pet run around gleefully.

Each one of these folks had some story to them. They all have their own background, why they ended up at the point they did, and why they keep going.

People run on a thread. If that thread snaps, their desire or will to live runs dry. That thread can be as simple as the next movie someone is excited to see. Or, perhaps that thread could be more complex than that. For example, a man who works 50-60 hours a week does so because he wants his family to be financially stable. All those grueling hours of working. His physical health is deteriorating, maybe his mental health too. Maybe he starts to feel back pain. At first, that pain starts off small, but as the years progress, it begins to hurt more and more. He might even take the overnight shifts or the early morning shifts. In return, he

gets less and less sleep. And maybe, just maybe this lack of sleep causes him to develop hallucinations.

However, he's willing to make those sacrifices so long as his tether remains. To destroy himself so long as he can keep his tether going. Snap that tether, then somebody has no reason to continue. It could snap for any reason. Perhaps he is physically unable to do his job because of the growing back pain. That leaves his family with a chunk of their income missing. Maybe, just maybe his wife decides to cheat on him with somebody else. Now there's a bygone relationship and children left with future divorced parents. For whatever reason that tether breaks, he is put into a position where he has no reason to keep going.

So, what does he do now? His goals, his "raison d'être", have completely vanished. Where does he end up? Does he turn that emptiness into violence? Does he turn it onto himself? Does he take it out on others? Or does he do nothing at all? Whatever the case is, it doesn't change what happened. Many, many people are like this. They

have these things, big or small, to keep them going. But shatter these things, and all hell will break loose.

Everyone's tether just seemed to unravel.

People were shattered. Politically. Economically. Socially. They've been split. Never making ends meet. Genuine connection is nigh impossible to find. Loneliness. Fear. Apathy. Everything felt trivial. Like there was no point to it all. It feels like all of this was bound to happen, that humanity as a whole will shatter and return to a more tribal era. A collision course for the sins of the world. An unavoidable punishment for the damned and innocent.

Now in return, there are no morals, there are no laws, there is no government, no families, no communities. There is no peace and only chaos running rampant. I wonder, what's better? A completely "free" world with none of these systems or a world where people are kept in check? Would things always end up this way regardless of what happened? Was the world doomed to its natural end point due to the

ignorance of humanity, the systems in place, the apathy, and the rising hatred of the common people?

I think too much, don't I?

Chapter 3

I had started my days as a soldier doing nothing more than helping civilians out. There was no "real exposure" to how awful the world was, yet. I simply showed the civilians where the shelters were, giving them food, and occasionally being a security guard for a camp. For all the destruction happening across the world, I had barely seen any of it. I was delegated to a peace officer and had the authorization to use force, but I had no need to. Still, I was trained on how to use firearms and close quarters combat if the situation called for it.

To be completely honest, I'm not exactly sure why I wanted to fight in the first place. I had a wife and a kid on the way. I don't particularly care for my country or defending it for that matter. I didn't really do it for honor or for the adventure. There was no raging desire for me to protect this world. But I had done so anyway.

This path of "heroism" had led me to my first kill. I was stationed somewhere in South America, where the riots began to take place. People had begun to burn stores down and loot anywhere in sight.

It didn't matter who, it could be small businesses or big corporate structures; everyone was caught in the crossfire regardless if they liked it or not. I remember the stench of fire and tear gas. The screams of a mob that never let up. I couldn't understand them. A cavalcade of useless noise. I had been "promoted" from a peacekeeper (of sorts) to riot controller. My squad leader had simply told me to only use lethal force if it is necessary. We were set up in a typical formation: make a large horizontal line full of soldiers and shove the other soldiers behind to keep the line symmetrical. At the very front would be those armed with clear shields. I was not in the front, it was a little further back and had my rifle ready (not aimed anywhere, but held in my hands) in case anything went south. The same went for the other soldiers next to me. For now, our main goal was crowd control. We would do our best not to harm anyone. Sadly, reality doesn't allow much room for peaceful intervention.

One member of the mob had hidden a makeshift explosive from under his sleeve and lobbed it at us. The bomb had landed towards the center of the formation. Luckily I was positioned on the far right

side, so the explosion had missed me. Twenty or so of my squad mates were blown to smithereens. Some men stood still in fear. Others (as if they had experience in this before) instantly snapped towards the direction of the mob and began to fire, including me. Though, I don't think I hit anything.

The explosion had made an opening for the mob to go in. Despite our superior firepower, they held the numbers advantage. They carelessly ran towards us, throwing their lives away at a moment's notice. One by one, I witnessed a swarm of people attack my so-called allies. One member of the mob held a steel pipe and began to swing wildly into the face of a soldier. He looks like a school teacher, someone I wouldn't think twice about committing such an act. When the pipe made contact, the soldier recoiled backwards as the helmet crashed into his teeth. It appeared as if he had put his whole mass into it when he swung.

He goes for another swing.

He missed.

A soldier fired and shot the man with the pipe in the back of the chest.

A woman with a makeshift spear appeared to my right side. She looked like a college student. With her spear, she stabs my colleague in the chest and kicks him to the ground. As if she were a feral animal, she began to bite down into his throat. She's really trying to rip as much flesh off as she can.

Next to her is another man. This one looks like he eats too much. Parts of his shirt have been ripped off. I can see bits of his over-sized stomach hanging out. This man is armed with an overtly-sized blade. It's as if he had wanted an excuse to use a highly impractical but cool-looking weapon. The blade dug into the throat of another soldier. Then he struck again into the same wound.

I saw a faint orange glow from further back. A small chunk of people began to light Molotov cocktails. It would only be a matter of time before a large chunk of them came crashing down on us. I attempted to warn other soldiers nearby, but the commotion had blocked any sense of noise. My attempt at a warning proved useless.

Fire began to reign down on top of us. My comrades began screaming. Actually, they started screaming a while ago. I could feel the heat surrounding me and my vision began to blur. I felt dizzy.

A crescendo of shrieks. An orange haze engulfing all. I could no longer tell who was an enemy or an ally. Everything began to blend together like a spill on an oil painting. My ears were ringing. Gunshots rang from every crevice of this place. My eyes hurt. In front, civilians repeatedly stab and beat a dead man. On the right, soldiers accidentally shooting each other in the chaos. They're as confused as I am. To my left, a soldier realizes he's out of bullets before a swarm of mobsters surrounds him. He's knocked to the floor as the blobs of flesh have their way with him. I then looked behind me.

Before me, I see the silhouette of a man with his knife raised high. I can barely make out any specific details. My vision is a blur from the fire. He swings the knife downwards. I have enough energy to dodge the attack. I could feel bits of myself coming back here and there. Something swishes around his chest. It's a tie. He looks like an office worker.

He swings again.

I evade the attack once more.

He seemed frustrated, mumbling something from under his breath.

His back is turned against me.

I remove the pistol from my holster and aim it at him.

He turns around.

His eyes open wide and in one last bit of rage, he screams and charges at me like a bull.

I pull the trigger.

The bullet tore through his throat. He didn't register the pain at first, but his physical body reacted appropriately soon after. The knife fell from his hands and he fell down to the floor. I saw his hands curl and grasp at the wound. Blood spurted out from the open hole. He attempted to breathe but all that came out was raspy noises and gurgles. The man continued to writhe around and flail helplessly. Fear rang in his eyes. Any sign of life from him began to dissipate. His arms swung around, then his legs moved on the floor like a newborn baby. The

movements began as erratic, but he gradually slowed down and stopped moving altogether.

I took a step back and took a look around me. There was an even bigger hell scape. Numerous bodies began to pile up on the floor. Soldiers and civilians painted the concrete ground. Those that were alive kept fighting. Some even took advantage of the chaos. A group of men surrounded a female soldier. Her clothes had been partially ripped, revealing her breasts. As if a demon possessed man, one began to unbuckle his belt and smiled gleefully at the sight of her squirming. I looked to my right. More explosions went off a bit further back. I see soldiers shooting as much of the mob as they can. Their eyes were tainted with fear. One soldier kept missing despite the attacker being right in front of him. The mob member jabbed a knife in his eye. A soldier close by turned to his direction and attempted to open fire. Another member of the mob came from behind him and swung a bat towards the back of his skull. Then his leg, then his face.

From behind, I could hear the sound of someone screaming coming closer. I turned around and noticed a man with a knife charging

at me. I swayed to the right, but he managed to get a stab in my shoulder. He seemed frail. He then motioned to strike again. I dodged again, successfully evading his attack this time. He's wide open. I grab his arm from behind and toss him onto the ground. His face hits the concrete first. Blood splatters on the floor and his arms and legs began to shake ever so slightly. He appeared to be a teenager at second glance.

I looked around once more. The same destruction ensued from all sides. Fire had engulfed a good chunk of the area at this point. Many of my squad mates were in danger but after checking my ammo, I realized it would be foolish to save them. We were dropping like flies. The smartest thing to do here would be to run away. Part of me still wanted to help. That woman being assaulted, soldiers being held by mobsters and repeatedly stabbed for fun, a man begging for his life as a mobster takes the gun he stole and points it to his forehead. I had noticed something beyond the flames. People held pikes with the decapitated heads of soldiers I recognized. I wasn't friends with any of them, but I would remember stories they would tell me. How some didn't believe the world became this way. Others just wanted to do some

good. There were others too, with wives, husbands, children, and family they had wanted to protect. Now, they were nothing but a prop for show.

I realized now I'd been standing still for a while. My dizziness and the scene's commotion had gotten the better of me. I had a feeling part of me had gotten lucky with how I had gotten away mostly unscathed. But soon, my luck would run out.

This horde of unearthly beings all set their sights on me. I saw them, as they turned their heads towards my direction. I had been one of the few soldiers remaining at this point. A couple of them picked up their spears. Some picked up their bats, some had knives. Others pointed stolen firearms at me. They had pistols, rifles, and tear gas stolen from my dead squad mates. Without hesitation, I turned the other direction and began to run.

The gear I was carrying was heavy and slowed me down. I began to strip myself from this equipment one by one. First, I get rid of my helmet. But as I ran, a small group from the mob had formed and began to chase me. Gunshots fired in my direction. I was a fair distance

out, which made me a smaller target. I also doubt the average civilian could aim properly. However, I am not foolish enough to risk it. In front of me, was a park that contained various bushes and trees. These make a suitable place to hide.

The city's power had cut out and nighttime had dawned. None of the streetlights remained on. As I ran towards the park, I noticed the sound of mass footsteps approaching me beginning to slow down. These were civilians at the end of the day and I doubt they would possess the same stamina as I do. Still, there's no way I could handle all of them. They possessed a severe numbers advantage.

I ducked into one of the bushes and began to take off my vest. It was heavy and I heard the sound of footsteps growing louder. I needed to unbuckle it quietly. The back buckle was the first to be removed, but as I pulled, something was caught in between. The footsteps grew in noise. I tried to keep it quiet, but it's better off to rip it quickly. I stopped caring about how much noise I made. The strap had finally released and the vest was doffed. Those footsteps became louder and I quietly snuck to an adjacent bush.

The mob approached. I took notice of their equipment. Some had torches, tagging along with someone carrying a firearm. Smart. Others had flashlights and a melee weapon on the other hand. They were looking around by themselves. I needed to keep away from the ones with guns.

From the bush, I was able to observe parts of the mob. There were six to my left and four to my right. The four to my right were grouped up in pairs. Each pair had someone with a firearm, the other person had a torch. On my left, they were split up in threes. One had a gun, the other with a flashlight, and another with a torch. All those without firearms all held a melee weapon of some sort.

I needed a distraction, some way to make them turn around so I can get out of this spot. I looked nearby for something. Next to me, I found an empty soda can on the floor. This could get their attention. Quietly, I removed my head from the bush and crouched over to the soda can. Slowly, I picked it up, watching my left and right as I did. Nobody had noticed me. I carefully looked around where to aim and decided to throw it in the center of both groups.

It had hit the concrete floor, causing both groups to walk over to that location. However, two of them decided to stay behind in case they saw anything. They were in the way. As I saw the other eight moving towards the can, I noticed the two of them walking opposite of my direction. My left side was open, and they kept moving to my right. It was my chance to move.

My eyes could barely adjust to the darkness, but I made sure the ground didn't have anything I could step over. Glass, cans, branches, etc. I remained crouched and moved slowly towards the left. As I did, I made sure to glance behind me in case they noticed me. The eight had moved to where the can was. The other two were still walking.

I made it to a tree, which was wide enough to hide my body. I laid my back against it and caught my breath. Most of my heavy gear is off at this point. All I was wearing now was a sweater, pants, and boots. They were still searching for me. I peered over to the left and saw a small building. My guess was that this was the park's bathroom. The eight guards from earlier headed towards the direction of the small building. I had no idea where the other two were.

With this in mind, I checked my belongings for anything I could use as a weapon. First and foremost, I checked my ammunition. Silently, I ejected the magazine and inspected how many bullets remained.

Three.

I check my pockets for any other magazines. In my left pocket was one spare magazine. The gun I have holds 17 rounds. Doing the math, I have 20 bullets remaining. Quite a bit. But I'd rather not risk a firefight. It also doesn't help that my shoulder still aches from being stabbed earlier.

I peered from the tree again and saw the eight guards motioning them to go inside the building. Four of them accepted and decided to go in. I kept watch for the other two I lost track of. The four who stayed outside had two guns and two torches. I could take them out now. But, I also don't know if there is more nearby.

To my right, are two men from an earlier rendezvous with the four of them outside. From what I can tell, the four men were filling them in on where the other four had gone. The two men nodded.

Soon enough, the four mob members came outside. They were speaking to the other six now. I was close enough to make out who they were. It comprised of eight men and two women. Some of the men were rather skinny, two of them seemed to be physically strong, others appeared to be of a normal body weight. The two women appeared to be petite. They were all grouped up now. I aimed my pistol towards them.

Twenty rounds. Two bullets for each of them. If I miss one, then I have at least one other round to hit them. Is it worth the risk? They're still talking. They're distracted. I can pull the trigger now and hit them. I was a good shot at the range, but this is a different story. I have never shot a person until today. There's ten of them. Four of them have guns. Can I beat them like this? I just need to focus on those with guns. Then that gives me some leeway to deal with those with melee weapons. I can beat them hand to hand. They don't seem trained. I'm physically stronger than them. Though there are six of them. I'm not some superhero. The ones who look physically fit are the ones with guns anyway. But, what if they pick up the guns and start to shoot me? Do they even know how to properly shoot a gun? How to properly aim?

Where to place their hand? How to hold it? How to handle recoil? Is it even worth the risk?

My pistol is still aimed at them. I haven't pulled the trigger. I set my target on the bald man with a rifle.

Suddenly, they decided to turn around and walk in the opposite direction from me. I put my pistol down.

I observe them for a little longer. Making sure there's enough distance for me to move again. The surrounding streets are engulfed in fire. Smoke is piercing my nostrils. There's still explosions going off a fair bit away. I can still hear it. What do I do now?

Suddenly, they stop. All ten of them stop. They begin to split up. I need to make a decision now. They're still looking for me. Still hunting, treating me like prey. I have to find some place to hide. Would the building they just checked be enough to dupe them?

I saw a couple of them move left, some move right, and some of them continuing to walk forward. However, none of them moved backward in my direction. If there was a time to move, it was now. I moved quickly and quietly towards the bathroom, making sure to look

on the ground in case I could step on anything. I also made quick glances in all directions in case some of them decided to change trajectory. None of them did.

I reached the door to the bathroom and opened it silently. My hands slowly shut it, careful not to make any noise. There's no way I can lock it, it needs a key. Poor luck I suppose. Near the top of the wall, I noticed a small window on the top emanating from moonlight. The wall itself was near the corner stall, but not in it. I moved towards it.

I hid inside, locked the door, and placed myself above the toilet. I would wait here until they would pass. I checked my watch. The time read 10:47 PM. I remained silent as the time passed, paying no mind as to the time itself. Though, the sound of the second hand ticking bothered me. My focus was on listening to the surrounding environment. Any footsteps, talking, or shuffling. I began to hear my breath more than anything. It felt like hours had passed. I would lean over and check the window to see if I could scout for anything. Even if I was high enough, the window itself was too far out for me to peer through. I checked my watch again. The time read 10:55. Eight minutes

had passed. The sound of footsteps came close. I remained vigilant. From the noises, I could discern that it was only one pair of footsteps. Whoever it was, they were alone. I could hear the sound of a group of people being more distant. It appears they have grown tired of searching the area. However, somebody here was close. Does this person insist on finding me?

Somebody approaches the door. It appears to be one person, I could handle it. I quietly stepped down from the toilet. The person outside was still approaching the door. This stall door was still locked. I began to crawl underneath to the other stall. Now, the bathroom itself only had two stalls. The corner one (which is the one I was hiding in) and a smaller stall in the center. I crawled to the center stall. My back lays against the side wall. With this angle, I wouldn't be very visible through the open door. I removed the knife from my sheath.

The door to the bathroom had finally opened. I hear it creak. Somebody had finally entered. A few more footsteps, and my hunch is confirmed. It was one person after all.

Good.

The door to the bathroom closed and I hear a flashlight click. Those footsteps grow closer to me. I gripped my knife tighter. The footsteps pass me and whoever it was begins to pull open the corner stall. He or she took the bait.

I peered my head over to the stall quietly so I could get a look at who I was up against. It appeared to be a petite woman, armed with nothing but a knife. She kept knocking on the stall and decided to take a peek underneath. Her flashlight shines around the stall. I ran towards her.

I removed the knife from her hand, flipped her over, and put my hand over her mouth. My blade plunges into her chest. She tries to scream. I push my left hand deeper into her face. Her screams muffle. At this point, I doubt anyone is here. They would have heard the commotion at this point and intervened. I stabbed her again. She keeps trying to scream, even kicked me and fought back. Her head jerks around and she tries to punch me. I aim for her heart this time. It's best to end it swiftly; there's no sense in prolonging it.

My hand is still over her mouth. I begin to plunge the blade in deeper. Her kicks and punches cease, as did her head jerking around. Blood pooled around the center of the wound, bleeding through her sweater. Her eyes roll to the back of her head. It was over.

I removed the blade from her corpse and wiped the blood off of it. The moonlight from the bathroom window gave me just enough to see. I took a second to peer at the body laid in front of me. Something seemed off.

Perhaps it was the shape of her face.

Or her hair.

She looked like my wife.

Chapter 4

Most people (particularly men) have dreams wherein they meet this beautiful woman and connect with her. As time passes, the two of them grow closer and closer until eventually they get together. What do couples do? Spend time with each other, whisper sweet nothings, and have sex. Once they've reached this point in their life, they now have one more goal in mind: to get married.

Thousands of dollars are spent on a dress, a nice suit, and tie, a beautiful venue, the whole nine yards. From here, everybody gets invited: the bride's family and friends and the same goes for the groom. It's a big old party where everybody gets to be happy. The newly pronounced husband and wife call it a night where they have a lovely bed waiting just for them. And then, they have the most passionate sex of their entire lives. He thrusts inside of her, she moans in return.

Some of it is rough.

Some of it is soft and gentle.

He holds her tightly.

She holds him back.

Isn't romance swell?

From here, where do they go? For some, this is it. The end goal. They have a beautiful wife, married and now can live comfortably. But, there is just one more thing left to accomplish: making a baby. Why stop at marriage? It's time to populate the planet with their seed. Once this is done, they can call it. They'd still have to spend 18 extra years raising said child and maybe more along the way. But they won in life. Should they get a medal?

I have no qualms with this idea itself. In fact, I have had this "fairy tale" ending myself, for the most part. I am a walking cliché military story of a man being sent to war while his beautiful wife stays behind with his kid on the way. But to be perfectly honest, it's not as grandiose as one may think. I care for both of them, truly I do. I met her at a time in my life where I wasn't necessarily looking for romance. We had simply met each other because I just so happened to be in the park, sitting on the bench and taking in my surroundings. She was walking by

and asked if she could sit next to me. From there we hit it off. It was a "meet cute".

In an ideal world, everybody would get a moment like this. Then, this moment transforms into something beautiful: a partner, a soulmate, "true love" even. It sounds swell. The cacophony of emotions that come with a feeling such as romance. If one were to ponder it, then love is merely nothing more than a series of unchecked, unfiltered emotions running rampant. It can ruin your life. It can also give you so many reasons to keep going. There is simply nothing else like it.

The endorphin rush. The opera singing in your head as your first kiss is laid upon you. A choir of happiness and bliss in your mind. And at the very core of the world, somehow, some way. Through generations of people reproducing, swapping spit and sperm, thousands if not millions of souls bonding through generation after generation, someone's life popped out. Think about it a little deeper, and one might start to wonder how they got here. Perhaps they believe themselves to be a mistake. An accident that spawned life. Yet, maybe that life is a masterful work of art or a pitiful sack of shame.

I recall my first love so well. In fact, I'm rather lucky to have a girl like her be my first and later become my wife. The same went with her. We had never dated anyone prior nor seen anyone prior. We had crushes in the past, sure, but those were high school and middle school days. Never once did either of us act on that feeling.

I live in that moment again and again. It's not a frequent feeling. In fact, it's been so long since I've genuinely felt that sense of "romance". From time to time, I think about our fateful first encounter, our almost dreamlike situation. It' was a pitch-perfect scenario that anyone would kill to be in, akin to a movie or a show where the main character wins in every conceivable way. All roads led to victory in the end, despite all the constant hardships.

Her face, her hair, the way she smiled in the Autumn breeze. She was so happy to see me for the first time. The leaves blew in the wind as we talked, occasionally blowing past either me or her. We would laugh a couple times when it happened. Laughing and smiling at each other's jokes. I'm not sure if we were laughing because we thought it was actually funny, or because we were nervous to talk to each other.

Either way, I recall that conversation so well. It started off with a simple compliment, about how she had liked what I was wearing (in retrospect, it was just an excuse to talk to me). Then, she had asked if she could sit next to me. I told her yes.

Me and her discussed bits and pieces of our lives. Where we went to school, where we grew up, what we're doing now, and what we plan to do for our future. Apparently, she had seen me around during high school. I never paid that much attention to her in all honesty. But as they say, "it's never too late to meet somebody" (ha). For a girl I never paid attention to, we certainly had a lot in common.

See, there was this one asshole in high school we both hated. Real douchebag. A womanizer. What was his name? It doesn't matter. It's been too long.

Regardless, we had a mutual dislike for the guy. He was in her friend group. Though, he was her best friend's boyfriend's best friend. She never liked the guy. He had always acted weird when he was around her group of friends. That guy tried to hit on her, then tried to hit on her

2 other friends. Sadly, there was this one girl in particular who was rather shy.

Of course, he aimed his sights on her. He was a total fuck rabbit. Wanting to have sex again and again and again. Love is but a fickle concept to people like him. After all, he could just get his dick wet, and that was enough for him. The girl herself had a modest appearance. She never intentionally stood out. Simple black clothes were all she wore. Though, some guys look at her outfit as if there was something more.

There were cliques in school who fell into different categories of course (as every school does). The jocks, the nerds, the outcasts, the goths, etc. This girl in question had black hair and glasses, but her most stunning feature of all: her massive boobs.

In his words, "shy girls give the best sex, even if they don't know it yet." He also thought she was goth, but it was just black hair (he couldn't tell the difference anyway). Now when she overheard that, a look of disgust hit her face. Her friend (though not the closest friend) was most likely going to be swept into something horrible. But for a socially inept and shy girl like her, any attention was good attention. Naturally, he took advantage of that.

He started off simple, playing all nice.

"Do you want to be friends?"

She accepts, they trade contacts.

For a while, things were normal. They texted for a couple of weeks. Talking about teachers they dislike, school drama (like two lesbians fingering each other in the hallway), hobbies, and homework. At an outsider's glance, this might even be a romcom between a jock and a social outcast. Unfortunately, life isn't as ideal as fantasy.

During lunchtime, where her whole friend group was there, she couldn't see anything off the mark between him and her. But looks are deceiving. For as friendly as the two of them seemed, his goals never changed.

One day he invites her to hang. This is the first time the two hung in person. They've known each other for a couple of weeks at this point. In his words, "I like to take it slow." The day rolls around. She comes over to his house. It starts off normal enough. He converses with her, and says his parents aren't home. The plan was simple: to watch a show they had mutually liked. He had snacks, drinks, and everything all planned out. Both of them lay on the couch in his living room.

They begin small talk.

How her day went.

How she's doing at her new job.

How she's been improving with her grades.

How proud she's feeling of herself.

He obviously doesn't care.

The conversation shifted to something more sexual. She gets uncomfortable. She's new to these experiences. He gets more specific with his sexual questions. She wants out. He wants in. He keeps pushing. He reaches out his hand. He reaches for her breast. She swats it away. He doesn't care. He does it again. She swats it away once more. It does nothing. He's got a hard-on. She's afraid.

He stops.

He says he's sorry.

She tells him to go.

A couple days pass. The two of them don't talk to each other. He tries to make it up to her and she isn't interested. Eventually, her friend group notices the two of them aren't talking anymore.

"Did something happen between you two?"

She doesn't bite. She remains quiet.

The group notices how uncomfortable the topic is. So, they lay off the subject. Someone wants to intervene though. Someone wants to make sure her friend is safe.

She tells me that she made plans to meet with that shy girl the following week. The two agreed to go "shopping." The plan was to "butter her up" so she can feel comfortable enough to talk. It worked. After they go around a couple stores and buy nothing, she eventually tells her why she wanted to meet her.

The shy girl tells her everything that happened that day. How the two planned to meet for the first time in person and what the plan was. She had no idea it was a "date" plan. It was her first experience with something like this. She tells her what happened next. How he touched her. How he tried

to get on top of her. How she told him to leave. But for some odd reason, she still liked him.

She tells her to drop him. Cut all contact. Report it to the police. She thought about that, but was conflicted. She wasn't really sure why he liked him as much as she did after he did that horrible thing to her. Was it infatuation? Romance? The first time somebody really got to know her? She couldn't tell.

This obviously infuriated her. A monster like that, now suddenly being let off the hook for some confused form of "forgiveness". Why would she allow something like that? For all of her interventions, the worst possible outcome happened.

As the weeks went on, the two gradually distanced themselves from one another. She wanted her to drop everything to do with him but she didn't want to. That girl and him got close. Real close. She began to notice, but she couldn't help her. She talked to staff about the situation and they glanced it over. What mattered more was managing the school's budget and having their outward image projected positively. It was hopeless.

On the other hand, she was getting closer to him. They began to text again. This all started after he had confronted her in person in school about it.

He practically begged for her to talk to him. The man kept saying that he changed. That he wanted to be a better person. She fell for it.

Text after text, night after night, day after day of constant meetings and communications, their bond grew closer. They had begun to see each other at the same table again in the cafeteria. The two had wormed their way back into the same friend group. All of them were happy about it, except for one. But, outside appearances fool everyone. Nobody else suspected a thing. That girl was happy. She may even look back on those days as the happiest days of her life, even if it was a faux romance. Simpler times, more naive even.

One day, he invites her over for the first time after that incident. Naturally, she's scared considering what happened in the past. But, part of her also wanted to give it a shot. In her eyes, he had changed for the better and if she denied him that day, it would've been wrong to diminish his progress.

It started out good.

They make small talk.

He talks to her about how her day went.

She tells him about class.

Her grades are doing better than ever.

She's comfortable.

He's comfortable.

They sit down on the couch.

They both agreed to watch a movie they mutually enjoy. He's got snacks, drinks, and everything set up. At first, they sat a fair distance apart. The movie plays in the background. The light reflects on both of their faces.

She slides closer to him. He notices and freezes. His heart is racing, his brain is going into overdrive, thinking of what's going to happen. For the first time in both of their lives, they have butterflies in their stomach. He slides closer to her. They're still a fair distance apart.

She moves closer to him. She's shaking. His face turns red. She wants to grab his hand. He wants to grab her hand. Their heart rates mutually spike.

"Can I move closer?"

She wants him to say yes. He doesn't say anything. Instead, he moves closer to her. Both of their hearts beat faster than ever.

She makes the first move. She puts her hand on his cheek. Her fingers are soft. She leans in for a kiss. He leans in as well. Their heads explode with joy. They pull apart their heads. She leans in for another kiss. He leans in again. Then another. Their faces have flushed to be bright red. A spit line has formed between the two of their lips.

"I love you."

She's dumbfounded upon hearing those words, but in the happiest sense.

"I love you too."

He's dumbfounded as well, but in the sickest sense.

They no longer pay attention to the movie. For all they care, it could have ended ages ago. They are making out on the couch. He's on top of her. He's kissing her on the lips, then the neck, then the shoulder. She feels so many

things at once. The adrenaline, the rush of love, and something from down under.

"Do you want to do it?"

He says yes, and removes her underwear. She removes his shirt. An article of clothing is removed, then another. She reaches out her hand. She moves his hair so she can see his face. To her, he's as beautiful as someone can be. He stares at her. He smiles. His nude body is on top of hers. This is her first time.

This is another Friday night for him.

Chapter 5

I remember one day in high school I was in the bathroom, taking a shit. When I walked in, there was a group of guys talking about something. I had paid no mind to the specific details. But I distinctly remember hearing only one voice from that group. He had talked about some girl he was with.

How he impregnated her on purpose.

How she was freaking out.

How she called him and yelled at him over the phone.

How she said she still loved him.

He kept laughing as he told the story. He didn't want to be a father at that age. He was bragging about how good it felt. How good her body looked. All about her ass, her tits, the way her face looked when she orgasmed, the way her face looked when she realized she was pregnant. It was all something to brag about. At some point, she kept calling him and texting him talking about their child.

"Our child?"

They laughed. They all kept laughing. He says he blocked her number after that. Said something about how that, "bitch felt good though." He even offered to one of his friends that she could convince him to fuck her. I forgot how the conversation ended. But after that, they had all left before I was done in the stall. In retrospect, I realized it was him.

I still think about what happened to her. Particularly, at the irony of her situation and mine. Someone loses out there in the world and someone else comes out on top. Do people lose so others can win? Is there punishment for those who deserve it? Is karma a fable made to cope with injustice? Is life too random to care for the various goods and evils in the world?

I had asked her what happened to her friend afterward. She tells me that she kept the baby and chose to raise the child as a single mother. At the time she and I met, that child had turned 5. Her parents didn't like the fact she was pregnant at that age. But, it didn't stop her

from wanting it all the same. Even if the father was a good-for-nothing deadbeat. Even if it would derail her life. Even if it may cost her everything. She had vowed to keep and protect her child, no matter what. Admirable.

We had talked for what felt like hours, but in reality only 30 minutes had passed. She asked me if it was alright to keep in touch. I said yes, of course, and gave her my number. We shared stories about friends we once knew, paying off our finances, and how different it was adjusting from high school to adults. She had been the same grade as me, a sophomore in college. I wasn't sure if the career path I'd chosen was right for me. She was in the same boat. When I asked what college she went to, it was the same as mine. When I think about it, there's a possibility that we have passed by each other a couple of times. I had a feeling she noticed me and wanted to talk, but never had the guts until now. I was imagining it, like some idiot teenager falling in love for the first time. She was probably taking glances at me in college while I was all the more oblivious to it. She was probably thinking to herself all the

various ways to approach me. But yet, that day of all days is when it all began between me and her. Perhaps, it could have happened earlier.

I had a feeling that moment would go well. My paranoia was cast aside and I talked to her as if I knew her for years prior. We had both met here at the same place and the same time, coincidentally had similar interests, struggles, and backgrounds. As if the universe itself twisted certain situations to get us to meet right then and there. How adorable it all was.

This first meeting of ours led to a domino effect. Day by day, we'd talk via texting. How our day went, what we did for our classes, what we do for our jobs, what we're interested in, etc. It all flowed nicely together. I was in no stress to rush anything, each day had passed with bits and pieces of my happiness remaining in check. Even if someone new had entered my life, I felt as if I had no need to put anything on pause. I admit, I have had days where I was stressed. But having someone to talk to, about anything really, feels nice.

Eventually, I had built enough courage to meet her in person again. We'd been talking for a week at this point and it felt natural that I

would ask her to get a cup of coffee. It wasn't elaborate or anything. Just simple enough that even if it went south, we could both agree that it didn't mean much.

She agreed immediately.

The day had arrived for me and her to meet. I arrived about fifteen minutes early, waiting outside at the entrance of the coffee shop. My outfit was nothing to write home about: just a grey hoodie, some jeans, a beanie, and some black sneakers. 5 minutes had passed, then 10, then 15. Part of me thought she stood me up. But, as I looked around for the last time, I could see her walking towards me a bit far off in the distance. She waved at me when she noticed me and I returned the favor. When she finally came to the entrance of the coffee shop, I noticed the light amounts of makeup on her face. The last time I had seen her, I remember there wasn't any. She was wearing a white sweater, jeans, white beanie, white sneakers, and tied her hair up in a ponytail.

We were both quite nervous. She had stumbled on her words here and there and so did I. It was getting awkward, so I opened the

door and motioned her to go inside so we could at least have some kind of distraction.

The line to the coffee shop was meager. It was usually busy during this time, but I suppose that day was the outlier. 4 people were ahead of us, giving me and her some time to think about what to say. I asked her what she was thinking of getting, just because I had no idea what to say. She said something along the lines of an iced coffee and a blueberry muffin. I told her I'd just get a black coffee and cherry pastry.

We sat down after we got our orders and for the first minute or so, laughed nervously instead of uttering a word. Eventually, I just decided to ask how her day went. From there, she started to open up to me. Just some classwork and a call from her boss asking her to pick up a shift today. She, of course, declined, so she can meet with me today. I thought that was sweet.

The scent of coffee pierced my nostrils. I realized I didn't even sip my drink nor take a bite out of my pastry. I only bought it so the moment wouldn't be awkward. Apparently, she had the same idea. Her food wasn't touched at all. I finally opened my mouth.

I asked her if she had been up to anything else during our one week of texting. She told me she had omitted some details. Like dealing with a new group project for one of her classes or one of her classmates trying to befriend her, but she herself wasn't interested. From there, we started to talk the way we used to, just like the day we met in the park. It was easy, not like lines that were rehearsed from a script. It didn't feel like a forced conversation and not at all like a painful one where you just wanted to get it over with. No, we were just talking like old buddies. I had found it strange how well we connected despite only knowing each other for a week.

At some point, she started to laugh. Not the fake kind of laugh to blend into an awkward conversation, but because we were talking about things legitimately funny. Part of her was embarrassed by how much she laughed, sometimes she would cover her mouth in an attempt to hide it. But the more we talked, the less she did so. We loosened up in terms of topics. At some point, the conversation stopped being surface level.

Our experiences with shitty classmates, old friends of ours that ended up hurting both of us, how much we dreaded how our future would go, and some more. She had asked me how long I intend to live for. I simply told her I didn't know. She asked again if I was sure. I responded by saying it would be nice if I could live past the age of 50. We joked about how neither of us were sure if we could even get that far. She told me her concerns of waking up day by day, doing the same thing and having that become so monotonous to the point where she doesn't know if she can ever really be at a point in her life where she is truly "satisfied." I told her most days are boring to me and that I find happiness in very brief moments, but then those moments go right back to the way they were. She was confused when I said that. As if her brain got scrambled. I had to clarify that I wasn't depressed or miserable, just that I find most of life to be mundane. Waking up, brushing your teeth, doing your laundry, going to work, meeting friends, etc. They're pretty normal things, tasks most people do (though, I'm aware not everyone gets such opportunities). Not everything is grandiose or fills me with joy when I do it, it's just something I do. It's not a bad thing or a good

thing. It's just something that happens. She told me that she never really saw it like that. To her, the world is rather scary. Not knowing when you could die, the people around you being a possible threat, and failure arriving at a moment's notice. But at the same time, she knows that parts of her life make her happy. Those things include: her father, her pet dog, her hobby consisting of drinking tea and reading books, sewing clothes, and me. That last part made me smile. Hell, I even tried to hide it. But I couldn't. She took notice of it and chuckled nervously in return. To me, the world is neutral.

I walked her back to her car that evening. Apparently, this downtown coffee shop has a whopping four parking spots. I had taken the last one. So, she had to park five minutes away. Oh, how long that walk must've been for her when she arrived. On that walk, we discussed if either me or her had any plans for next week. I told her I was free all of next Wednesday and she asked if she could meet me that day. As to what we were gonna do, we didn't figure that out yet. So, we both decided it was best to figure that out through text.

When we finally arrived at her car, I felt the cold air hitting my face. The wind decided to pick up, and I could see a nearby tree shed with red leaves. It looked beautiful. She noticed that I was staring at the tree and asked if I could take a photo of her standing next to it. I said yes, and she ran towards the tree and smiled next to it. In that photo, she had shyly thrown up a peace sign. I think I still have that photograph somewhere.

We ended up talking for a bit more, essentially about nothing at this point. The conversation had stalled here and neither of us wanted to force it. She asked me if I was still free next Wednesday, just to double-check. I told her I was and had no intention of flaking out on her. She smiled and walked towards me. Her arms wrapped around my chest. My face blushed red. It wasn't a very long hug, but it was just enough to stick with me.

"You smell nice."

Those days have long since passed.

Chapter 6

The sun beams down on my head. I see the overgrowth of vines far off in the distance, above the barbed wire fence. It's hot outside. My uniform isn't helping. I am slumped on a bench taking in my surroundings.

In front of me are a couple talking.

They seem to be talking about how their day is going.

I look to my right.

Two children are playing patty cake.

I glance to my left.

The guard watching the entrance looks as bored as ever.

Today will be a fun day.

I often recall various memories from years ago. From my first kill and meeting my wife for the first time. All of which clash heavily. Some are sweet, some bitter, some angry, and some jading. There's not

much else to do to pass the time. Maybe I can play cards, talk to some of the people here, make some friends, but I'm much older than a vast majority of them. I live in a different era entirely. But, I also know living down memory lane doesn't really do anything for me. The world can never truly go back to the way it was.

It's been decades since all of that occurred. The world has changed so much since then. There's been communities formed, all of which attempt to mirror the echoes of the old world. School for children, jobs for the adults (they obviously don't pay, but are used for keeping the premises organized), "hospitals" for the sick, and military and police for public protection. There's been attempts to form some kinds of political parties, but they never get any traction.

Even with these in place, none of these are technically "official". People still take advantage of the fact that this is a wasteland. Stories of an extreme nature tend to travel around. Because of this, I've developed an inclination to eavesdrop on others. Whenever I'm eating lunch or walking around in some pseudo-recreational center, there's

always some kind of news to be heard. Today, a conversation between two teenage boys pique my ear.

"Did you hear what happened to that chick?"

"What chick?"

"That brunette. You know the one I'm talking about."

"Wait, was she the one with the massive tits?"

"No, the one with the flat chest."

"I don't know who that is."

"They raped her."

"Who raped her?"

"I don't know, some group of guys did. You think I know them by name?"

"No."

"Then stop asking stupid questions."

"Well, of all the women here, why not choose one with massive tits?"

"What the fuck is wrong with you?"

A lot of horrible events just end up being gossip. Common conversation topics for people to talk about. Someone in their respective community ends up dead, raped, or cannibalized. It's ugly, but people seem to have adjusted to it for the most part. News is heard through word of mouth or through the radio. Radios themselves were set up via repaired radio towers and different camps correlated to different stations.

From here, those with a walkie-talkie are able to chat with others. People were also able to get electricity around the area. As to how, I would assume that someone is smart enough to generate some kind of power. Perhaps they used generators or found some alternate method.

My particular community calls itself *"Sanctuary"* (a very unoriginal name). I volunteered to be a guard due to my prior experience in the military. Add the other things I've seen past that, then this job would pretty much be the only thing I'm qualified for. Teaching, nursing, gardening, and cooking are not my strong suit.

The nice perk of being a guard is having your own living quarters isolated from everyone. Sure, I share the same building as other guards. But, I'd rather take pseudo-military gossip any day of the week over what I hear anywhere else (especially in our hospital section).

The other guards often make fun of me for my age. How I'm old and should have kids and all that. They are joking, of course. Most of the guards here are from the new world, born after society had collapsed. Technically, the age to become a guard is 18. However, since we have no official forms of ID, people often lie about their age.

I could personally care less in this regard. The more people here, the merrier I suppose. And, if they end up dying, then that's on them. This role is voluntary and we've forced anyone to be a guard. There's been a couple of times where we've had the occasional stragglers attempt to raid and get us, but we're more armed and have the numbers advantage. So, they usually back off.

If anything, this is all for show. Not everyone here actually knows how to shoot a gun, let alone aim properly. However, if we show an intimidating enough presence, people won't mess with us. It's just a

psychological tactic at the end of the day and a nice way to keep everyone here safe without wasting resources or risking anyone being injured.

Most of my days are spent walking around here and taking in the scenery. Currently, it's summer. Spring had just passed, so the sun came out to scorch us all. Though, this season makes it especially nice to grow crops.

I pass by the garden. It's rather massive, and it's quite a shame I don't know much about plants. I just enjoy looking at the various crops and vegetables they grow here. Years and years of having no phone or internet and I have slowly started to become the old man who enjoys looking at the natural beauty of the world with my hands behind my back. Funny.

I then pass by the hospital. This is home to various people who volunteered to be nurses, doctors, or any medical professional. Though there is a different building dedicated to teaching people how to learn this sort of stuff. The only instructors there are three doctors, one surgeon, and four nurses from the old world. Some of the alumni there

(we don't do official graduation by any means) have volunteered to take their place after they pass. A way to introduce this concept to the next generation. Cute.

Thankfully, the hospital is located next to the cafeteria. As a guard, I don't really have time to clock in or out. It's rather free. So long as I scout the area, I can walk and do what I want. That means I don't have a set lunchtime.

There's a long line formed in front of me. It's just another day here I suppose. The cafeteria itself is open 12 hours a day. However, what they prepare varies based on the time. 9-12 is breakfast. 1-5 is lunch. 6-9 is dinner. Currently, it's lunchtime and I have a tendency to skip breakfast.

On the menu today is some chicken and vegetables (mainly mashed potatoes, carrots, and broccoli). Food supplies have been low as of late. The farm here is attempting to breed more chickens, and we ran out of cows for steak and milk. All we're left with now is water, chicken, and vegetables. I'm not one to bicker about food though. I take what I can get.

I grabbed my plate and headed outside to eat. Inside, there were plenty of seats available, but I enjoy looking at the scenery as I eat. It's peaceful. Inside is too noisy anyway.

I set my glass of water on a table and stand my back against the outside wall of the cafeteria. There's a couple kids playing soccer, some people growing crops, and what appears to be two young people I recognize. A man and a woman, both look like teenagers. From my view, it seems both of them like each other but are afraid to say anything about it. How sweet.

After my meal, I headed back inside to the cafeteria and left the dirty dishes to the resident dishwasher. I thanked the person there and wished him well. When I stepped outside, I figured I would take a walk around to kill some time. Things were pretty normal at the camp today. There was no cause for concern anywhere.

I reached the entrance of Sanctuary and told the guard I was headed out to go for a walk. The girl there recognized me (as I have done this numerous times before) and said to enjoy myself. I told her I would, and wished her a good day.

There's not much of anything outside. Just abandoned buildings and trees all around. There would be the occasional animal that I pass (like a deer) but I don't think there are any birds any more. I haven't seen anything fly in years. Sometimes, I look up in hopes to see that, but I know it's just false hope.

I kept walking down the road and passed by a familiar building, a run-down convenience store. By this point, I had already made 1 mile past camp. This is my usual route, and I've designated certain landmarks that tell me how far I've walked.

Just for curiosity's sake, I decided to head inside. It was swarmed with overgrown moss and vines. The shelves were tipped over and clear doors that once stored drinks were shattered. Empty glass bottles are laid on the floor below. Some of it was cola, some were alcohol, and others were empty energy drinks. The register was covered in cobwebs and moss. The plexiglass displaying that same old sign that said, "DON'T EVEN BOTHER SHOPLIFTING. WE'LL KNOW," had been chipped away. Tears and scratches were on it. I moved over to the

back and checked the storage closet and manager's room. Ransacked as well. Nothing here, as per usual.

I hear the sound of rain tapping against the rooftop, and it was just sunny outside as well. First, the noise started off light. But in a flash, the sound became heavier as the rain engulfed the building. Hopefully it passes quickly. From the sounds of it, it seems to be a hell of a downpour today. I walk out of the manager's room and peer at the front windows. Water hits the glass.

Tap.

Tap.

Tap.

The sky is gray, but it doesn't look like it will thunder. A sudden shift in the weather, huh. I'd rather not go outside in that, even if it is just water. The rain will end at some point and I have a feeling it won't be long. Next to me are more of those empty shelves and the register counter. As uninviting as this place is, I might as well get comfortable. I could be here for a while. I head to the manager's office just in case there's someone out there who would see me in the open

and make sure the door to the manager's office is closed. Thankfully, this door can be locked without a key. I lay down on the floor and put my backpack under my head as a pillow. I could use the rest.

My eyes slowly pry open. The sun beams heavily after the rain. The yellow glow is nice, I just wish I heard the chirping of birds again. Still, the outside world is as beautiful as ever. I get up from the floor and leave the store.

I'm down on my usual path again. This time I cross another landmark. A statue of a broken angel. This one had its head torn off. I stare at the statue for a little while. I wish I could take a picture of it, but a camera is hard to come by nowadays. Actually, I'd like to take a picture of a lot of things on my route. Maybe when I amass enough photos, I would be able to hang them around the living quarters for the guards and explain what each of these things were. I'd be like a cool uncle showing his nephews his favorite memorabilia from past times. A good chunk of them never leave Sanctuary their whole life anyway. It's dangerous and unknown out here, so I don't blame them. It'd be nice, but I also know that's just fantasy.

I continue on my route and decide to veer off course. I had passed a previous landmark of a park fountain and decided to move to the left. Usually, my route consists of a straight line, say for the

occasional left or right turn. I've done it so many times, walking to and from here has become second nature to me. However, today I wanted to explore more. Maybe it was the inner child inside of me wanting adventure around or my boring adult life forcing me to find some kind of entertainment in anything. Regardless of what it was, I decided to go into the woods for the first time.

Now, this was obviously dangerous. I had memorized my route so as to not intervene in any territory that is considered "hazardous" or "suspicious." Some places nearby are known for being a spot where corpses are found. Nobody has any idea how they end up there. Some people guess it's a popular suicide spot. Other people say a serial killer lurks. It doesn't matter either way, as I still remain cautious. There are other places that I've marked as "dangerous" territory. But this is because they are unknown to me. For once, I need to see something else. A change of pace. This was itching in the back of my head.

I move past the trees and take in the scenery on display. The sun was still out. I kept on moving and passed more woods and trees. My feet had started to hurt from walking so long. I realized now that I

don't really have a backup plan to come home. However, I was too far in to be stopped now.

I continued forward and passed what seemed to be a near endless maze of leaves and branches. They scraped against my uniform as I moved. Eventually, I stopped.

In front of me was a river I'd never seen before. My eye caught it immediately. For a world so run down and filthy, the river contained water so clear and beautiful. It flowed quietly amongst the banks and the pale sky reflected above me. I had gotten so used to run down, overgrown buildings, and trees caused by neglect. Everything was sick. Everything was tiresome.

This was different.

The water looked pure.

I couldn't even recall the last time I had seen something like it.

I rushed downhill to get a better look.

As I ran, I noticed something sticking out from the dirt.

The light seemed faint.

It was red.

I tried to stop myself downhill,

but I had too much momentum.

My foot hit something.

I felt something from beneath hit me.

I rose up in the air for a brief moment.

My limbs moved away from me.

For a minute there, I was in the sky.

What do they say?

That curiosity killed the cat?

I'm just amazed that I survived this long.

Section 2:

Chrysalis

Chapter 7

Rain taps gently along the roof of the farmhouse.

I stare at my reflection in the cracked bathroom mirror.

On the sink, there's lipstick, a hairbrush, and mascara.

I'm not sure why I bother.

No one is coming here.

No one ever does.

Still, I gently apply the mascara to my face.

My hand is steady from practicing.

They used to shake a year ago when I did this.

I lean closer to the mirror.

Not bad.

I grab the hairbrush next to me.

My hair is tangled after my nap.

A few strokes later and it straightens out.

I look average.

Maybe in another life someone might have said something nice.

It doesn't matter now.

I wipe the small smudge from my cheek and take a listen.

The house is quiet.

No footsteps outside.

No voices.

No gunshots.

Everything's good.

I move into the hallway and step over the loose board near the door. This one creaks if someone steps on it. My bedroom holds the rest of my supplies. The bell on top is still intact. The wire is pulled tight and untouched. Guns are scattered around this room. Some up top in the closet, others in hidden areas in places only I know. If any incident were to occur, I'd be prepared regardless of the room I'm in.

I grab the duffel bag from the closet and remove the guns inside. An AK-47, a 1911, and an M18. All three use a different type of ammunition. Just my luck. I usually scavenge for supplies. Different camps carry different weapons. Hence, I find different ammo types. It'd be easier to just have one ammo type to worry about, but this world isn't very simple. Bullets are piled up on the floor. I've been slacking. I need to organize them.

3 rough piles of 7.62, .45 ACP, and 9mm. I've amassed so much ammo. Yet, I can't remember how they all got here. These days keep blending in as I've been outside on scavenging runs as of late. I can't even recall a single day when I wasn't walking outside or staying in this place. I prefer staying on the move. Sitting still and lying here is something I usually avoid. But still, I need to rest.

I play with the guns sometimes. Slide the rack back, squeeze the trigger, fire at non-existent targets. Aiming at random parts of the house is one of my favorite pastimes. For example, there's a small

hole in the wall located in the kitchen that I pretend is someone's skull.

I like to use my head in most situations. How much ammunition I have in the magazine. If there's a spare bullet in the chamber already (making it 7+1 rounds in the gun rather than just the 7 rounds in the magazine). And, while I like to pretend the hole in the wall is someone's head, it's better to aim for center mass. The chest is the bigger target, and head shots may kill instantly. However, in a stressful situation, it's preferable to hit the easier shots than the harder ones. Unless I myself were to be a psychopath and score imaginary points based on where you hit my target. Still, I prefer living and would rather take the path of least resistance in a life or death situation.

I'll say though, my favorite gun to shoot is the 1911. It just sucks that the magazine is only 7 rounds. I tried searching for extended mags for it, but I couldn't find any. Just a bunch of spare magazines that all hold 7. In a weird way though, it forced me to be more accurate due to the limited capacity. Still, it's better to carry the M18 though, since it holds 17 rounds and 9mm is a common ammo type to find around here.

God, I'm getting distracted. My intention was to organize bullets. Piles of them are still scattered around, all thrown carelessly on this wooden floor by yours truly. Great...

Thankfully, these three types of ammunition are easy to tell apart. 9mm is the smallest and .45 ACP is also small but wider. 7.62

rounds stick out like a sore thumb because they're bigger and taller than both types of ammunition. I just need to get them all into groups now.

I've sorted the 9mm towards the corner of the bedroom, near the window. Rain continues to tap against the house. It's been raining for a while. The sound of raindrops is peaceful when I'm organizing things like this. Apparently, there were these things called streaming services where people could listen to music whenever they felt like it. Music while cleaning. Folding clothes. Making the bed. That stuff was hard to come by after everything happened. People were more focused on getting their community in shape by growing crops, healing the wounded, and just making the place run as if the world was back to normal. Medical supplies, food, and weapons were the ideal resources to obtain. Music is just entertainment. Same with movies and books. Though, books at least don't need some sort of power supply to work. It's just text on paper. The only learning curve there is to learn how to read.

I've organized the 7.62 rounds in their own little pile now. The rain pours and trickle from the window. Outside, the clouds are gray and the grass blows in the wind. Nobody's out there. Nobody ever is.

There are other windows around the house. Two in the kitchen, one in the upstairs bathroom, two in the master bedroom, one in another bedroom, and one in this bedroom. This is the only window I really look out from. This room is small, but I prefer it this

way. The other bedroom is slightly bigger, and the master bedroom is much larger. However, that empty space just saddens me. The master bedroom especially. It's a place for multiple people. Sometimes I sleep there, but it just feels so empty. There's supposed to be other people in this house, other people in those bedrooms. Sleeping, laughing, talking, living, but no. It's all just phantoms and ghosts. Things that aren't there anymore.

At least this room feels like it's for one person. It makes more sense for me to stay in. To sleep here. To stay. To mess around. To talk to myself. I've been here for so long, I can't help but wonder what having company would be like. Most of my life has been running away. I'm not sure if there was ever really a chance for me to be with others, given the way the world turned out. I just wish it could've been different, you know?

But that's not in the cards for me. It never was. I know I can't change the environment I grew up in. I know I can't. I know I can't just have people around me, a family, a group of friends, this world is simply too dangerous for that. People use each other out here. They abuse and destroy any sense of goodwill from one another.

Kill.

Cannibalize.

Dissect.

Rape.

It doesn't matter.

If I let my guard down, even once, there's no telling what could happen to me. I hate it. I hate living this way. Living constantly on edge from everyone and everything. But I've seen what happens out there. What they're all capable of. If there was a way, if there was a way to just relax and live peacefully, I'd take it. I'd take it like a starving child getting scraps of food. It's tiresome. It's exhausting. I just want out. Just give me a break.

Something happens off in the distance. I hear it. It's not faint but not subtle either. I can't make out what it is exactly. The noise is moderately loud. Gunshots? That's normal. An explosion? Rare, but not impossible. Grenades are hard to come by. Regardless, I peer out the window and try to see where it's coming from, staring at the direction of the noise. I thought I would see something at least. Smoke, people, but it's nothing. Nothing at all. Still, it remains in my mind.

I'm just in my head again anyway. I need to clear my mind. Think and lean too hard into that perspective then I start to break. I need to remain strong, to have a clear mindset. I can't break, not here or now. But some days it does get to me.

The .45 ACP rounds are almost sorted. The 7.62 and 9mm rounds are organized and put into their respective areas. I've already put the 7.62 and 9mm rounds in bags in case I need them.

My head turns back to the window. The rain has stopped as the sun peers through the cloudy sky. At any rate, the sun will completely take over and the gloomy mood will lighten. What a

funny coincidence. It's like my hypothetical prayer has been answered. Time for a walk. But before I do, I make sure the traps on the bedroom door are set. The wire still looks good from here.

I'm not sure if I should even walk. Outside is safe, at least from the looks of it. Being inside here isn't much better either. Safer, but more boring. But boring is good, boring means nothing happens. Boring also means I don't die. Going outside is a risk. But I can't just keep holding myself up here out of paranoia. Most I do when I go outside is scavenge and that's it. It's safe. But that's all I do. Go out, raid, scavenge. It's a cycle I'm sick of. Why can't I just go outside and take the world in for what it is, even if it's awful? Why does everything feel like a risk? Why did the world end up like this? Was it always like this? Why did-

Ah, fuck it.

From a hidden panel inside the closet, I take out my backpack for my little voyage. I make sure not to pack much.

Four M18 magazines.

Three gauze bandage rolls.

Antiseptic.

Tourniquet.

A small canteen.

I toss in the bottle of half-empty painkillers nearby. These are scarce nowadays.

A lighter goes in next and then a flashlight.

I make sure a rag is still inside of one of the pockets.

I put a knife in my pocket, along with a pair of binoculars.

I sling my backpack on and check the weight. It's light enough to move around. Anything heavier might get me killed.

Finally, I strap the pistol to my hip.

I step over the wire located on the bedroom door and shut it. The other three doors in the hallway are closed. I head down the stairs and avoid the creak on the staircase in case anyone is near. The kitchen is clear, and it looks the same as usual. That same hole in the wall is there and no objects seemed to have been moved around. I check the living room. That somewhat dirty couch with bits of stains on it is the same as it always is. The grand piano sits there and collects dust. Music books lay on top of it. A mildly dirty kitchen table is in the middle. I look at the entrance to the kitchen, where the stove and window is and crouch down. The thin wire that lays there appears to be stable. I follow the wire as it connects overhead atop of the doorway's casing. The bell is still in order. I check towards the back entrance for the same thing. The wire there is also intact, along with the bell. As for any other entrances in this house, those are the only two. Everything is in its right place.

Avoiding the wire in the front entrance, I open the door and a bright haze of yellow hits my eye. The sun shines brightly on my face, and I put my hand out to block it. My eyes squint a little and take

a moment to adjust. The rain is gone and before me stands a dirt path. It's still damp as uneven puddles of water reflect the sun's light. The forest ahead of me looks almost inviting.

Almost.

I closed the door behind me, careful as to not trip the wire. The air smells... clean. There's no reek of blood or rot. No smoke to be inhaled or anything. All that's here is damp soil. This blissful atmosphere won't last, however. It never does.

I adjust the strap of my backpack so it's more comfortable to walk in and put my hand over my hip to feel the weight of the pistol. A force of habit. A few steps forward, and I feel the mud stick to my boots. I look across the fields in front of me.

It stretches farther than I could see. Rows and rows of crops were taken care of by multiple people at once. All that's left are just patches. I'm able to manage small sections without killing myself over it. The other parts of the crops? Overgrown, left to do whatever they want.

I started to walk down the path in front of me. A minute or two passes. At some point, the house is no longer in my vision. No voices can be heard. No footsteps that aren't mine. No movement in the trees. The only sounds are the mud squishing against my boots and the occasional whoosh of wind hitting the leaves. It's peaceful, but quiet.

Something is bothering me. It's not in front of me or around me. Just something in the back of my mind. A memory from earlier.

A sound, far off in the distance. I'm still not sure as to what it is, but I need to remain alert.

I walked down the path some more. I'm not sure what's driving me. Plain old human curiosity or stupidity, probably. If I let my curiosity get the better of me, I may just be getting myself killed. Though it's not like I'm the type to run head-first into danger any way. At least that's what I like to think of myself as. By this point, I'm not so sure as to how far I walked. There are markers I've written in chalk I made prior to gauge the distance. They're small little Xs written on trees, off to the side, or on the ground. I think though, I've walked past my markers. I began to look around for familiar landmarks. For the tree stump that's too far bent with an X on it. For the heavy dip in the ground off to the left side. They're not there. Before I realized it, I've walked too far with my head on autopilot.

I slow down and try to remember. I could choose to turn back now but that sound from earlier is nagging at me. Maybe someone needs help? No. I can't risk putting myself in a situation. What if it's a trap? Not directly for me. But what if the sound was the aftermath of a firefight? Are there hostages? Would people still be there? If there's too many people, there's no way I can handle all of that by myself. I'm just one person.

My heart begins to race. I'm not sure how far I've walked. I close my eyes for a minute and try to calm down. Let me think about this rationally. If it was a firefight, I'd certainly have seen someone by now, right? Unless it's further up. It could be further up. I can't

dissuade that as a possibility. It was a far off sound. Like a dull thud. It really could've been anything then, right? Maybe someone set something off? Turning back is the safer option. But something, something tells me it wasn't just a firefight. It was something else. A firefight would've had multiple sounds. This was just *one* really loud noise. I keep walking.

The trees are closer to me now, they feel bigger than usual. The wind feels heavier. Light breaks through the foliage above me. I put my hand on my pistol and drew it from my hip. I stop again. It's not a feeling this time. *Something's wrong.*

It's quiet.

Too quiet.

Something has shifted.

Not a sound, but something I see.

I look down.

The mud has been disturbed.

These aren't my bootprints.

They're bigger than mine.

These haven't been washed out by the rain.

It's recent.

I grip my pistol tight.

I look at the tree line.

Nothing.

It's just branches as light pierces through the leaves.

I follow the footprints.

This isn't the smartest idea.

That, I know.

I continue anyway.

Down the hill.

Down this slope.

Part of this is exhilarating, but also terrifying.

I'm careful enough not to run.

I remain at a walking pace.

I look ahead.

And now-

Now I see it.

Not clearly.

But something is there that shouldn't be there.

Farther down, near where the path bends at the trees.

A beautiful river flows.

The light glistens on it.

I'm not sure if I've ever seen nature so pure before.

But there's a break.

A break in the shape of things.

Something lies flat on the ground.

I don't move closer.

Not yet.

I watch.

I can't make out what it is.

I pull out the pair of binoculars from my pocket.

It's... a body.

The way it's laid out isn't right. It's too still, too flat. My foot presses into the mud silently. I take another step forward. Whatever it was looks like it was just dropped there. My hand holds tightly onto the grip of my pistol. I step forward. Colors begin to take form in my vision. It's not just mud and leaves. There's something darker.

Red.

The blood is soaked in the ground beneath him. It's spread out in uneven patches. Some blood is washed thin from the rain, others remain thick. My nerves begin to swell. I've seen bodies before, but something about this-

I take another step.

The torso appears to shift slightly in the light. It's not moving, just the angle changing as I get closer. It appears to be a well-built man.

Clothing. Torn. Burned in places all over.

Head. The right side appears to have been deformed.

Chest. A green uniform, ruined by fire.

Arms. Gone. The sleeves hang empty.

Legs. The same case. Torn.

A dismemberment.

Not clean.

Nor precise.

He shouldn't be alive.

No, no way-

A sound.

Small.

A breath.

My head snaps to his face.

His eyes are open.

Not wide, nor panicked.

It's open.

Looking.

At.

Me.

I don't move or speak.

He doesn't either.

I'm not sure if he can.

For a moment, the world is completely still.

Chapter 8

In front of me, the limbless man lies. His arms and legs have been scattered in various areas nearby. He gasps for breaths weakly. A small bit of blood gushes out from each and every one of his stumps. I put my backpack down and pull out the antiseptic and rag. Carefully, I put moderate amounts of antiseptic onto it. As rude as this sounds, I'm not wasting any supplies. I apply it gently to each of his stumps. First his arms, then his legs. At least, where they used to be. Each time I apply it, he weakly moans. His face grimaces a little, but he himself isn't very audible.

His eyes shake violently. As I apply pressure to his stubs, he looks around frantically. Sometimes at me, at the dirt, at the blood spatters on the floor, or his limbs scattered around. I put my hand on his shoulder to comfort him. He nods his head up and down. I continue applying it.

As I put pressure on the stub of his leg, I take a good look at my surroundings, at the tree lines and in between them. All I see are leaves blowing in the gust of wind. If anyone were to be here, I'm sure I'd be able to hear them as there lay a large number of branches on the ground. I've made sure not to step on any prior and noticed them on the way here. It appears to be safe.

I take out my bag once more and pull out a roll of gauze bandages. It should be good to apply now. Hopefully there's no risk of infection. I stretch the gauze bandage out and begin wrapping his

arm. Starting off at the center of his stump, I gently roll around his arm. Then, once it's covered all around, I slant diagonally downwards to cover the stump again, then diagonally upwards in the opposite direction to form an X-shape. I wrap around once more, continuing the same pattern until a good chunk of his stump is covered and roll the gauze horizontally, covering him a little below his elbow. He twitches his eye a little. I guess it hurts. Blood seeped through the bandage once it was done. I repeat the same process for the other three limbs.

My eyes returned to the man before me. He appears to be well-built. His chest is very big and muscular. At least, bigger than what I usually see around here. He takes care of himself quite well. I suppose it makes sense, he is a soldier after all. Well, appears to be one anyway. Part of his hair appears to be gray, particularly towards the bottom of his scalp. The rest of his hair is black and resembles a classic crew cut. I take a good look at his face. His right eye has been burned as the skin surrounding the same side is charred all over. It's black but bits of red seep through as muscle is exposed. I put the rag on there as well. He grimaces once more. The left side of his face is surprisingly normal, as if everything was left intact in this end. Though, it's far from injured. His throat is charred, mainly on the right side, nothing is lodged in it, but a patch of flesh remains loose. Parts of his muscles are visible. His eyes lock onto me for a while. I'm not exactly sure what he's thinking. Perhaps he's grateful for my

assistance or looking at me lustfully. I doubt it's the latter though. At the same time, I wouldn't put that possibility past him.

He moves his head to his right. I follow where he's looking and see in the distance a torn backpack sandwiched between some trees. I point to it and stare at him. He nods his head up and down. I suppose he wants me to get it.

The backpack isn't very far. In fact, it's not on the other side of the river. It's been turned sideways and stuck halfway in the mud. It appears to be full, possibly full of weapons and ammo. I crouch down and pull the backpack from the mud, my boots make a loud squishing sound in the process.

Upon grabbing it, it seems rather heavy. Not heavy enough to the point where it's difficult to carry, but heavy enough that something feels valuable inside of it. I look back to where the man lies. He's staring at me with that same gaze. Not lifeless, not cold, just empty. It's as if he's judging me, wondering what I'm going to do with his belongings.

A thought crosses my mind. To check what's in the backpack and see for myself what's in there. It might even be good stuff. More ammunition (that I might not even need), water, medical supplies, food, extra flashlights and knives. Who knows what could be in this bag of goodies? I could use these if that's the case. It would save me from endangering myself on further scavenges. In the long run, these supplies might last me a while. Not for an indefinite amount of time, but enough to keep me afloat. But at the same time, that would be

wrong, wouldn't it? A man is left injured here in a state that's as close to death as it gets. He couldn't even stop me even if he tried. As helpful as it would be to take his supplies and leave, it wouldn't be right. This world has taken enough out of everyone anyway. For all I know, this was all just an unfortunate accident.

As I pull the backpack out of the mud, I notice something etched onto the ground. A small shard is stuck inside the dirt. It's black. The shape of it appears to be split off from something. Is it shrapnel? I take another look around my surroundings again, particularly at the floor. I walk to my right to see if there's any other pieces similar to this one. Mud sticks to my boots as I begin to crouch down. There's other other pieces of shrapnel sticking out. They're all various sizes. Some smaller and some bigger than others.

Was it an explosive that did this to him. A grenade most likely. But is a grenade capable of doing that much damage? Where was it located when it hit him? Directly beneath his legs? I'm not too sure. But regardless of what it was, there's still someone who needs help.

I change my direction and walk towards the man. As I looked for shrapnel, I was looking for anything else in the area that could've hurt him. But to my knowledge, it appeared to be just this. A singular explosive. He appears to be staring at me.

I crouch down towards him and put the bag beside him. I don't open it, I don't think he wants me to. A small noise emanates from his mouth. I can barely hear it. He stops himself.

"Do you want me to give it back to you?"

He nods his head up and down. Then he looks at his body. He looks at his legs, at least where they used to be. He moves the right one up and down. Nothing's there, sadly. He does the same with the left. He can't walk. He can't move. I think this realization has just hit him. He grits his teeth. I walk towards him and try to lift him up.

Despite his muscular build, he was rather light when it came to moving him. As wrong as this sounds, the loss of his limbs made him quite easy to carry. I sat him up straight and lifted his uniform up. His chest was in good shape, surprisingly. There's some burn marks here and there but it's nothing too severe. Nothing here needs any medical attention. I shift my attention to his back and see burn marks on the upper part of his spine through the ripped uniform. Towards the center of his back, I notice something else. Part of his spinal cord is exposed. The explosive had burned through skin and muscle, leaving bone unaffected. It's not a big patch of exposed bone, but it's not small either. The man moans weakly.

I considered wrapping the bandage around his chest horizontally to cover the exposed spine. However, when I pulled out the gauze roll again, I realized the amount left was too low to cover. I have some more at home. More medical equipment, more supplies to stabilize and let him heal. He might not get his limbs back again, but I can still help him. It's the least I can do.

I hear him breathe quietly. Part of him is still taking in what's happened. Slowly and carefully, I put the backpack on his back, careful as not to touch the exposed spine or put too much pressure on the burn marks on his shoulders. He quietly exhales as I do so, trying to numb the pain as best as he can. Time for the test.

His backpack was "heavy" and he himself was lighter than I expected when I lifted him up. I grab him underneath both of his shoulders and try to lift him up.

Nope.

Too heavy.

I know I'm not exactly as strong as a man, but I'm not exactly a petite woman either. Well, I'm not too sure how small has to be to classify as "petite" anyway. My judgment of myself could be wrong. Regardless, it's not like I can lift him. Perhaps I can drag him? It's not like his stumps would be hit when he's dragged. I just don't want him having any rashes when I drag him, particularly on his butt. The road here was mainly dirt, so it's smooth enough to not injure him. But after a long period of time, it might. He's already injured enough as is, but it's not like the rash could kill him. Leaving him here isn't exactly an option either, he's completely defenseless. I could look for someone, but that means I'd have to gamble for someone good to come along. I've learned the hard way that people can be rather two-faced and deceitful. A persona of someone angelic with the intentions

of a demon is common. Those who fall for it get baited into being human food, stuck in a sex ring, or kept as a prisoner for God knows what. Too risky. The walk here couldn't have been an hour. It's not exactly nighttime and the sun isn't down. I had left when the sun was shining brightly. Dragging him would slow me down, yes. But it'll get more dangerous when it gets dark. Well, I don't have many options anyway.

"I'm sorry in advance, but I don't have many options. I think you can tell I'm not exactly the strongest and I can't lift you. I'll have to drag you to my place. If it starts to hurt anywhere I'll do my best to help. I don't know how far out my place is, but it couldn't have been more than an hour out. You'll slow me down as I have to drag you, but I don't want to risk it being dark outside. Especially with how it is nowadays. I don't want to leave you here, especially when you're in a state like this. Are you gonna be okay?"

He stares ahead at him, particularly at his limbs that have been scattered about.

His right leg is near the river.

His left leg is in the hole of a tree.

His right arm is in a patch of dirt in the ground.

And his left arm is closeby,

On top of a tree branch slightly high up.

He nods.

I get to moving.

Chapter 9

In my bag was a sweater I had kept in spare, in case it ever got cold out. I had wrapped the arms of the sweater around him and lifted them up below his armpits to make it easier for me to drag. It'd be a lot easier if I had someone helping me, but that's just wishful thinking. I've been carrying him for a while now. Not sure how long, but my arms are beginning to feel tired. Well, they've been tired for a while now. It's getting sore I suppose. This whole time, I've been dragging him on the side of the dirt road. If I were to drag him towards the center, we'd both be too exposed if a conflict ever ensued. I'd have to drop him first, then pull out my pistol. At least on the side, I am able to scout the place out first from safety. Well, relative "safety" anyway. There's always a possibility that there's someone lurking in the woods, waiting to strike. But on my way here, nothing seemed out of the ordinary. I'll remain alert still.

I believe I'm at the halfway point to my place. Perhaps a little more than halfway. The X markers are now visible on the ground again. I'd have to be a fair distance from my house. I check in on the man again.

"Are you alright?"

He raises the stump on his right arm. I'm perplexed.

"Is that supposed to be a thumbs up?"

He nods his head. I suppose he's fine.

As I drag him, I feel my arms begin to tire out. I'm already close enough to my house anyways and need to take a rest. I drag him a little further into the woods, deeper into the side of the road.

"I need a while to rest. I can feel my arms getting tired. Don't worry, we're close by to my house. When I get there, I'll take you in and we'll be safe. As for now, I'm gonna rest for a while. Maybe ten minutes. The sun appears to be going down soon, it was bright earlier. I won't rest for too long. In the meantime I'll stay alert for us. Sounds good to you?"

His head shakes up and down.

I drop him gently onto the floor and lay his head onto my sweater as a cushion, of sorts. I sit down next to him and lay my backpack down on the floor. I realized he may be uncomfortable, as I left him laying down with his backpack still on.

"Did you want me to take your backpack off? Sorry, I forgot about that."

His head shakes left and right.

The man gazes at the sky. The leaves blow in the wind, the last bit of sunlight pierces through the leaves as sundown will soon arrive. The only sound I hear is the sound of me trying to get comfortable. My head lays back against a tree. My right hand hovers over the grip of my pistol.

"You're enjoying the scenery, I take it? This world is beautiful. At least, when there's not something horrible happening around the corner."

A small smile appears across his face.

"I'll let you be. You seem to be in the moment. I won't ruin that for you."

His head turns behind to look at me. His eyes move up, then down. I tilt my head to meet his gaze. His lips form a slight smile as he looks at me. His head returns to look at the sky.

I look in front of me. There's more dirt roads and trees. Same old path. Just need to continue that when I get the chance. I don't really need to worry about that now. I just need to relax for a little. The man rolls his shoulders up and down. I guess he's trying to get as

comfortable as he can. I tilt my head up towards the sky and see nothing but the leaves blowing from atop of the trees. Maybe birds would fly above me. But I've never seen a bird in my life. I learned about them when they were younger. There were common animals that would fly around in places like this. But alas, they appear to be no longer here.

I suppose I'm taking in the moment now. All the years of my life that led to this point. The escapes, the scavenges, the betrayal by others who I've had to run from. I don't think I've killed anyone. I've shot people, stabbed them, bit into them, but I'm not sure if I've ever taken a life. Honestly, this would be a nice place to read a book. A nice bit of sun and the sound of slight wind (though having the pages turn by themselves might be annoying) create this nice sense of atmosphere. I remember when I was a kid in school. The closest thing this world had to school, anyway. Other people my age learned the same thing. Some learned it faster than others (like me) while others struggled to learn it at all. Reading was not a universal skill, at least to my knowledge. Speaking and communicating were. More often than not, people just chattered. Books were fairly common as ways to pass the time. As were meeting with "friends." Sure, not everyone could read, but those who could took great leisure in it. I did as well when I was younger. Though, I don't do much reading anymore. I've been too caught up living solo like this to ever truly relax. But that's the nature of this world, isn't it? At least now, at this moment, it's peaceful, it's quiet. I wonder what he's thinking.

I'm not sure if ten minutes had passed, but regardless, I felt ready to drag him again. My arms still felt sore but the sooner I get this done, the safer both of us would be. I grab the arms of my sweater from beneath him and pull it under his armpits. He's still smiling. I guess he's feeling at ease, despite his situation. I take notice of him shutting his eyes. I'd do that too if I were him.

On the way back, the X markers were more constant. A good sign, as this means I'm getting closer to my place. In fact, a little far off in the distance, I could make out my little crop area. All I really have to do is turn the corner here, and it's a straight shot. The more I dragged him, the more I really felt the pain in my arms and legs. Still, I persisted and dragged him to my house.

I had reached the point where I could see the front door. The man had taken notice of the crops on the sides of the entrance as he moved his head left and right. I'm not sure if he could believe his eyes. I dragged him a little further to the front of my door and stopped, laying his head down gently beneath my sweater. I still had a wire at the front entrance I had to disassemble first.

I opened the front door and carefully looked down at the wire; It remained tight and intact. As far as I can tell, nobody has been here. Of course, even if it gets tripped I wouldn't know since I haven't been in the house, but it still appears to be undisturbed. No change in the thickness of it, no cuts or anything. I step over the wire carefully, entered the house, and shut the door. As I did, I saw the man's eyes

widen. I'm not gonna leave him there, but I also should've told him what I was doing.

I did a quick scan of the inside and walked over to the wire in the kitchen. My eyes gaze at the back entrance. Both appear to be undisturbed. The first floor seems to be clear. I turned around and began to undo the wire on the front door. Carefully, I untangle the knot at the bell located up top and lay it down on the floor. I didn't want the man to hit the wire as I dragged him. I didn't know if anyone was here. Plus, I can't lift him over it anyway.

I open the front door and see the man still gazing at the sky. The sun had finally set as night began to form. I pick up the arms of my sweater again and drag. Hoisting him over the slight elevation of the front door was a bit of a hassle, but it wasn't too bad. When I finally got him inside of here, I shut the door and made sure it was locked. I turned my attention over to him and dragged him to a more open area of the living room. This way, I don't accidentally hit him when I reattach the wire.

I crouch down on the floor and pick up the wire, making sure the string is still intact. On my tippy-toes, I thread the string through the clapper and make a knot. I reach down and slightly pull at the string to make sure it works and the bell chimes as I want it to.

The man is laying on the living room floor. His eyes are darting all over the place as he tries to get used to his surroundings.

"I'm gonna check upstairs. This floor is safe. Don't worry, I'll be back. Like I said earlier, I'm not just going to leave you."

I turn around and remove the pistol from my holster. Slowly, I walk up the stairs. This time I don't bother avoiding the creak on the floor. If someone were here, they'd hear the commotion downstairs of me moving the man and hitting the bell. As I approach the end of the steps, I take a good look at the hallway. There are four doors total. Two on the left are the bedrooms. One on the right is the bathroom. Dead straight is the master bedroom. I make sure all the doors are closed when I leave and, judging from the sight of it, no one appears to be here. Every door is shut. Still, I want to make sure.

The first door on my right is the bathroom. This is the easiest to check. I open the door slowly and through the small opening and see nothing. In the bathroom, to the left is a sink, in front is a toilet, and to the right is a shower. I walk slowly towards the shower. This is the only part of the room outside of my vision. As I approach, I lean my head to the side to see if anyone's there. There's no shower curtain, so I don't need to bother sliding it out of the way. Nothing's there. This room is clean.

I repeat the same process to the first bedroom on the left. This is the one that I had exited out of prior and contains my equipment. The door is opened fully and it appears empty. The only place in the room yet to check is the closet on the left side. However, the door to this one is one I leave open, in case anyone tries to hide.

No one appears to be there as well. I peer my head to the left side and right, in case anyone tries to hide there. Nothing. There's no bed here to check either.

For the next bedroom, the layout is much the same. This time, the closet is on the right instead of the left. The closet door is still open and I peer inside of it. The left and right side appear to be empty. Nothing here either. I step outside of the room and approach the master bedroom.

Finally, I have reached the last room. I creak it open slowly, doing the same procedure. This place is mostly empty, but still substantially bigger than the other rooms. There's nothing on the left side. The center just has a bed and on the right side are two doors. A walk-in closet and a bathroom. The bathroom is the room closest to the door. I check there first. I walk slowly towards the entrance of it and find nothing to be there. The bathroom consists of a sink in the center, a toilet to the left side, and a shower to the right. Unlike the bathroom in the hallway, it's less confined and I'm able to see the shower from the entrance of the room. This is fine as well. The last place to check now is the closet. I approach it, slowly open the door, and point my pistol towards the opening. Once the door opens fully I point my gun in the center. As expected, this place is empty. The whole house appears to be safe.

I put the gun back in my holster and walked down the stairs. As I do, I take notice of the man on the floor. His eyes are repeatedly shutting and opening. Is he sleepy?

"Hey. The house is clear, I'll take you upstairs so you can sleep safely. That's alright with you?"

His eyes open. He nods up and down. I drag him by the arms of my sweater once more. Up the steps. I make sure to be gentle, his spinal cord is still exposed. It's a little difficult because of the elevation. I'm partially afraid I might hit him on the way up. The stairs are rather cramped.

I open the door to the first bedroom on the left, my room. I drag him to the left side of the room, towards the closet and lay him flat. As gentle as always, I lay him down. From the top rack of the closet, I grab a pillow and put it beside him. I sit him up briefly and remove his backpack, leaning it up against the wall next to him. He can't grab it. He can't reach it. But as long as it's in his sight it should give him a peace of mind. I lift his head up and remove my sweater from behind him. I then put the sweater over him as a blanket. It's not cold out and I should give him a change of clothes, but I doubt I have anything that could fit him. As I lay him down, I put the pillow below his head. Its soft cushion makes him smile. Bits of charred skin and dried blood stick to the white pillowcase. He can rest now, and so can I.

I drop the bag on the wall, near my side and grab a pillow. I shut the door of the bedroom and lock it. The house is safe and secure. I put the pillow on the floor and lay down. The wood is hard

and annoying to sleep on, but my fatigue is overbearing. So long as I can shut my eyes, I don't care where I rest. I can feel the soreness of my arms now. After such a long day, the physical wear has finally gotten to me. I guess I didn't notice until now. My eyes begin to open and close. I take notice of the window. It's finally nighttime. The sky is black and moonlight peers through the window. It illuminates both sides of the room. I feel it laying onto me and onto the man as well. I turn over to the man and see his eyes are still open. There was something I wanted to ask him.

"What's your name?"

Something comes out of his mouth.
His voice is quiet and soft.
I can tell speaking hurts his throat.

"Johnny."

Chapter 10

I knew already. Even before I opened my eyes, I knew. There was nothing to move. Each time I move my limbs, any of them, it feels like it's there. I know they're not. The memory of it, of trying, of failing, and each time I feel less of my own body. The right side of my vision is blurred. At least the left side appears to be fine. The sun peers from the window behind me. The light shines on my body. I see my legs first. Bandaged and bloodied. I kick it up and down. My mind fills in the visual gap. Sometimes I see my legs there, other times I don't. I know it's a trick. I don't actually see anything. Hell, even when I move there's a delay. A delay between thought and action. I know something is missing, but my body hasn't caught up to that idea yet.

I turn my head to the right. Same bandaged stumps as my legs were. I move it side to side, as if I'm waving. I'm picturing my right hand, all five of my fingers spread out, waving. But that's not reality. Nothing's there. Just a phantom limb. The illusion of an appendage.

I hear the sound of my own raspy breath. The room is quiet. I'm the loudest thing here. It bothers me. I know that's because it's the least concerning thing I can focus on. So, in the opposite sense, it gets on my nerves. My throat aches, but only slightly. I attempt to mutter something.

"Mo-th-er".

The word is broken down into different pieces. I feel a burn in my throat as I pronounce it. I can barely finish a singular word in one go. Last night, I told the woman my name. I think she told me hers. I can't remember. Yesterday was so much.

I stop trying to move. It all ends in the same result anyway. My focus shifts towards the room. It's small. Enclosed. A singular window is located behind me. The backpack to my left is still there. Her things are organized. She's cautious, that much is clear. The door in front of me is closed. That woman. She's keeping me alive. Why? I don't get it. I'm dead weight. She'd have been better off leaving me.

Something feels wet beneath me. I know what it is. With as much strength as I could, I flip over to my side. A loud thud comes from the floorboard.

"Shit."

I hear the woman from earlier on the floor below me. She drops something, presumably on a counter. Her footsteps climb up the stairs. I hear her running up. The door opens.

I hear her scurry over to me. She mumbles something under her breath.

"Ew."

The stench of my own urine fills the room. Even in my injured state, my sense of smell appears to be perfectly intact. I wish I couldn't smell at this very moment though.

"Sorry, I didn't mean to say that. It's just... this is the first time I've seen something like this. The urine I mean, I'm not talking about you."

She's trying her best to sympathize with me. She didn't hesitate to help me. Didn't flinch either. People like this don't survive very long. But, she's got a good heart. She saved me. A woman of her size dragged me pretty far to get to safety. People like that in this world are hard to come by. It's admirable. Whether or not it was a stupid idea, it doesn't matter now. I'm still in her house, presumably here to be taken care of.

"Hey, you're tilted on your side. Let me get you."

She grabs me from under both armpits and takes me to the opposite side of the room, where her bag is. I feel how soft her hand is. Her skin is smooth and pale. Mine has been blackened and roughed up. She gently lays me down, but before putting my head on the floor, she puts the same pillow I slept on underneath me. She swapped out her pillow with mine. I get it, she wants to sleep on a clean pillow. That's okay with me.

"Listen... I will be right back. I have to go get some stuff downstairs to clean this up. Then I'll have to get you a change of clothes. I assume those are soiled too?"

I nod my head up and down.

"Okay. I won't take too long, I promise."

She smiles at me before turning around and opening the door. I hear her go down the stairs and a creak at the top of the staircase. There are more sounds coming from the floor below me. A cabinet opens, then shuts. Something else opens, presumably another cabinet. I guess she's searching all over for something to wipe the mess.

"God, where is it?"

I hear her talk to herself from up here. The footsteps from below get a little faster. She's in a rush to help me. I take it she doesn't wanna leave me in this piss-stenched room for very long.

"Finally."

I hear a pitch of relief from her voice. Footsteps approach the staircase as she moves up. The same creak at the top of the staircase happens again. She swings the door open.

"I got it."

In her hand is a rag and a bottle. I take it, there's some kind of cleaning chemical in there. A homemade one from what I can guess. Those kinds of chemicals are difficult to find nowadays. She begins to spray the rag with it and begins to scrub onto the floor. The stain comes off rather easily. If it were feces, it'd be a different story. Speaking of which, if she is serious about taking care of me. I would have to eat solid food at some point. That would mean I'd have to defecate. Would I just do it on the floor or what? Maybe she's got something planned, or maybe she didn't think this through. At least, when it comes to taking care of me long term. I see her scrubbing the piss still. She seems rather

calm about it for the first time. At least, it seems to be her first time dealing with this anyway.

The woman stands up and wipes the sweat from her brow. I notice she doesn't have any gloves. She clenches her face as she puts her elbow near her nose. I take it she got an accidental whiff of it. Her head turns to me.

"Alright the mess is cleaned up. Your clothes are still wet huh?"

I look down at my pants. The pant legs hang empty from the ends. In fact, it's torn off. I still feel how wet it is on my asscrack. It's uncomfortable.

She opens the closet door and looks up and down. She didn't find anything and stands still for a while. I think she's confused. Her head spins towards my direction.

"I don't think I have any clothes for you here. But maybe the other rooms have some. I'll go check. Be right back."

She turns around and opens the door, this time going to the left. I hear a door being opened, a little further down the hallway. Her foot steps echo inside of the room. She's rummaging around.

"Ah-hah. This should work."

The lady seems to be relieved.

I hear footsteps coming in my direction. As expected, the door swings open as a pair of pants, a shirt, and a different rag are in her hand. She walks towards me and crouches down, placing the two articles of clothing next to her. Her hand reaches towards my pants, then stops. She notices the dark spots near my crotch area. I see her face grimace a little bit. She begins to move her hands again, her hand undoes my button, and she pulls the zipper down. From the waist, she gently pulls the pants downwards, attempting to avoid the wet spots as she does so. Eventually, she takes the pants off of me.

"Uh..."

A look of discomfort hits her face. She glances at my penis briefly. I blink at her a couple times.

"Sorry, It's my first time doing this. I don't mean to offend you."

I continue to stare at her. I'm not sure what I can do in this situation. She gets the rag and wipes my perineal area. There's some kind of liquid on it. My guess is just plain water. Chemical supplies would be for the house, antiseptic is common, I doubt wet wipes of any kind are even available anymore. I take notice of my crotch area. Despite everything, it seems to be oddly unharmed by the explosion.

"I wish I had adult diapers, that'd help you a lot wouldn't you think?"

She tries to break the ice. At least, I think she is. I take a good look at her face. This time, without the sun in my eye or the threat of being outside messing with me, I can really see her. She seems awfully

young. Not a teenager, but more of a young adult. I'm not sure how she knows what adult diapers are. Those haven't been around in decades. No one has a need for it. Though, I guess she was taught in one of those schools. She grabs the pair of pants next to her and realizes that the leg holes would be too long for me.

"Do you want me to cut it?"

I shake my head left and right.

"Okay then."

"Really, it's fine."

I'd like to tell her that if I could.

The leg holes would be nice. It'd almost be like I had legs again. The illusion of legs, at least. She begins to pull the pants onto me. A pair of gray sweatpants. One leg at a time. The right hole goes in first.

It gets caught on my stump. I twitch my eye. She apologizes for it. She grabs the right pant leg from the bottom and pushes it up carefully. The process repeats for the left leg. All she has to do now is grab the top of the pants and pull it forward. She does so with ease, even with my butt on the floor. I guess the loss of limbs makes this easier, huh?

The bottom of my shirt is still soiled. She gently sits me up and lifts the shirt off me. Sitting here, I see my chest. Say for some burnt patches here and there, my chest seems to be mostly fine as well. As for the woman, she stretches out the shirt and begins to put the bottom of the shirt through my head. She stops for a little while, though I see her clenching her teeth with her eyes slightly wide. She's looking past me. Is she looking at my back? Regardless, she continues to put on my shirt and puts the sleeves through my arms. The sleeves dangle with nothing on their ends. She begins to lie me down on the floor and takes the soiled clothes and rags with her.

"I'll find you something to eat alright? I'm not sure when the last time you ate was, but I want to make sure you're at least fed. I'll be back soon."

She stands up and heads out of the door. I take notice of my new clothes. An olive shirt and gray sweatpants. I wonder if she knows how I'll defecate. Or maybe she doesn't know and refuses to think too far ahead. Regardless, I'm back to the room, all to myself. The sun shines brightly on my body. I see specks of dust fly out through the rays of light. I spin my head around and look behind me at the window. I don't get to see much as I'm lying on the floor. All I can witness is the top of a tree, its leaves blowing on the left side. Besides that, the sun itself isn't directly in my vision, it appears to be blocked out from the top, at least from this angle.

The pain from my right eye begins to subside. It still irritates me, but it's not painful. It's a slight burn if anything. I blink it a couple times to numb the irritation. Doesn't do much. I begin to hum.

What melody is this?

I can't remember.

Perhaps it's something random.

My throat stings a little as I do.

Though, it doesn't hurt as much as it did before.

I take a look at my chest again.

My shirt covers the damage.

I still see my shoulders, charred and exposed.

Bits of red peek through the burn marks.

I see the outer layer of muscle.

Bits of snot hit my nostril.

I have to sneeze.

Maybe.

It feels like it has to come out, but it doesn't.

Even if I did, I couldn't wipe it.

My pant legs are still hollow past the thigh.

I kick up and down.

The flaps at the end follow the rhythm of my legs.

I see it flow accordingly.

The same goes for my arms.

Something feels hot in the center of my right stump.

The sleeves hang loose at the end.

I dangle my arms around.

I imagine I'm waving hi.

Or giving a high-five.

I don't have that luxury.

I look at the window again.

There's no birds chirping outside.

But I like to pretend there are some,

And replay the sound in my mind.

I rest my eyes.

Black engulfs my vision.

The room is quiet.

The light is warm.

For a moment, my mind is at ease.

Still, I can't move.

I realize it now.

I can no longer do anything on my own.

Chapter 11

I feel someone touching my shoulder. My eyes slowly open in response.

"Hey, you awake? I didn't want to disturb you when you're sleeping, but I think you should eat."

The young woman stares at me. Her long hair makes contact with my cheek. My eyes open wide to signal that I'm awake.

"You ready to eat?"

I nod my head up and down.

She puts her hand on my shoulder and her other hand on the center of my back. Something about it stings, particularly in the center. My face clenches in response. I'm not sure what it is though. I look over to the woman again. Her eyes appear to be wide and her head quickly turns towards me.

"Sorry about that. You've got a pretty bad injury on your spine. I should've told you earlier. I'll be more gentle next time, I promise."

I'm curious to see what this "injury" is. I'm injured all over, so the severity of it probably doesn't matter. It's just a shame I can't see it. If she had a mirror or something she could use that to show me. God, I can't even ask that. Part of my throat still stings. Maybe I could say a full sentence, but even speaking one word stings my throat. It also leaves an afterburn after I talk. I can't even use sign language.

She grabs a spoon and dips it into a bowl. I turn my head down to see what it is. It's some kind of liquid. A soup, probably. It's yellow, with noodles and bits of what appear to be chicken and carrots in there. It's chicken noodle soup, isn't it? Not bad. I'm rather hungry anyway. I could eat anything right now. Part of me misses the food from Sanctuary, but beggars cannot be choosers.

Her hand moves towards my mouth, spoon in hand. I open my mouth to eat it. It's almost like I'm a child, having my mother spoon-

feed me. Ah, I'm imagining it. I'm a little toddler, sitting in a booster seat on the kitchen chair. My mother is talking to me, ready to give me soup or some kind of purée. I'm playing with my little plastic toy. Maybe it's a toy car or a toy train. Most likely a car though, I played with those when it was younger. I'm crashing them into each other repeatedly, not knowing what the names are for either objects in my hands. Our kitchen window is in the center, above our sink. The dishes have piled up, all dirty and need to be washed. My father is on the other chair, watching my mother feed me. He was always a busy man. On his phone for work-related reasons. When I was born, he had to pick up more shifts to pay for all the expenses I created. But here, in this moment, his eyes gaze away from his phone. He puts his attention directly towards my mother and watches lovingly as his wife feeds me. I don't know what went through his head during that. Perhaps a sense of peace or fulfillment. My mother spins the spoon around in a circle, saying something about an airplane coming. I open my mouth wide and smile as I cease playing with my toys for a little while. Eventually, the bowl of soup is emptied. My mother walks away to clean the dishes or maybe do some other task.

Maybe do something for work, make a call. She always had to make phone calls for her work. Then, my father gets up as well and sits in the same chair my mother used to sit. He sits directly across from me and pulls out more toy cars in his pocket. They're different models and I smile and giggle gleefully as he hands them towards me. I clap with my hands over my head and reach my hand forward to grab it.

The thought of this makes me smile. I look at the woman in front of me. A spoon is in her hand as she feeds me another spoonful of soup. By this point, a good chunk of the bowl is empty. A little less than half remains. She's been doing this same process for a while now. Dipping the spoon into the bowl and waiting for my mouth to open so I can be fed. The room glows with an orange haze from the sun and I taste the bland but satisfying flavor of the soup. In front of me, the young woman shines a wry smile. She dips the spoon into the bowl again. I open my mouth once more. My mouth closes as I feel the swish of the soup go down my throat. It's not too hot, not too cold. I hear the clank of the spoon hitting the bowl as she gets another scoop. The process repeats, and I will continue until the bowl is empty.

Something about this is... peaceful. I am being taken care of. Being guarded by a woman who, from what I can tell, has good intentions. I don't know her story, or how or as to why she's so kind. Yet, I can't help but feel at ease from it. Despite what's happened to me, despite my pathetic state, despite everything that was taken from me, this... is nice.

Yet, the cold reality of my situation sets in regardless. Decades have passed since those days. People are not who they used to be. I've seen things, done things, all of which have hurt me in more ways than one. My sense of paranoia is constant and never-ending. My distrust of others is at an extreme. This world disgusts me and forces me to do terrible things. All of those things destroy me, little by little. Other times, I have no choice but to be a bystander to the revolting events surrounding me. I so badly want to revolt, to strike back at everyone and everything that I see. To destroy everything that has done this. To rid the evils of this world that are persistent. The small bits of atrocity and the unforgivable, mass amounts of sin that plague humanity. All of it is a pestilence. I want to release my hate somewhere, somehow. Is this

"lashing out?" That term seems like something a teenager does. Except it's not adolescent confusion. It's the rising, revolting, abhorrent filth that this world has become. Yet, I know I can do nothing to stop it. There's nothing I can do to ever truly redirect my sense of hate.

And despite all of that, in front of me, is the warmth and care of a woman. This stranger, who picked me up in the middle of the woods, when I should've died, took me in. She put me in her home, cleaned me up, patched my wounds, gave me new clothes, and is now feeding me. I don't get it. How can someone in this world be so kind? After everything that's happened, she is still going out of her way to help me. Perhaps it's to her detriment. From what I can tell, she's living here by herself.

I wish I could ask her what her living situation was. To get to know her more. She fascinates me, intrigues me. How someone of this character has survived so long and so alone is something I want to know. I applaud her for her tenacity. Yet, I know myself that I am physically restricted from such a thing. Confined to a body that can no longer service me. I am a machine. No, a machine is too generous. At

least a machine works. I am a mere object. I have no specifics as to what I can be described as. I am a blank slate of atoms and molecules. A being that has outlived his purpose, whose punishment is to live in a physical cocoon. No, not even live. Living is a privilege. I am in my own form of hell.

"Alright, you've finished your food. Good to know your appetite is still fine after... you know. I'll have to head downstairs again, I have something that I think would help you."

She gets up and leaves.

Once more, I am alone in this room. A room with one window and one closet. My head lies gently on the singular pillow, stained by my blood and charred flesh. I don't know what time of day it is. My best estimate is that it's morning. However, it could very well be the afternoon. I'm not exactly sure how long I slept. Though, it's not like that matters. All that remains here is a quiet, empty space. I have nothing to do but to occupy myself. The only way to do so is with my

thoughts. To breed my ideas further. To untangle everything that comes to mind. Yet, I am also aware that I cannot do anything beyond that. If the human body could do more with just their brain, I would be in a better spot as of now.

I can raise my arms. I can raise my legs. Calling either of those two appendages by their respective names is laughable. The most I can do is pretend they're still there. Oh, I can also blink my eyes. My right eye still stings. Those are the limits to my physical capabilities. Perhaps I can force myself to trick my mind. To see legs and arms that were once a part of me. I could imagine wiggling my toes and curling my fingers. Perhaps, I could crack my knuckles. Is it possible to delude my own vision? To force my mind to feed me hallucinations so I can live in a lie? Lying, in this instance, wouldn't be a terrible thing to do. It'd give me a sense of happiness. Isn't that what everyone wants at the end of the day? It's what I want. What I no longer have. What I lost and can never gain again. It was stripped from me. Taken away. But when, when did that happen, I wonder?

Was it when I was a soldier? When I had killed for the first time? Seen the limits to human atrocities during and after the world's sudden implosion? Or was it when I foolishly stepped on that landmine in the woods. A gullible man, such as me, in awe of the beauty of nature. Duped by the inherent elegance of the world. Led like a horse drawn to a carrot, into a man-made trap. Sure, I couldn't have known about the landmine on the floor. But I still should've been cautious. Yet, at that moment, I acted like a child. A child who saw something graceful for the first time. Perhaps, like an initial exposure to their favorite cartoon or their favorite superhero. Ha. I'm imagining myself in that situation again. Stars glimmering in my eyes as I run down the slope and step straight into an explosive. This accident, all for a chance to see beauty again. Real beauty.

In the end though, I know thinking about this doesn't matter. It won't change what's happened. It won't change what I've become. All that's left for me, is to watch the walls of this room and stare out of the window. Maybe I can take notice of the intricate patterns of repeating floorboards. Or maybe, stare hard at the broken crack in the closet door.

I could use my imagination to fill in the gaps. To think about how that crack into the wall came to be. Maybe the people who lived here before fought. A husband and wife perhaps? Was the husband beating on her? Was the closet door collateral damage? Or maybe, this was a child's room and he or she foolishly broke one of the panels of the closet door. Actually, was this that woman's childhood home? Was she raised here by parents who are no longer around? How'd she get this place? How long has she stayed here? She's by herself, that's for sure. If she wasn't, then somebody would've been here and stayed the night. But it's just her, only her. Me and her are alone here.

Footsteps approach the door in front of me. In her hand, are two pieces of heavily blended cloth. I have no idea what they're for. In fact, they could be towels. It looks torn. Perhaps it was from something heavier and she had stripped a layer from it.

"I was thinking about this for a while and didn't know what to do. Luckily, something clicked in my mind while I was feeding you. Since you ate, you'll have to defecate at some point. And well since you're in a certain... state, I'd have to use these as makeshift diapers. I'll show you."

She walks over to my direction and begins to take my pants off. The same procedure occurs, except this time she isn't irked at the sight of my genitalia. She begins to fold the cloth in a certain shape. It's folded into a U. One of her arms goes under my legs and lifts me up. From underneath, she centers the folded cloth and aligns it appropriately. She gently places the lower half of my body down and straightens out the cloth. She makes it wide enough to cover my perineal area in the front and in the back, lifting me up again to make sure that's in the right spot.

"Alright, since there's no diapers, I had to improvise. When you defecate or urinate, these will get stained. They'll go underneath your pants and I'll be able to wash it out with the water from the well on the outside of the house. I'll toss out any solid feces in the disposal spot outside on the ground. Probably somewhere a little past the backyard. I'll leave this other piece of cloth here just so it's around and I can use it. Got it?"

I nod my head yes. She walks over to the other side of the room and slumps down at the wall, exhaling heavily as she does. Her head turns to the window behind me. Her eyes lock towards the leaves on the left side, she seems to have focused her train of thought on there. I wonder what she's thinking of.

Her head glances towards my direction from time to time. She never takes a look at me very long when she does. I don't blame her, I know what I look like already. Her hand goes over her knee. I watch as she wiggles her fingers around. She turns her head towards the ceiling, gazing at a crack in the wall. I've gotten familiar with little imperfections in this room already.

A crack on the bottom right corner of the room.

A broken panel on the right side of the closet door.

A small tear within a wall on my left.

A tiny rip in the ceiling, though no water comes down from it.

A piece of paint peeling on the wall on the right of the window.

A tiny crack within the bottom left of the window itself.

Though, no hole has formed.

I wonder if she notices these things as well. Perhaps she doesn't pay attention to it as much as I do. She doesn't have to. She can maneuver around anywhere in the house. Sure, she may see it from time to time. But she doesn't need to fix it. It's just something that exists in this house. There's no need to put her focus on it. I'm a different story. All I see are these walls. The same imperfections. The same things that are broken. I am powerless to do a single thing.

All I have power over, is my own mind and vision. Nothing else. I wonder how long I can remain like this without breaking.

Perhaps I've already broken. This is it. This is the life I have to live now. I have to accept it, I have no other choice. I don't want to. God knows this is the last thing I want. I can't get her to kill me. There's no way I can even kill myself. Death would be an escape from this. My body has turned into a prison. There is no release. No peaceful exit. Only a cacophony of hateful thoughts and a constant reminder of my own physical disabilities. Every time I look down, I am reminded of the person I've turned into. A blob of flesh who has lost the privilege to do something as simple as moving. I have become a painting of permanent scars and damage. What have I done to deserve such a fate?

Has God punished me specifically for a sin I've committed? Or was I an unfortunate victim of fate? Why... Why was I turned into this? What was the reason? Is there even one at all? Has life just rolled the dice and chosen to ruin me and me alone? It would be sick, revolting if there was no reason for this. No reason as to why I've become this. This... freak of nature. This worm. This insect. No, even insects get to move. I suppose it's not about who deserves what right? It's about who

wins and who loses in the game of life. I just happened to draw a bad hand.

I turn my head to the woman. Her head is put between her knees and pointed downwards. Her long hair covers a good chunk of her legs. I see her chest expand in and out. I'm not sure if she's sleeping or thinking. My guess is the latter. A gray jacket covers her arms. It seems a little big for her. I pick up on the sound of her breathing. It feels like it echoes, but I only know that's because of this quiet room. Her hands are wrapped around her legs, her fingers are interlocked together. She begins to tap her left foot on the floor ever so slightly.

I feel something. A scourge of heat wraps around the right side of my throat. It doesn't hurt, oddly. I can feel my airway get clearer. The sounds of my breathing become less raspy. I exhale from my mouth to see how it feels. It's as if something has opened up. I start to hum. It doesn't hurt. I stop, then try again. The sound comes out clearer. Not perfect, but not entirely broken. This wasn't how it felt before. I noticed the burning sensation had dissipated. The pain... it seemed to have stopped.

I take notice of the woman to my right. Her head begins to look up and her hair begins to move away from her knees. Her arms spread out to the side as she leans her head back. She cracks her neck from side to side. I see her head centering towards me. The woman looks at me in awe. Her eyes begin to widen. She approaches me.

"Wait."

She leans a little closer towards me.

"Your throat..."

Her eyes shift between my throat and my face.

"H-how?"

"What?"

Chapter 12

It doesn't hurt. My throat doesn't hurt. I don't feel the sting nor burn as I did when I talked before. The woman looks at me with her mouth slightly agape. I'm as perplexed as she is. None of this makes any sense. She looks at me and inspects the skin on my throat. Her head leans closer to me.

"I don't get it. I don't get it at all. When I found you a day ago, there was a patch of skin hanging loose. There was a large area of red. Your muscles were exposed. Even besides that, part of your throat was charred with burn marks surrounding it. Now, it just looks like your regular skin tone. It's as if nothing happened. You have completely healed. Your throat, at least."

Her voice was higher pitched as she said this. She seemed to be astonished by the whole situation. I watch as she extends her fingers forward, aiming at my throat.

"Would it be alright if I... you know, touch it?"

"Yes."

My voice sounded as clear as ever. It's as if it was back to normal. Her hand inches closer to my throat. I feel her soft fingers press against it. It's rather... delicate.

"It's smooth. It feels smooth. There's no burn marks whatsoever, no rough feeling anywhere. Damage like this, it should be permanent. But, it's not. It healed- you healed in the span of a day. The human body doesn't do this. It can't regenerate that fast. It can't regenerate like this at all actually. It doesn't heal like this. How... how is this possible? This shouldn't happen. It shouldn't..."

She's repeating her words as she talks, stumbling over herself. If I were her, I'd most likely do the same.

"I'm not sure. You're shocked, and from what I can tell, you seem to be well-informed when it comes to taking care of someone else. Were you a nurse before? Some kind of medical worker? At least, in the new world. After the world had ended. You seem young. I know you're

taking in everything and still figuring out what's happened. Hell, I know asking all these questions is a little much considering what just happened. But, I can't tell you how any of this occurred. Truthfully, I have no idea what's going on. This is as confusing to me as it is to you."

Her face remained still. No expressions or anything of the sort. I had talked. Fully. With my voice. A voice that was fully mine. That had returned to normal. At least, it seems that way. I didn't have to worry about the pain. Her eyes squint at me. I watch as her hand slowly moves away from my throat. As I spoke, I could feel my Adam's Apple move along her with her fingers. I'm surprised her fingers didn't move away earlier.

"You can talk... you can talk just fine. Your voice sounds a lot more clear than before. Granted, you only spoke to me once and that was the night where you told me your name. Then, I could tell that speaking hurt your throat. At least, I assume it did. It sounded coarse, like gravel or something. Well tell me, did speaking hurt your throat? How's it feeling now?"

She catches on quick.

"Before, I had this burning sensation whenever I spoke. That night, when I told you my name, it felt like fire had erupted on the inside as I did. Afterwards, my throat began to burn. It didn't hurt as much as I did when I spoke but it lingered for a while and remained until I woke up the following morning. It was an afterburn, for lack of a better term. The following day, you had decided to feed me. As you were prepping food downstairs, I tried to hum. To see how much it would hurt. It still did, still left that same burning feeling. I tried to speak after to see if anything changed. I only said one word again. The pain was about the same. Now though, it seems to have subsided. In fact, last night I felt that same burning sensation. It was... different. It didn't hurt. I had felt it rising and expanding in the center of my throat. I didn't know what that feeling entailed. Now though, I guess that's what it meant. Tell me, does my breath smell bad?"

"You are... oddly calm. And yes, it smells bad. But given the condition you were in, I wasn't going to say anything regarding that. It would've been rude, you know? And to answer your other question, yes, I was a nurse. Well, taught to be one anyway. That's how I knew how to bandage your stumps and clean your wounds. From the looks of it, you're a soldier, aren't you? Wearing green, combat boots, physically in shape, short crew cut, carrying a backpack full of stuff. I haven't opened it by the way. I figured you wouldn't want me to. If you are a soldier, where's your weapon? Where's your gun? Were you carrying one, and it got lost in the explosion? Unless there's one in your backpack. Well... are you a soldier?"

"Technically, a guard. But back then I was a soldier. I was alive before the world ended. That should be obvious. Just look at me, I'm old. But I did have a gun on me at that time. There was a rifle I had slung on my back and a handgun in my backpack. I don't know if it's damaged now. It might not be, but the bag looks fine. How'd you know it was an explosion anyway?"

"I saw bits of shrapnel lying around. Some stuck onto the dirt, some into the trees. I walked around slowly to make sure my

suspicions were right. If you don't mind telling me, how did... how did this happen?"

"It was a landmine. I stepped on a landmine. I saw you that day. Looking around when you first took notice of that shrapnel. I wanted to warn you about the landmine, that there could be others laid in the dirt. But I couldn't. I tried, and my voice wouldn't come out. Each time I tried to speak, the only thing that would come out of my mouth were rasps and moans. It hurt to even try to talk. It was as if a bullet had ejected from inside my mouth. Eventually, I ended up just staying silent. I was afraid you'd end up like me if you kept looking around. Thankfully, you didn't step on one. As for me? Well... take a good look."

Her face gazes upon me. Her focus, which once was centered on my throat, had shifted towards taking a look at the rest of my body. I notice as her eyelids tighten and expand ever so slightly as she does. She has this apologetic look to her. Her hair begins to cover her face as she begins to look downwards, towards the lower half of my body.

"Tell me, why did you help me? You look like you know how this world operates. Saving me, taking that risk, if you encountered the wrong person you'd end up captured or even dead. It was a stupid idea, no offense. The risk there was too high. What was the reward? Saving a limbless man who might as well be better off dead? In what ways does that help you? It'd only create more problems. That day, when I had lost my limbs, I should've died. Like a child, I saw that river, how beautiful it was, and ran downhill towards it. I saw a red light and right there, when I stepped on it, that's when it all hit me. By then, it was too late. Next thing I know, I'm in the sky, and my body parts separate from me. I hit the floor and started bleeding out from each and every stump. My eyes began to blink in and out. I was going in and out of consciousness. I saw the sky and the clouds for what I believed would be my final time. And yet, after some time had passed, could've been hours or even shorter, I saw you. I don't know what your first thought was when you saw me. But when I first saw you, I was scared. Scared you'd end up like me. That you'd step on a landmine as well. But you didn't. I was relieved

that there was no other landmine there. The only unfortunate person in this, is me. Why? Why did you save me?"

Her eyes shift towards mine. Her head tilts slightly to the right. She blinks a couple times and stares at me. She's thinking of what to say. I watch as she repeatedly opens and closes her right hand. Finally, she decides to speak.

"I- I don't know. I'm not sure why I saved you. Even when I think about it, not a single thing comes to mind. I just... did it. I saw you lying there. I remember the way you looked at me for the first time. You had this look on your face. It wasn't cold or malicious. You looked... lifeless."

She's starting to get upset. I can tell by the tone of her voice.

"More than anything, you needed help. So, I did it. It felt like my body just moved by itself that day. I hurried over to you and opened my backpack to mend your wounds. I didn't think about much of the "risk" you were talking about. Sure, I remained cautious. I'd look around and take note of my surroundings in case anyone came near. But, my focus was on helping you."

Her voice begins to rise in volume.

"And yeah, I admit it was a partially stupid idea. Risking my life for someone, someone I don't even know, probably getting captured, or raped, or killed. But what? Was I supposed to leave you there?"

She screamed that at me. I look at her eyes. Her face was wincing before, but now shifted towards a look of realization. She backs her head away from me and steps back, just a little. I prepare to say something.

"I would've preferred it if you did."

Her head points down at the floor, away from me. I upset her, that I know.

"What you did was admirable. You saved my life. I can never thank you enough for that. You've done something no one else in this

world would do. I don't want to diminish what you did, or make you feel awful for doing so. What you did was good. More than good. But just... just look at me. What life do I have? What can I even do? I can't move, I can't feed myself, can't even take a leak or shit without getting my pants stained. I lived, sure. But at what cost? To remain in a vegetative state for the rest of my days? To do nothing except stare at the same old walls? The same cracks? The same floor day in and day out? You take care of me, and I really cannot express enough how much I appreciate you for doing so. But this... this isn't a life. It's not living. You can't even call it that. I can't... I can't even do a single thing by myself."

I stop myself from talking. The woman remains staring at the floor. Her head remains still. I realize what I've done. I know what I said wasn't right but-

A single tear begins to form beneath my left eye. At first, I barely noticed it. But I stopped myself from talking when I realized. It starts off as one. Then two. Then three. Then they keep coming. My right eye begins to tear up as well. This side hurts. Each teardrop falling feels like acid pressed against my skin. But, I can't stop it. I can't help myself.

I try to wipe it off with my elbows. But they're not there. I had instinctively done so. My eyes gaze at my two arms, in the center of my vision. My right side is blurry, my left side is normal. I feel a burn underneath my eyelid. It's constant, and happens so often. I can't stop it... I can't...

Johnny appears to have stopped talking. My gaze remains locked on the floor. Deep down, I know part of what he's saying is right. I know it was a stupid plan. I know in his state he can't live the way he wants to.

I know. I know. I know. I know.

But it didn't want him to die. I don't want anybody to die. This world is full of awful people. Full of atrocities that happen every day. Things I can't control. Innocent people who get hurt, who don't deserve the fate they end up having. I've seen it. The horrible things that happen to other people. I don't want to be like them. Those... monsters. Those filth that call themselves "people". They hurt others for their own reasons. Reasons I can't understand, can't fathom. I don't want to. They're low.

Scum.

Filth.

Bottomfeeders.

Insects.

That's what they are.

Even still, I want to help people. I want to help them as best as I can. I know they suffered. I know I can only do so much. I'm only one person. I can't fix everything. I know why people get upset, I know why they get angry. I don't hold it against them. I don't want to. But it still hurts. Hurts to see them as angry as they are. Unable to do anything. I'm not sure why this world turned out this way. Part of me is curious as to why it happened. The other part of me knows that

won't change a thing about my life. Knowing won't change what's happened to me.

I look up.

Johnny's there.

He's staring at the stumps of his arms.

Tears drop down from his face.

Clear tears drop from the left side.

Dark yellow tears drop from the right.

He tries desperately to wipe his own face with elbows that aren't there.

I get up off of the floor and approach him.

His face looks up to me.

One step at a time, I approach him.

I see the window behind him.

The sun is bright today.

Rays of light shine through the partially broken window.

I get closer to him.

My arms spread open.

I embrace his body.

What remains.

What's there.

What he has left.

I wrap my arms around him tightly.

His tears start to drop a little faster.

I hold him tighter this time.

I stroke the back of his head and comfort him.

I feel the sun's heat as it hits my back.

He doesn't deserve this.

No one does.

His lips part.

Nothing comes out at first.

Then, quietly-

"Thank you."

Chapter 13

I look down at Johnny. He's cradled in my arms. The rasp in his breath has disappeared. The sun hits both of us. My back feels its heat. My sleeves are wet from wiping his face so much. I was careful around the right side of his face. Johnny's left eye is fully open. His right eye isn't. His direction gazes at the window behind me. He's humming something.

"What are you humming?"

"*Corcovado - Quiet Nights of Quiet Stars.* Are you familiar with jazz by any chance?"

"I can't say that I am. That's a genre of music, isn't it? I never got around to listening to music much when I was younger. That was mainly because there was no way to play them. I've heard you could play them digitally back in the day. Through some kind of streaming service or something. But before that, things such as vinyl and CDs existed, correct?"

"Yes, you'd be right, but I collected a lot of vinyl back then. There was no reason for doing so, considering the fact that playing it

digitally was more convenient. We had something called phones. Communicating with other people from anywhere in the world was the main intention for it. But as time went on, that idea kind of got lost on everybody. Technology got so advanced, it became more than a means of communication. You could use it to watch movies, listen to music, and much more. Everybody had a hold of one at some point. Adults, teenagers, children. News and a plethora of information were at everybody's fingertips. On paper, that's good. But in execution, not so much. If you ask me, people had the most convenient means to learn and do anything because of it. Things like that came at a price. It was easy to spread false information, to lie and defame others by any means necessary. Something small could be blown out of proportion, with the means to destroy someone's life. Then, that could be spread far and wide. Even when not considering how it impacts someone at an individual level, it still affects everyone on a mass scale. Governments had access to it, as did the regular people. In a way, they could use and abuse each other. People had used this technology, not just phones I should say, but computers and much more to turn on the other person.

At some point, people had lost faith with each other, the government, and the systems in place. It all collapsed under the weight of itself. Technology only assisted in speeding up their destruction."

The look on his face dims. His smile is gone. His right eye opens; he blinks a couple of times. He's told me before how much his right eye stings. Blinking helps in numbing the pain or shutting it entirely makes it go away. I asked him before if he would like an eye patch, but he keeps saying no. His eyes stare directly into the window behind me. He stopped humming his song. All I hear is his breathing.

"I never understood how technology worked. Most of my knowledge about what happened prior are from books and things I overheard when I was living in my own community. Part of me wishes I could listen to music, discover who made them and explore what that's like. I know I can't, but that would be nice."

His eyes look to mine.

"It might be rude to change the subject, but I wanted to ask you something. I remember the first night I was here. I told you my name. The sound of it was weak. I could barely get the words out of my

mouth. But you told me yours as well. When you did tell me, I didn't pay attention to it. I had fallen asleep by then and that day had exhausted me to an extreme degree. I always wanted to ask what your name was. And now, I have an opportunity to. You saved me. I can never truly thank you enough for doing so. So tell me, what's your name?"

I smile at him warmly. His eyes still gaze into me. He seems to have warmed up since he's gotten here. Despite his condition and circumstance, he seems to be at ease. At least, at this very moment.

"My name is Jane. Though I was given a different name when I was born. As to what that was, I have no idea. My parents had died shortly after I was born. At least, that's what one of my teachers told me when I was a child. When my teacher took me in, my mother had given me away to that community for safety. My father had died at that point, leaving my mother alone to protect me. However, she later took her own life shortly after I was taken in. I don't think they ever saw me take my first step, let alone crawl. I'm not even sure what they look like. My teacher became my official guardian at that point. I was taught to read and write. She had called me by a name when I grew to be a toddler, but by that point I never paid attention to it. She would call me, but I never responded to it. In retrospect, I think I just had no clue what my name was, let alone what names even meant. At an early

age, I began to get into reading and drawing. Drawing was something I was never the best at. In all honesty, I'm terrible at it. All it's delegated to now is a way to kill time. I can't even bear to look at my own sketches and drawings. They make me wince at the sight of it. The proportions of the faces and angle to draw at were always wrong, at least to me. Though, my teacher always said it looked good. I think she was just trying to encourage me. Reading, on the other hand, was something I could never get rid of. Learning about how the world used to be, the stories people could come up with. It all fascinated me. It still does even now. Sometimes it's fantasies, like a dragon who breathes fire fighting a knight with a sword. Other times, I would just learn about different careers the world had. This one book had pictures of people in outfits. They were police officers, firefighters, doctors, chefs, train conductors, astronauts, construction workers. Those don't exist anymore. Well, to a certain extent. But I was always keen on learning what the world was like before I was born. How all those careers and jobs meshed together for everyone. How those careers gave people structure and some kind of meaning. To me, it seemed rather heartwarming. Though at the time, I had no idea the extent of how terrible or great each career was. I had only an idealized version of them in a myriad of picture books and later down the line in life, read books about specific parts of that field. Which parts of the human body did this for nursing, for example. But as for my name, I had read about this thing, this alias. Apparently, women who are unidentified are called "Jane Doe". So, I began to call myself Jane

because of it. When I was a kid, other children my age would ask what my name was when they wanted to play tag or tic-tac-toe. I always responded with "Jane." Eventually all the kids started to call me by it and that sort of stuck. The teachers began to call me that as well."

"Interesting story. You do seem like a bookworm. Plus, you're rather quiet and reserved. At least, to me."

"Really? I come off that way? What gave it away?"

"The day you dragged me here, we stopped on the side. You leaned up against the tree to rest. I saw you, pondering to yourself. You may have seen me close my eyes and do the same. The look on your face when you're at ease... it's the same as mine. The few moments where life is truly peaceful are ones to revel in, aren't they?"

"You certainly are a bit of an oddball. You're kind of blunt about things. I was just messing with you when I asked that. I'm not sure if you could tell. But to answer your question, they are. It's hard to find peace and quiet nowadays, and when there is... it's beautiful. I don't think there's a word that can ever truly describe that feeling of its peace. I've also been told I come off as a quiet individual. Most

people didn't think I wanted to be bothered, or when they did talk to me, they felt like I wanted to brush them off. Truth be told, I just sucked at communicating when I was younger. Though, when people are around I usually don't mind talking to them. It can get especially lonely nowadays, you know?"

"I get where you're coming from. It's difficult for me to relate to anyone, especially at my age. The older you get, the less people care about you. I envy those younger than me, they have something I don't have: time. But nowadays, that gift doesn't mean much. Though before any of this happened, I had always kept to myself. But people come along here and there that you can't forget. Sometimes, people stick around in your mind, long after you see them. Even if they pass away or only exist in your life for mere months or weeks, people will always find some way to be with you one way or another. In that regard, it's very beautiful the effect people have on you. They can hurt you or they can love you. Sometimes it's both. The good and the bad hit you at once. I tend to let both of those coexist in my memories. I've met a lot of people in my life. People I think I may never see again. Part of me is scared for that very reason. Deep down, I don't want to accept it. Accept the fact

that there is no realistic or feasible way I can ever meet the people who were in my life once more. That's a dream, a fantasy. A fantasy I want so badly to be true, but it could never be. The reality of the situation is much more cold. They could be dead, end up as sex slaves, cannibalized, or whatever else. I'll miss them. I really will. And if they are truly gone, then I accept it."

He begins to hum a song once more. It's a new tune for my ears. One that I am slowly becoming more familiar with the more he hums it. This song means something to him. His eyes shut and a smile forms upon his face. Through everything, part of him still maintains a sense of peace. That's... admirable.

"The song you're humming, it's *Corcovado*, right? Is there something about *Corcovado* specifically that you like? What does it sound like? I'm not the most musically-knowledgeable, but I'd like to be, even if I may never get the chance to listen to it myself."

His eyes stare back onto mine. The sun surrounds his body as his smile shines towards the light.

"It's just... the feeling it gives off. It's quiet. Calming. I listened to it for the first time when I was in high school. I was in my school's jazz band, as a pianist. *Corcovado* was one of the songs we had to play for a gig. I was given sheet music and looked over how to play it. It wasn't terribly difficult. The song is slow-paced. When I went home that day to listen to the song, I remember being entranced by it. Something about that lady's voice is just so... soothing. The song itself is only sung in English for the first part, which is where the girl sings. After that, it's sung in Portuguese by a male singer. A guitar comp rhythm happens throughout the song, which actually has one of my favorite chord progressions. In the middle, there are two solos that happen. The first solo is done by a saxophone. The other is by a piano. That was the one I learned to play, in addition to the rhythm of the rest of the song. I remember rehearsing it quite a bit along with the rest of the band. I always did my part well, the guitarist was off time here, same with the bassist. After a bit of practice though, everybody synced up well. Then, there was the vocalist. We only had a female vocalist in our band and, of course, we kept all the lyrics in English when it came to performing. But

she had this beautiful voice. I could never forget it. She was cute too. Apparently, she had a thing for me. I did as well, but I was too nervous to approach her. I remember after we performed that song for the first time, at our high school's own auditorium, she came up to me. When everybody was packing up their instruments, she asked if she could talk to me outside for a moment, just the two of us. I was shocked, this girl was popular, especially around guys, and she was talking to me. Obviously, I agreed. I was 16 at the time, so was she. People begin to fall in love for the first time around this age. God... it was so innocent."

A smile on his face begins to form. Sun surrounds his face. My arms remain still as I hold him. He's rather heavy. I can feel my arms starting to get tired. But this moment... it's nice.

"I remember that moment so well. She was waiting for her dad to pick her up from our school. I didn't have a car either, so it ended up with both of us just waiting in the front entrance. At some point, everyone else in the band went home, but our teacher stayed behind to

make sure both of us would get a ride at some point. He stayed inside, at the front office. A glass window was in there, he could look on the outside. Our teacher knew me pretty well and saw what was happening. Guess that's why he stayed inside. Ha, what a wingman."

A tear begins to form on his left eye.

"It was dark out. Our performance started at 6:30. We played 8 songs if I remember correctly. The show had ended an hour after that. It was just the two of us, sitting on the curb, looking up at the moon. She sat next to me. I remember what she was wearing. A black dress, with the head of a rose pinned on the right side of her chest. She was... beautiful. I remember she was asking me when I started to play piano. She complimented me, telling me how good I was at it. She had wanted to learn how to play an instrument for the longest time, but was never good at any of the ones she picked up. Piano? Too hard. Guitar? Same ordeal. Bass guitar? She called that the easy guitar, but she could never play that either. She tried to play the drums. But each limb had to have

to work independently to play that. That was the most difficult instrument for her. But she told me that she was always good at singing. Her father encouraged her to do that. From there, she honed in her voice. How well to sing, how high, how low, how soft, how heavy. She always preferred softer songs. Those were more of her taste. She also told me that she struggled making friends growing up, never got along well with women and tried to make friends with men. However, men saw her in a romantic light. She never saw that in any of them. Even then, she struggled to relate to anyone, regardless of gender. But, something about me, she told me I always piqued her interest. She was just scared to talk to me. During our conversation, she would inch ever so closer."

His tears begin to hasten.

"She'd tell me about her mother. How she and her father divorced when she was in elementary school. She told me she sees how much her father tries to take care of her, how many shifts he takes just

to keep both of them afloat. They were poor, and could barely afford anything. The few times they could go somewhere nice, it was always some commercial restaurant. That was their way of celebrating. They had planned to find some nice restaurant to eat that night, even though not many were open during that time. One of her dreams was to be a famous singer. She wanted to make it, for her father mainly. As a way to thank him for all he's done for her life. I saw her tear up a little. She apologized for talking about herself so much. I told her it was alright. She told me she always wanted to talk to me at some point, but she never did before as I had this look on my face where, "I didn't want to be bothered." I laughed at that, we both laughed, actually. I told her that's just the way I looked. She said she wished she could've talked to me sooner, but she also said that it was nice, nice that the two of us were finally talking. She sat closer to me until eventually there was barely any space left between us. My hand was on the ground, next to hers. My face was blushing. I'm not even sure if I hid it that well. She looks at me. I remember how kind her face looked. It was innocent, pure, not a sense of malice in sight. She put her hand over mine and interlocked her

fingers with me. Her face had leaned closer to mine, and she kissed me on my lips. Her lips tasted like cherries. I remember being taken aback. I didn't say anything after that. She just looked at me and smiled. She kept holding my hand after. A little bit later, her dad finally came. He saw the both of us holding hands on the curb. I saw him grinning ear to ear at the sight of both of us. She asked me if anyone was coming to pick me up. I told her my dad hadn't texted me back in 30 minutes. So, she offered to give me a ride. I thought about it for a bit before deciding to text my dad that a friend would drop me off at home and rode along with her instead. She grabbed me by the hand and stood up with me. Her hand reached for the car door and motioned me to go inside. When I did, she sat next to me, holding my hand once more. I asked her if she was still going to go to her restaurant with her father. She said no and asked her dad to take me home. He obliged and asked where I lived. I gave him my address and I saw him smile once more. The ride itself was 20 minutes. She had laid her head on my shoulder and begun to fall asleep. Her hand was still holding mine. Her dad didn't say anything, he was quiet. Occasionally, I would see his smile flash in the rearview

mirror. Once we arrived at my place, I had to wake her up. Her hair was slightly disheveled. She rubbed her eyes. I watched as she smiled at me before I had to leave. I stood up and she followed. Before I walked towards my front door, she hugged me tightly. That night was a Friday night. She said she was looking forward to seeing me on Monday at school, and kissed me on my lips. I tasted cherry for what would be the final time."

His tears keep flowing now. Once more, his face is smothered in a mix of clear and yellow. I notice his voice cracking ever so slightly.

"When I got to school on Monday, everyone seemed to be in a sad mood. I didn't know why at first. Jazz band was my first class of the day. I took notice of everybody there. Everybody was present, except for her. I had put the pieces together already, but I didn't want to accept it. My teacher came up to me and put his hand on my shoulder. He asked me to step outside. It was just me and him in the hallway. He filled me in on what happened. On her way home that Friday night, a drunk

driver crashed into them. She died instantly, along with her father. The man who killed them lived with minor injuries and was in the hospital being treated. I cried. I cried so much when I heard that. He hugged me. I sobbed into his chest when he did. I couldn't stop crying. I was upset at her death. I was upset that the man who killed her got to live. I was upset that this happened in the first place. That any of this happened at all. Yet, I couldn't do a thing about it. All I could do was cry."

I feel like I should say something.

"I'm- I'm sorry."

"It's alright. You have nothing to apologize for. It's just... something that happened. Decades ago. It hurts, just hurts to think about. I miss her. I miss her a lot."

"May I... may I ask what her name was?"

He sniffles a bit. His voice begins to clear up slightly.

"Ah- ah, that's right. I never told her name. It was Claire. Her name was Claire. She had a beautiful name. It fit her very well."

"That is a beautiful name. I'm still sorry to hear what happened between you and her. She didn't deserve that, not at all. I apologize for not being able to articulate what I feel very well and for repeating myself. It just... saddens me."

His eyes, which once gazed empty at the window behind me as he told the story, shifted towards my face. His tears began to stop. A slight smile appeared on his face.

"It's okay. There's no need for you to apologize. That was decades ago. There was nothing you or I could've done to stop that. Still, you're very sweet and sympathetic. That's a good thing. Please, don't take that away from yourself, regardless of what happens. As for me, I still miss her, even after everything. After her death, I stuck with my jazz band for the next two years, up until my graduation. Though, even when I played piano, part of my mind drifted to Claire. At a performance, I would often slip up on some notes and chords when we were in front of an audience. It wasn't noticeable, but my jazz teacher

could tell. He knew I never stopped thinking about her. He'd always tell me I could exit the jazz ensemble if it was too much to bear. I always declined, and we'd have talks about Claire from time to time. My jazz teacher talked about how talented she was, how she out shined a good chunk of the singers that came before. She was the most talented vocalist he'd ever seen up until that point. I told him how beautiful her voice was and how I would've liked to be with her. Sometimes, I'd tear up just from talking about her. Not all the time, but at certain points. He always reassured me that it would be alright. Those conversations with him saddened me then, even now."

I'd visit her gravestone every year, on her birthday. She was buried next to her father. I'd show up by myself with a rose and stick it into the ground, right where she was buried. I sat down in front of it. I'd talk to her, her gravestone, and I'd tell her how everyone in the jazz band missed her, how everyone in that band was doing, and how I was holding up in my life. I'd keep her updated with my graduation and where I was going to college. Of course, I was talking to nothing. It was just me talking to dirt and stone. But I always looked straight at it, her

epitaph. It said, *"To my little angel, shine brightly amongst the stars and keep singing. I'll always miss you."* Her mother had written that for her. I met her at the funeral. Nothing was on the gravestone at that time. And to be honest, I'm not sure why they divorced, but she seemed remorseful that she was barely present in her daughter's life. And now, after years of not seeing her, she had passed away. She had no idea who I was when I came up to her. I filled her in on how I knew her daughter. I told her about the jazz band, how she picked up singing, and how much that meant to her. She wasn't around when Claire picked up singing, but I offered to show videos of her singing on my phone. We were recorded at each performance we did. I remember when I showed it to her. She began to tear up. There were only a few performances to choose from, and when I got to *Corcovado,* I began to cry as well. It was her final performance. Her last day she was alive. All the memories came flooding through by then. She thanked me for showing it to her, and asked if she could have the videos. I emailed it to her and from there, she had someone etch that epitaph into her gravestone. Eventually, I stopped visiting during my second year of college."

He stops talking for a moment. I see his chest rise and fall again. Water around his eyes started to form. Though, not a single tear is shed.

"Truthfully, I could never bring myself to play *Corcovado* again. Even playing the opening chords just brought back painful memories of mine. I kept the sheet music of it somewhere in my room. But I just never had the guts to get it from my folder. After that, I gave up on my musical abilities as I grew older. Claire's death wasn't the trigger for why I stopped playing. I stopped playing piano because of... life. Got busy with work, with college, and I had set my dream aside of being a musician to be an architect. That was more feasible and paid more money. It hurt to let that dream of mine go, but if it weren't for that, I wouldn't have met my wife. It's kind of funny how that worked out."

His voice begins to choke up a little bit. His smile begins to fade, ever so slightly.

"You had a wife? How'd you two meet? What was she like?"

His voice gets a little more clearer.

"Ha, that was on a whim. I remember I was sitting in a park one day. This was during the time I was in college. She came up to me and asked to sit next to me. I remember being shocked when she came up to me. But... it just ended up with me and her talking for quite a while. Funny thing, me and her actually went to the same high school together. We were never in the same class. However, she took notice of me in the hallway. I was her little hallway crush. This bled over to college as well. We were both in the same college and the same thing happened. I never paid attention to her though. But, I guess that day we ended up meeting regardless. Life just brings people together out of the blue, I suppose. Oddly enough, we clicked well. I felt as if I could talk to her about anything. We shared a lot in common and bounced around from topic to topic. All of it just felt natural. I didn't feel stressed about screwing up when I talked to her. She just kind of... came into my life at the right time. Though, I never told her about Claire when we first met. That memory of mine just lingered and never went away. At that time, 5 years had passed since Claire died. During those 5 years, I met other women, went on dates, but nothing ever clicked. Ended up with me just

never talking to any of them again. They had all called me "disinterested" or "boring." But her? She talked to me like an old friend. It's like both of us knew each other for years at that point. She had the same smile Claire had. Innocent, pure, not an inch of malice in sight. It reminded me of her. Part of me was sad during our first encounter because of that. But still, I really liked her. We talked for about 30 minutes, but it felt like hours. Eventually, she had to leave but asked for my phone number to keep in touch with me. I gave her my contact information and we planned another date. But I never... I never told her about Claire."

He began to look sad once more. I could tell from the way his eyes looked. I should change the subject.

"I'm going to head downstairs. I have to feed you something. I have to feed myself too. Neither of us have eaten in a while, especially me. You can fill me in on your other stories when I come back. It was... nice to hear about what's happened to you, even if all of it wasn't pleasant. I'm going to put you down on the floor, alright?"

"I was talking your ear off a bunch anyway. You can take a break, you know? You don't have to feed me right at this moment. Eat downstairs if you want. It's not like I'm going anywhere."

I flash a smile at him and put him down gently on the floor. I make sure he's centered on the pillow.

"Thanks, Johnny. But, I'll still feed you anyway. The sun's about to set, it's almost dinner time. There's not much, but I can make something warm. Would stew be alright? I got potatoes and carrots I could toss into it, along with bits of cabbage. Though my options for protein are far more limited. You seem like you need quite a bit of that, soldier boy. The most I got in terms of protein is canned chicken noodle soup, the same thing I gave you from earlier. But, I do have a bunch of canned sardines. I don't eat them though because I hate the taste. I'll have to scavenge again at some point anyway. What would you like?"

"I'll stick with the stew. Don't worry so much about giving me the chicken noodle soup. It's better off if you save that for yourself. Besides, I won't be needing protein much. I'm still... limbless. Though, if

you do have an abundance of canned sardines, I don't mind having them. Thank you at least for offering that to me."

"Of course. I'll be back in a bit."

I turn around and walk away from Johnny. He smiles as I leave. Through the kitchen window, I can see the sky turning orange ever so slightly. There's a limited window to cook, safely anyway. I grab a pot from the cabinet. On my left is the cutting board along with a block of kitchen knives. I set one knife and the cutting board on the counter.

I grab the bucket I use to collect water and take it with me outside, making sure not to trip the wire on it. I head towards it, attach the hook to the bucket via its handle, and hoist it down to collect the water. As I turn the handle, I look down and make sure the water looks clean. As usual, it's about as clear as it could get. Regardless, I'll boil it. I collect it and take it back inside the kitchen. Oh, right. I still have to cook the vegetables.

I head back out and take a good look at the crops. I crouch down and take a good look at the best ones to choose from. A lot of them look good, guess all that matters is size. I take 4 potatoes and 4 carrots with me and head inside. I begin to chop the vegetables into round pieces. First the potatoes, then the carrots. Afterwards, I dump them into the pot, along with the water I collected earlier. Looks like

there's still enough water to boil, I could use this to drink. Actually, more like *we* could use it.

A thought crosses my mind. I've been making the same bland stew for a while now. I'd like more flavor of course, but it's not like I have much of a choice. The most I can do is add salt. However, Johnny said he wouldn't mind taking the sardines. Perhaps, I could mix the sardines with the stew. The tomato sauce might help by adding flavor. But, what if it doesn't taste good? It's not like that matters really. Eating is more about survival than preference anyway.

I grab two cans of sardines from the pantry. I should eat these more, but I don't like the taste. Still, I should probably suck it up.

Back to the counter I open both cans. The smell is rancid, the contents somehow less appetizing to look at. Regardless, I dump them into the pot and toss the cans away. Behind me, I grab a wooden spoon and mix it all together. Hopefully this tastes good.

Outside, I collect the wood I chopped earlier to boil water. I strike the last two pieces together until sparks finally catch. After a few moments, flames begin to rise. I set the pot over the fire and wait.

The sky begins to turn a darker orange. Though, I don't have to stay out here for long. It'll take 30 minutes for it to be ready.

Part of me considers going back upstairs to keep Johnny company while I wait. Still, I don't want the food to be taken when I'm gone. If someone took the food, that'd be a waste. It wouldn't terribly

upset me if it was, I still have food to go. I'm more concerned if someone came here at all.

The fire crackles beneath the pot as the stew boils. Smoke drifts into my face. I've always hated that smell. It clings onto my clothes and hair no matter how long I stay away from it. But compared to everything else, it's a minor inconvenience. There's more pressing matters to mull over.

Now that I'm thinking about it, this is the first time I'm cooking for someone else. I've really never had company before. It usually is just me. I eat enough to stay alive. Save whatever remains. Repeat the next day. But this feels different. I found myself trying to make the food taste decent. Perhaps it's just basic manners. If someone stays under my roof, I should take care of them. At least, that's what I remember people telling me a long time ago.

I wonder, will I ever see some of them again? Are they dead? That would hurt me if they were. But I wouldn't know for sure. It's just... been a while since I've had contact with anyone, let alone conversation. It's been years I think since I've talked to someone properly. Maybe two. I gave up trying to keep track about the time. Johnny's... different.

He's someone who I don't have to be paranoid about. I don't have to feel so tense around him. I'm not waiting for him to pull a weapon or try something stupid when my guard's down. He's just a normal person. Or about as normal as anyone can still be now. That itself is hard to come by. A lot of people I have to be so cautious

about, to raise my gun at them, to be ready to hurt them because I simply cannot risk it. But this is one of the first times in a while where I don't have to risk a thing. I can... relax. Even thinking about that is strange.

In a way, I had gotten my wish for human company. And now that I finally have, it comes attached to suffering. He's been through hell. Still, he seems earnest. Honest. Someone I trust.

Maybe I do pity him.

Eventually, the stew finished cooking. I take it off the fire and put the remaining water in the bucket to boil instead. Water boils quickly and by the time I'm done putting the stew in their bowls, it should be ready.

I carry the pot and set it on the kitchen counter. Behind me, I get two bowls and place them on the same counter, along with two spoons I grab from the nearby drawer. Carefully, I pour the stew into each bowl trying my best to make sure an equal amount is poured. After I do so, some leftovers remain in the pot. I put the lid on it and leave it on the stove. I'll leave these for tomorrow.

Once the bowls are set, I leave them on the counter and head outside to check on the water. Only a few minutes have passed, so I sit near the fire to wait.

Night has fully settled in now. The light emanates from the fire, though the bucket drowns out the glow. I lower my head onto my knee and close my eyes for a moment.

I'm tired.

Eventually, the water finishes boiling. I grab the bucket and pour water into two glasses. Some water remains in the bucket, I'll pour this into my canteen some other time. I believe I left it upstairs. Right now, I'm more focused on getting the food upstairs before it gets cold.

I head upstairs and open the door to the room. Johnny is there, laying still with his eyes wide open. He smiles faintly at the sight of me.

"Hey, I'll have to head back down and get our drinks. I'll be back soon to feed you."

"Sounds good."

It's still nice to hear his voice sounding clear. I leave both bowls next to him and walk back down to the kitchen to retrieve both of our glasses. I took a good look at each of them, at first I thought there was something floating in there. Upon closer inspection, there was nothing there. Guess I'm more exhausted than I thought.

I head upstairs and nudge the door open with my foot. I left it slightly cracked so I wouldn't have to turn the knob. I sit down, next to Johnny.

"Alright, I'm gonna sit you up now. You ready?"

He nods his head and I put my hand on his shoulder. As I lift him up, I put my other hand on his back to support him. He can sit upright pretty well. I begin to feed him by putting a spoonful of stew. One scoop at a time, he gets fed. Sometimes, I put pieces of potato on it, other times the carrots, and chop a small piece of sardine with a spoon for him to eat. Sardines tend to have bones in the center, but he tells me he doesn't mind eating the bone as it's soft and he can chew through it. As much as he insists, I still avoid giving the bone regardless.

"I'm surprised you put sardines in with the stew. I figured you'd make 'em separate. Are you gonna eat the sardines?"

"I might as well. This is the first time I've had company here. Figured this was a good time to force myself to get used to eating it. There's an abundance of them anyway. How's the stew by the way?"

"Honestly? Pretty good. Especially with what you had to work with. But I've always been a sucker for pretty much any food. I'm not too much of a picky eater, never have been. Even before the world ended up like this, I ate food straight out of the can. Corned beef. Spam. Sardines. Tuna. I didn't really care. Combining it with stew is new for me, but it's not exactly out of my palate. You did a good job."

"Thanks, I just wonder if I'll like it now."

He chuckles a little bit as I give him his last spoonful of stew.

I lean him back down gently onto the pillow and watch as he lays flat on the floor. The large window behind us glows a black sky. He begins to shut his eyes. I move the empty bowl away from him, into the corner of the room so I can leave it for later. Now it's my turn to eat.

I grab a spoonful of food and decide to bite into the sardines first. I hate the smell, but I still have to eat it regardless. Surprisingly, the taste isn't nearly as awful as I expected. Maybe mixing it into the stew helped. Or maybe it's different eating with someone else nearby. I probably wouldn't have eaten it if he hadn't asked to have some.

I continue eating while staring out the window. My eyes dart towards the window. The stars of the night sky take on different shapes. There's no big dipper to be found. That one looks like a random square. I think I see Hercules. That one to the right might be Pegasus. There's one with a triangle. Above it all hangs a full moon. That's rare.

I barely notice myself finishing the food. Once I finished, I pit the empty bowl and plate next to Johnny's. Tomorrow morning, I'll get it and clean it.

I stretch my arms and begin to lay onto the floor. My head sits comfortably on the pillow. I feel exhausted, but none of my limbs feel sore. It's just my head I guess. As my head sinks into the pillow I turn to the left and see Johnny. His chest moves up and down as he breathes. He looks comfortable. The temperature of this room is nice as well. Not too hot. Not too cold. Just quiet.

As my eyes close in and out,
Darkness engulfs my vision.
But something catches my eye.
Something is in Johnny's sleeve.
A faint bit of red.
It's shaped like a cylinder.
In fact, it looks like muscle the more I glance at it.
I'm too tired to think straight.
I shut my eyes and keep them closed this time.

As I do,

I hear the sound of something wet, stretching beneath skin.

Section 3:

Molting

Chapter 14

I recall the face of the woman I once loved. I would lie in bed next to her, her hand touching mine. Her lips would press against mine and I would move over top of her, still grasping her hand. At times, I would pull away just to see her face. There was this look on her. Her eyes would lock onto mine. She smiled at me, and I saw the dimples across her face form. She had insecurities about it, but I always thought it was cute. A tear fell down her cheek, but her mouth still cracked a wry smile. I asked her what was wrong. She said it was nothing and told me I was beautiful. Her hand reached out to my cheek. As she caressed my face, a tear began to form on her eye. Her face grimaced a tad bit as she did, still keeping the smile up. Even before this, I knew something was wrong. She wants to say something. I can tell. We look at each other for a while, staring into each other's eyes. I want to hear what's going on in her head. Eventually, she speaks.

"I don't... I don't want to lose something this good. You mean so much to me and I'm afraid... I'm scared of losing you. You're the best thing that's ever happened in my life and I want to stay like this forever. I don't know.

I don't know why I'm so scared. There's nothing wrong going on between you and me. I can't put my finger on why I feel this way. It's a feeling I can't shake. I don't want to upset you because you matter so much to me and I guess I'm scared this can't last."

Tears began to pour out. Her hand caresses my cheek again. The girl laid in front of me on the bed, my wife, the woman I love so much, is scared. Just as anyone else is. In an odd way this is good, it's something genuine. She didn't have to explain how she felt to me. I understood where she was getting at. An indescribable, existential fear of losing out on something, no, someone good. I felt the same. I loved her and she loved me. Who would want to lose this? She had been crying for a while. It was silent, perhaps for a couple seconds or even a full minute.

"You don't have to explain it to me. I know what you're getting at. I feel the same, you know? I love you so much and I want this to last. Losing you would be the worst thing to happen to me. You mean so much to me, so much. I'm not sure if I can ever truly put that into words. I just... I want to be with you for the rest of my life."

Her facial expression lightened up. What was once a pained smile turned into a genuine look of warmth and happiness. Her face was still tearful, but a look of joy shone through. She was still staring at me, a hand still gently laid on my cheek. With her other hand, she grabbed my hand and locked her fingers with mine. I lock my eyes onto her, she does the same. For a moment, it stays like that. Both of us remain in thought for only a short span.

My hand is raised up by her, then lowered. Her hand stopped interlocking between my fingers and my hand lay flat against her thigh. I feel how soft her skin is. She then moves my hand slowly to her stomach, then lower. My fingers brush up against her pubes, until eventually, my hand is between her legs. She lets go of my hand. I take my middle and ring finger and slowly insert it in her vagina. Once inside, I begin to roll it up and down, making sure to hit the walls of her canal. A small moan exits from her mouth. I put my lips over hers. Both of her arms wrap around me and she pulls me closer. She sticks her tongue out as her lips touch mine, I stick my tongue out in response. My fingers are still rolling up and down slowly. I get her juices on

my finger and carefully rub around her swelling clitoris. I feel my hand getting progressively more wet. Her soft voice whispers in my ear.

"Go *a little faster.*"

I pick up the pace. I begin to straighten out my fingers and move it back and forth. She puts her lips against mine again, moving her head wildly as we kiss. I close my eyes. Something presses on the back of my head. I feel her fingers pulling at my hair. The roots of my hair begin to hurt. I feel my scalp start to bleed a little. However, it feels pleasurable. Her hand squeezes tighter. My hand goes over her right breast. I squeeze tightly. She stops kissing me for a brief moment as she moans loudly. Her lips quickly lock back onto mine. My fingers pinch on her nipple, but as I do, I feel her hand touching my wrist. She redirects my hand to throat. I begin to choke her.

"Harder."

I tighten my grasp.

As I do, I hear weak breaths coming out of her. I lay my head back for a moment and watch as her eyes roll back into her head. I move my head a little and notice the white bed cover stained below where my hand is. She grabs my hand that was inside of her and removes it. Her hand then moves over to my erect penis. Bodily fluids flow down my fingers. I feel her touch my urethra, it leaks a bit of pre-cum out. She rubs and pinches the tip for a little while before guiding it around her opening and sticking it in. I can feel the liquid wrap around my member. I don't think she's ever been this wet before. Her arms wrap around me. I thrust slowly and stare directly at her face. Her eyes lock onto mine. I feel her arms push me down against her face as she sinks her lips into me. A pain emanates from my lower lip, she bites down hard into it. Blood rushes downwards as her tongue drags upwards onto mine, licking the red liquid as she does. I meet her tongue with mine as we lash aggressively inside each other's mouths. I pick up the pace on the inside of her.

I move faster this time, pushing deeper with each thrust. My phallus remains firmly erect and a surge of slime surrounds it as I penetrate. I look at her as both of her hands reach back and grab the pillow beneath her. Sweat pours down my chest onto hers. I place my hands on her hips and penetrate

deeper. A loud moan exits from her mouth. Quickly, she decides to put both of her hands on my back and digs her nails into it. I feel as they slowly drag across my skin. Even if it hurts, I can't help but to find enjoyment out of it. She attempts to say something through pained and pleasured moans.

"Are you almost done yet? Please... don't tell me you are..."

I grab her by both of the ankles and lift her legs up. A smile lights up across her face as I do so. I penetrate deeper. Faster. Then slow down. Then speed up again. I'm far from getting tired. Her legs spread apart and rest on my shoulders. Her ankles go past my ears. It feels a little more open this time. I massage my clit with her fingers as I thrust. Sometimes, I switch positions and try to jam my ring and pointer finger in the space above my shaft. I can't roll my fingers much, but I can thrust it back and forth. My other hand rests upon her stomach. I squeeze upon the small bit of fat there. Women with a bit of meat on them are nice.

I'm not sure how long we'd been at it for. Perhaps 30 minutes, maybe an hour. I'm not even close to climaxing yet. Neither is she. We've been in different positions. Missionary, then doggy, then spooning. Sometimes, we even did anal. I would stick my thumb in her anus as I penetrated her. Plugging both holes at once was pleasurable to her. She wondered why she didn't purchase a butt plug sooner. At some point, she had encouraged me to stick it in the other hole. I did as she asked. The lubrication from her vaginal discharge allowed easy access to her anus. Sticking it in wasn't as difficult as I thought it would be, at least from last time. Moving around was a different story. It felt tight and almost as if a vacuum seal had formed around my cock. It hurt to move around in. She quickly said to remove it as it felt like she had to shit when it was in there. I did as she asked and tried to wipe my shaft with a tissue. When I tried, she grabbed my wrist. With her other hand, she inserted my penis inside of her once again. It felt much better than before. I could actually move around and feel pleasure. Plus, it was more loose. I hear her say something softly.

"Ah... Just. Like. That"

A smile lights up across her face. The room reeked of our own sweat and fluids. Pillows and bed covers had been tossed around carelessly on the floor. I feel the scratches against my back start to settle. It still hurt, but the intercourse distracted me from the pain. She told me her vagina began to hurt. However, she insisted that I finish. If it still hurts, then she told me to use lube until I climaxed. I obliged, of course. This felt good for the both of us.

I move my head a little and notice the white bed cover stained below where my hand is. In addition to the bed covers on the floor, the remaining bed sheets were stained. Her discharge had leaked out to the bedsheets and I felt the sweat on both of our bodies. We were both exhausted, but still wanted to keep going. By this point, I was at my climax.

As I'm on top of her, I peer my head down and drag my tongue against her neck. Her hand reaches out to mine as she places my hand on her breast. I squeeze it and pinch the top of her nipple. Her hand goes over mine as she presses hard into both my hand and her own breast. Her other hand reaches down her clit as she rubs it in a circular motion. As I penetrate, I feel her hand hit the top of my shaft from time to time. I notice her middle and ring finger are covered in liquid. That same hand moves away from her clit

and inches towards my face. I open my mouth and lick them. A taste of salt and umami strike my tongue. Her fingers shift in my mouth a little, until it's just her thumb in there.

"Bite it."

I do as she asks and bite lightly into her thumb.

"Harder."

I clench down with more force. Bits of blood ooze out from it. The blood from her thumb drips onto my tongue. I'm too preoccupied to do anything but swallow it. As I do, I lighten up on how forceful I am. I don't wanna break a bone.

Still, I feel myself about to finish. I feel my sperm rushing to my urethra. Part of me wants to hold it in, to savor this moment. The other part of me wants to release it out of pleasure. Oh... I just can't choose. But I can't deny how good this feels. I start to go faster. She moans louder, screaming actually. Her nails dig even deeper into my back. I squeeze harder onto her

breast and pick up the pace even more. She leans forward and kisses me on the lips, sticking her tongue out once again. I don't want to cum inside of her. But I have a feeling I don't have a choice here. She can tell I'm about to finish. I don't even need to say anything. I feel it now, the height of my orgasm. I try to pull out, but she wraps her legs around my back.

My sperm is released inside of her.

We climaxed at the same time. My body laid on top of her immediately after. I feel my sweaty chest against hers. My cock is still inside of her, leaking small traces into her vagina. I don't feel like removing it. Neither does she. The scent of both of our fluids pierces my nostrils. It smells terrible, but also pleasurable. My phallus feels slimy. I'm starting to feel the pain against my back. The sperm oozes out of the opening of her vagina, even with my penis still inserted. Some of it makes contact with the bed sheets underneath her. My body lays flat against the bed. She shuffles around the bed to get a little more comfortable. I feel her finger lightly drag across my spine.

"I scratched a little too hard, didn't I?"

She giggles a little after saying that.

I turn around to grab tissues. She grabs me by the arm and plants a kiss on me as both of her hands touch my cheeks. A soft whisper comes out of her mouth.

"Stay with me, alright?"

Human beings are such liars, aren't they?

I awake to the sight of a horrified Jane. Her eyes are opened wide and her mouth is slightly agape.

"What, what is it?"

"Johnny... your... your arm."

I raise both of my stumps to the center of my eyes. There's nothing on my left. It looks the same as usual. However, my right stump...

My arm is back to its full size.

Fuzzy hair extends to my elbow.

I touch them with the stump where my left arm used to be.

Despite the soft look, the texture of it is hard.

The top of it is sharp, it pricks my skin.

A small green liquid oozes from the tip.

It makes contact with my left stump, it burns my skin a little.

Past my elbow and into my wrist, are rows of scabs and blisters.

I see yellow in their bubbles.

They look ready to pop at a moment's notice.

My hand is bright red and each finger is a different size.

My ring finger is abnormally large.

My pointer finger is substantially smaller.

I notice my fingernails are missing, replaced with a mass of bubbling red flesh.

I flip my hand to see my palm.

A small red spike exits from the center of it.

It appears to be covered in a slimy, clear substance.

A wound forms around it, the color of it is a dark black.

The wound and spike pulsate ever so slightly.

I feel my heart rate spike up. My breathing increases rapidly. My chest expands and compresses faster and faster. My vision blurs on both my eyes. I notice I see a yellow tint on my right eye. Something wet

comes from under that eyelid. I wipe it with my left stump, a yellow puddle dries up on my bandage. My left eye remains clear. I feel my eyes squinting in and out on their own. I'm not sure if I can control it.

"JOHNNY!"

Jane rushes towards me. Her hand places itself onto the center of my chest. I feel her other hand touch my shoulder. I keep staring at it. My right arm. What's supposed to be my right arm. But now it's just... it's just....

I feel his heart rate through the palm of my hand. It's accelerating rapidly. My eyes shift towards his face and I see his cheeks covered in yellow and clear tears. His right eye has turned a dark yellow.

"Johnny... look at me alright? Please, just look at me. I know, I know you're scared but please... Please just calm down. As best as you can."

I feel him start to hyperventilate. His voice begins to raise.

"Calm down? You want me to calm down? Look at me. Look at my fucking arm, if you can even call it an arm. Do you know what this feels like? What it's even remotely like in my position? I thought I would heal. Like some miracle was happening to me. I believed it. I don't know how it happened. How I started to regenerate but I thought... I thought I could go back to normal. To the way I was before. I could walk again. I could hold my own spoon and feed myself. I could walk to the bathroom and use the toilet. Not shit myself in my own pants. I could move the fingers on my hands individually. Curl my hand into a fist and spread my fingers out. Give someone a high-five or a handshake. I could wiggle my toes. I could put my own clothes on. I could jump, I could run, I could walk. But I get... this? My arm is... it turned into.... Look at it. What would you do if you were me? What could you do? I had hope earlier when my throat healed. It felt as if I had the opportunity to live life again. But God... I don't know anymore. What if... what if my other limbs regenerate the same way? What if I never turn back to normal? What if I'm stuck like this? What if I can't stop it? This

is a joke. A sick joke. I don't know what to do. I don't know. I don't know. I don't know. I don't know. I don't know. I don't know."

His tears reached his mouth as he spoke. He had choked on it slightly as he did. Midway through his screaming, his voice lowered down in volume. His pupils flicker in and out rapidly. His right arm shakes violently. I hear his breathing increase in volume. Sweat pours from his forehead. His eyes remain locked at his right arm.

I know he's angry. I know he's upset. His hatred is pointed towards me, but I understand why it is. He has nothing else to turn to, no one else for that matter. All he can do is be upset at the state of himself, and that redirects towards me. I'm not upset at him. I don't think I can be.

"Johnny..."

I whisper into his ear. My arms wrap around him tightly.

"I'm sorry. I'm truly sorry. I wish I could tell you what happens after. But I truly... I truly don't know. I don't know what's happening to you either. And you're right. I'll never know what it's like to be in your position. I may never understand. But I still want... I still want to help you all the same. Please... I know you're upset. Hell,

upset doesn't even begin to describe it. You have every right to be. But please... let me help you as best as I can."

I feel his breathing begin to slow down. His heart rate lowers as I feel it pulsate through my hand.

"Do you... Do you ever think I can go back to the way I was before?"

His tone of voice is calm. His head tilts up towards me.

"I don't think I can give you an answer for that."

"I know. I only asked for my own peace of mind. Though deep down, I think I know what the answer is. What do you... what do you think I did to deserve this?"

His left stump wraps around my arm, as if to embrace me as much as he can. He moves his right arm as far away from me as he can. Even now, he's doing his best to remain calm. He doesn't want to hurt me.

"Maybe... maybe you've done nothing at all."

His face dims away from mine. He seems disappointed but also accepting of my response.

"You're probably right."

His head lays onto my shoulder. I feel his stump tighten against my arm more. Despite the way his arm looks, the left side of his face remains normal. I wish the rest of him looked like this. I wish he regenerated back to normal. I hope this isn't just wishful thinking. Please...

Please...

I see the hairs on his arms vibrate, along with the one on his palm. The left side of his face lays softly onto my shoulder. Johnny opens his mouth. His voice is soft.

"Can you stay with me for a little while longer?"

"I can."

Chapter 15

I move my right arm in a circle. My fingers spread apart before curling into a fist. Despite the exposed flesh on my fingernails, I don't feel any pain. Jane sits in front of me. She's staring at my arm.

"How's it feel?"

"It doesn't hurt. Even my fingernails don't sting.

It just looks and feels revolting. Just wondering if the blisters on my arm might pop. Plus, there's green liquid seeping from the hair of my arm. I had pricked it by accident earlier with my stump. It hurt a little, but nothing's happened as of yet."

About an hour had passed since I had woken up. My shock from before has mostly worn off. Jane appears to be in bewilderment. I still dread the sight of my own body.

"What about your right eye? It's become a darker yellow."

"Ah, right. All I see from it is a yellow tint. It doesn't hurt, unlike how it did earlier. Just a pain to see, that's all."

"That's good to hear. Your left eye is still fine, I take it?"

"Yeah, still normal despite the rest of my body."

There's a concerning look on Jane's face. Her mouth squirms from side to side a little bit.

"Last night, I saw something.... You were sleeping and I was too tired to focus on it."

Her gaze dims towards the floor. In between us is a slight crack in the floorboards.

"Your arm... there was something red forming around it. It was dark so I couldn't make out the exact details. But I saw it, something forming, for a brief moment. I wasn't sure what it was, my

eyes had shut by then. I had heard it too. The sound of squishing and writhing. Like something wet. Did you... did you feel anything?"

My eyes lock onto her. I blink a few times. Neither of us say a word. I'm trying to recall anything from that night. The most I can remember is being tired and falling fast asleep. Actually-

"That night, I didn't feel anything. I take it that's when my arm regenerated. But...I felt something. Not my arm, but in my throat. Before it had healed back to normal, I felt this surge of heat. It didn't hurt, it was like something was cauterizing my wound. I didn't think much of it at the time, but the following day that's when you pointed it out to me. My throat healed. The patch of skin that was once burned and charred returned to its smooth texture. That's when I spoke for the first time. It didn't... it didn't hurt."

Her face looks up to me. She stares into my eyes with a dead expression. I can tell she's thinking of what to say.

"What do you think... what do you think happens now?"

"I don't know. Part of me wants the regeneration to stop. I despise the way my body looks. I don't want to turn into some freak of nature. Like I'm mutating to some sort of genetic monstrosity. The more and more this goes on, *if* it goes on, I don't want to be something less than human, or inhuman at all. I want to be back to the way I was before, more than anything. But every single time I look at my arm or my stumps, I can't help but feel angry. Angry that what I lost can no longer be obtained. For that reason alone, the other part of me wishes for it to continue. I envy you, for being able to walk and hold things. You're not a terrible person. But when I see you move, feed me, and hold things. Basic, simple tasks I should be able to do, that I've done before. I can't help but feel *awful.* It feels like a mockery. And I know, I know that's just how it is, and I can't do a thing about it on my end. You can't either. I know the extent of how much you can assist me here. But I don't hold anything against you for any of this. It's just... a cruel joke played on me and me alone. In a funny way, I got my wish. And of course, the monkey's paw curls. Maybe, I regain the ability to walk and

move my fingers. To hold things with my own hand. To feel the texture of the floor I'm laying on or the dirt outside or to even read books again or hold a plate of food. I feel like an infant learning how to move and grasp things for the first time. But at the cost of what? Look. At. Me."

Her eyes look at mine. There's no hatred or malice in those eyes. No sense of disgust at the sight of me. Perhaps, just remorse. She exhales heavily. Her look is as calm as ever. I watch as her mouth opens.

"I know Johnny. I know. I know how much it hurts you to see me do the things you can no longer do. All you can do physically, is just lay there. Maybe just wait for your limbs to come back. Maybe you turn into something gross, or maybe you don't. I don't know. But I see it all the same. I see how much it eats at you. The look on your eyes. The dead expression as you stare at random things in this room. And you and I both know there's only so much I can accommodate you for. It's a feeling of hate, isn't it? You can say it, it's alright. I don't blame you for feeling that way. Not at all. You lost your limbs to a landmine. You lived in the world that existed before I was even born. You got to experience what life was like before everything ended. And you got to experience it when it did. I can't imagine, let alone know, what that's like for someone. What that's like for *you*. And I know all

you can do now is lay there with your memories replaying in your mind of everything that's happened up until this point. How much you've lost. And you've lost a lot. That's not something against you, it's just life. I don't know the extent of how much you've suffered. And I want to do so much more because I see you in this state. You and I barely know each other. But that's not a bad thing. You've got your limbs regenerating. And I hope... *I hope* that it heals back to the way it did before. But that's all I can do. Hope and wait for it to work out. That's all you can do as well. In that way, we're both on the same boat. But if it gets to where you become monstrous then I know, I know we'll both suffer. More you than me. But... neither of us know that yet. And if it does, I'll tell you this."

I see her clenching her fists. Her voice begins to deepen.

"I'm not abandoning you. I'm not going to leave you, not in the state that you're in. That would be cruel for me to do. This world is cruel enough as is already. I'm not doing that to someone. I *refuse*. So get angry with me, get upset, *hate* me for that matter. You have every right to. So go right ahead. But I won't hold any of it against you. Because you know what? You didn't deserve any of this. None of the suffering you went through. The people you lost, the things you've seen and possibly dealt with. You didn't deserve to lose that much. And I don't know the extent to which you lost, but I'm not going to be someone who hurts you."

I don't say a word. I can do nothing but stare at the woman who's only ever exerted kindness towards me. She stares directly into me, almost as if she's expecting me to say something. I don't have anything to say at all. Both of us laid out how we feel. All the fears, the guilt, the shame, and the intentions of it. I've been cruel. I'm aware of it. For the first time in my life, it's never been so... direct. Reflected towards me in such a manner. I know she's right. There's nothing I can say to make it better.

This room's never felt so quiet before. It's raining. I'm not sure if it was raining prior. I wasn't paying attention. The floorboard creaks underneath her heel as she puts pressure on it. She rocks her foot back and forth. I hear the rain tap against the rooftop. I see the tree blowing in the wind through the window. Droplets hit the glass. It smears downwards slowly. I feel... ashamed.

"I'll get us something to eat."

Jane stands up and heads towards the door. There's something on my mind.

"Hey Jane, wait..."

She stops herself at the door frame. Her hand cusps the door. Her head turns towards me. I hear her soft voice.

"Yeah?"

"I'm sorry... for what I said earlier."

I see a small smile form.

"It's alright Johnny. You don't have to apologize."

She smiles from ear to ear this time. Her head nods ever so slightly. Her hand lets go of the door frame. I hear as her footsteps echo down the stairs.

Moonlight gazes through the window. I lay against the same dirty pillow. The back of my head sinks into the soft cushion. My backpack remains to my left. It hasn't been opened yet. To my right, Jane has fallen asleep. She's a fair distance away from me. I see her chest rise up and down slowly. Her right hand lays gently upon her heart. Her other hand lays flat on the floor. The blanket she lays in doesn't cover her up properly. It extends up to her stomach. I hear her breathe quietly.

Behind me is a desk she had moved into the back of the room. She figured it was best to have something there so not everything is put onto the floor. It came from the other bedroom next to this one. Her backpack and empty bowls from earlier are the only things on it.

I exhale. I can't fall asleep. My eyes stare directly into the cracks and tears of the ceiling. I've been looking at it for a while now. I'm not sure how much time has passed. I can barely switch the positions I lay in. Laying down on my side would hurt my stump or prick my chest, depending on the side. I also hate sleeping on my stomach. This is the only position I can be remotely comfortable in.

My throat feels dry. I can't tell if it's because I'm thirsty or because of something else. I don't care at this point. My left stump starts to hurt. The pain varies. Sometimes it feels like someone's stabbing at it. Other times it feels like an electrical shock or a very thin needle poking in the center and running through into my shoulder. It feels like it's still there. As if I still have it. I move it around in a circle. It itches, particularly in the center. It's starting to get on my nerves. I have to scratch it. I have to. I have to. I have to.

I move my right hand onto my left stump. My face avoids the sharp hairs near the top of my arms. With my fingers, I rub into the center of my stump and start scratching. My bandage is still there. I'm making contact and trying to scratch through it. I'm not doing it hard enough. I press deeper in. I feel my finger hitting the bone of my stump. It still itches. Why isn't it working? Why not? Why not?

Oh right. I don't have any fingernails.

It's just bubbly exposed flesh scratching against the inside of the muscles. It feels rubbery. The red on where my fingernails used to be bubble up. That part doesn't hurt. It's just slippery, smooth contact against another surface of the same texture. The only thing that feels remotely rough is the bandage itself. It scrapes against the inner part of my arm. I feel my bone roughen up against the interior of the bandage. Through the darkness, I am able to see red bleed through it. I just want the itch to go away. It's annoying. It's obnoxious. I hate it. I hate it. I hate it. It's not helping. It's not working. I stop for now.

Just then, it starts to feel different. Warmth. Not a burning sensation. Not one of pain. It's... changing. My stump begins to twitch on its own. Particularly from the center. It vibrates ever so slightly. Pressure builds from within. As if someone is squeezing it from the inside out. Something bulges through the bandage. It's small and coming out slowly. The sound of it... it's wet. Almost as if I were stepping on a puddle.

The pressure of it rips through the bandage from the inside. It slowly pulls each layer away from it. I see the muscle of my arm stick through. Red muscle forms a cylinder and pushes outward. A layer of skin forms over top of it. As it does, it begins to split. It extends towards my wrist, causing the strands of muscle and skin to form together. The bone in the center begins to expand in width and length. Eventually, it extends towards my hand. Copious amounts of red bubbles form over it. It starts off as one mound of flesh, shaped into an over-sized ball. Four incisions happen in between, and I see my fingers start to take form. Except, the skin over top of it doesn't appear. It remains red as bubbles

pulsate and expand over it. Fingernails form where they're supposed to over top the layer of red flesh. Something sticks out.

None of this hurts.

I feel something. Something sprouting from within my wrist. One hair. Two hairs. Multiple of them. All begin to form one by one on the bottom part of my arm. It extends towards my elbow, the opposite of my other arm. Past that, towards my shoulder, a mix of red and black ooze forms. It ripples, just a little bit. A large scab forms over the black and red pattern. A bright green liquid is visible underneath the bubble.

I lay my arm flat against the floor. As flat as I can. The hairs only go on the palm side of my hand. I'm only able to lay my arm on the side opposite from it. The texture of it appears... hard. I extend my hand out and stare at it. My fingers are overtly bloated. It's bubbling. Each finger is pulsating heavily. At least this time my fingers are the same size.

I stretch my fingers out.

This is the hand where my wedding ring was before.

I close my eyes.

I picture her once more.

The woman I loved.

Before I left for the military.

When was the last time I saw her?

Ah... I remember it all now.

Eating dinner across from each other.

Touching her face.

Brushing her hair.

Dancing as she spins in my arms.

Laying in bed next to her.

Her holding my hand and smiling at me.

That's all gone now, isn't it?

I don't want to accept this.

Chapter 16

There was a time when my wife insisted on cutting my hair. She had done hair styling as a hobby she wanted to learn. At first, she practiced on herself, changing her hair in various ways. A bob with eye length bangs, a wolf cut, and even decided to try and get her hair curly. Most of the time, she had kept her hair long and straight. But there were times when my hair grew too long. Well, "too long" in her eyes. I had a tendency to keep my hair a decently long length. Long for a guy anyways. She would insist that I should cut my hair, but only when it reached my shoulders. I knew this was an excuse to try out her skills on someone else. This was also apart of her "love language". Of course, I played along. I sat down on the chair she had bought specifically for this moment and watched as she prepared the equipment. Bottles of various hair supplies were splayed on the table. Shampoo, conditioner, leave in stuff, curling cream, the whole nine yards. The room itself didn't have a big mirror like they do in barber shops. Instead, she had used a handheld one to cut my hair. Beforehand, she had asked how I wanted my hair styled. I told her that she could do it however she wanted. Her eyes lit up and she smiled so brightly

when I said that to her. She began to spray my hair with water. Wet hair is easier to cut than dry hair, or so she says. It had grown a little past my shoulders at this point. I usually don't like my hair this long.

With a comb, she began to try and layer parts of my hair, starting from the back. She had picked out these parts by hand and put a hair clip on the top of my head to make sure it stays in place. Then, she began to cut the layers with scissors. This process would repeat until she went around my head. As to how short she would cut it, my guess would be around neck length. And, as she cut my hair, I had a feeling she would cut it into a pseudo wolf cut, the exact same style as hers at the time. I recall her fingers softly grabbing parts of my hair, rummaging it around. She would pull parts of it softly, and cut it. Sometimes she would mess with me by ruffling my hair around mid cut. I would joke around and tell her how she wasn't very good at this. To which she threatened to shave me bald if I kept talking. But in between, she had also complimented how thick my hair was, which was beautiful to her, but also annoying to cut. I chuckled.

Eventually, she had finished cutting my hair. With her phone, she took a photo of me so I could see what my hair looked like. To my (non)

surprise, it was a pseudo wolf cut with the length reaching my neck. I pretended to act shocked at the hairstyle she chose. She, of course, did not fall for it. Her hand lightly slapped across my cheek in response. But after that, she took a little to admire her work. She began to inspect the front of my face, then tilted my head to the side, and eventually walked behind me to inspect the back. I could see how proud she was of herself. She didn't think she had it in her to cut someone else's hair, let alone this well. That whole time she was checking, she was quiet, but happy. I asked her what she thought of it, and she simply smiled and said it looked good on me.

She asked if I wanted to shower with her. I said yes and headed upstairs. We took our clothes off and I got the shower running. She had a tendency to wait for me to go first because she hates showering in cold water. I usually just stood there and waited for the water to turn warm. When it did, I told her she could come in and moved the curtain to the side. She came in and asked me if she could wash my hair. I said I didn't mind. She grabbed one of the shampoo bottles from the side and poured some onto her hand. The whole time, I stand there and smile as she rubs her hand across my head. Her touch is soft. It's delicate. It's caring. It's warm. My eyes are shut to avoid the

chemicals from hitting my eyes, but I have a smile running across my face. I like to imagine she was smiling as well.

She tells me she's done and I move my head towards the water to wash it off. Her arms wrap around my chest from behind. Her head leans towards the back of mine. She holds me even tighter. I feel the water hitting my body. Something soft is whispered in my ear.

"I love you."

A shame I had to shave my head for the military.

I look down at Johnny. He's fast asleep. Daylight peers through the large circular window. It seems his other arm has grown. He's regenerating, fast. There's those same hairs on the other arm, but in an entirely different position on the one that has just grown. It opposes each other. The skin on it twitches. For a moment, I think he's waking up, but only his arm moves.

It's so... fascinating. The hairs on his arm, the scabs, the way his fingers have become a red jellied mass. I wonder how this all happened. I can never say this to him out loud, but I'm curious as to how this transformation of his has occurred.

Clearly it's impossible, at least in an anatomical and medical sense. I'm not sure if it's an infection either. Infections don't regrow arms. Is it supernatural? No... that stuff doesn't exist. Well, maybe? No use thinking about it regardless.

It's clearly getting to his head. I recall yesterday when he told me how he felt. I snapped back at him, but I never meant to. I'm just... tired. But in some sense, that doesn't feel fair to say. I'm not the one who lost limbs. Nor am I the one watching myself devolve into a monster in real time. I can move, I can hold things with my hand, I resemble a human being. It feels like I'm taking that for granted when I'm with him. He partially resents me for it. Maybe resent is too harsh of a term. I just wish I could do more. I know none of this is my fault.

But in a weird way, I can't help but feel guilty.

I crouch down and reach out towards Johnny's new arm. A giant scab has formed near his shoulder. Green liquid is visible underneath it. I'm so curious to touch it. My fingers extend towards it but... I stop myself. I don't want curiosity to get the better of me. It just doesn't feel right to do so. I'm not sure what that liquid is either.

He's still fast asleep. Part of him looks peaceful and at ease. I'm not sure if he's aware of his new limb or not. Either way, I'm not going to wake him. I've got a feeling sleeping is the only way he can relax. When he's awake, it just seems he's all too aware of the situation he's in. Nothing else he can really do except wait for time to pass. Still, he's under my care. All I do is feed him, change him, and clean him up. I'm just wondering if there's other ways to keep his mind occupied. For now, I should clear my head and let him rest. He's still knocked out.

I get the bowls from the desk and head downstairs. Moving the desk yesterday was a bit of a pain, considering the fact it was heavy and he was laying on the floor. It was difficult trying not to hit him, but he reassured me that it would be alright if I did. I had also asked him if he wanted to move to a different room, one with a bed. He declined my offer as he started to feel comfortable with the room. My guess is he likes the way the window looks. It's the only one in the house with a circular window, the rest have a square pattern. He has a tendency to look out of the window quite a bit. Usually when I return from cleaning up the place, he's always just staring at the outside, watching the leaves blow in the wind.

There's no soap or anything here. I just wash the bowls with the water from the well. It's about as clean as it can get, and rub the stuck on food off with a rag. This wasn't too hard to do. As for what else to do, I'm not too sure. I'm here to kill time for the most part. I just wonder when Johnny wakes up. Him sleeping gives me a bit of free time.

I walk towards the hole in the kitchen. This was where I practiced "aiming" when I was bored. Looking at it now, it's almost funny. I don't feel the need to aim as much here to kill time. Let alone bring a gun to screw with. Oddly, Johnny has kept my mind occupied off of anything paranoid within these last few days. Has it been a week already? Now that I think about it, I'm not too sure. So much has happened within that short amount of time. Taking him in, feeding him, getting to know him. Of course, there's him regenerating. Deep down, I want his regeneration to continue. But not for him to suffer, but because it gives him the ability to get his life back. As horrible as his transformation is, he's been given the ability to use his arms again. But still, I can't fault him for not using them. I notice he doesn't even do as much as squeeze or move his fingers. He often lies there and looks at the ceiling or window, pretending as if his arm wasn't there. Now that he has his other arm, I wonder how he'll react.

I've been walking around in circles aimlessly for the past couple minutes. My mind has been racing heavily but I can't seem to settle myself down. It just keeps dancing from random thought to thought. About how I met Johnny, about the fact that this is my first

human contact in a while, how this whole situation is a bit to process. His limbs healing still takes me by surprise. I'm just worried as to how he'll end up, if it continues. I need to sit down and take a breather.

My eyes take notice of the piano in the living room. I remember Johnny telling me about his days as a pianist. Back when he was in high school anyway. There's a book of sheet music atop of the piano. Songs composed by various artists such as Mozart and Beethoven fill the pages. There's other musicians in it whose names I'm unfamiliar with. Now that I think about it, he's got his arms back. Would he be alright with what I'm thinking?

I head up the stairs and swing the door open to the bedroom. To my surprise, Johnny is rotating his left arm and inspecting it. His right hand pokes at the scab near his left shoulder. He doesn't poke it all the way to avoid puncturing the liquid and having it seep out.

"Hey Johnny, I have something I'd like for you to do."

His head peers up towards me.

"Would you be alright coming downstairs?"

"What for?"

He squints one of his eyes. He seems confused by my suggestion.

"It's something to get your mind off of things. Trust me, alright?"

I flash a smile at him. His face still looks puzzled.

"Sure... yeah alright."

"Good. Here, I'll help you up."

His hand raises up at me. I see the bright red bubbles on his palm.

"Hey wait, I want to try something. Just stay there for now."

I halt. I'm surprised by him. He flips forward and puts his palm against the floor. Each time his hand slams onto the floor, red liquid is stained where it once was as he drags himself forward. He's... moving.

"Johnny... wait. Look, I can get you downstairs. It's alright. You're leaving stains on the floor anyways."

He shakes his head at me.

"Please just... let me do this alright? I haven't done much here except stay in this room the whole time. Just let me, okay?"

I can't really say no. This is probably one of the few things that gives him a peace of mind. Denying it would be rude.

"Alright yeah... yeah sure. You're leaving quite a bit of stains on the floor though."

"I know. We'll worry about it later, alright?"

I watch as he moves towards the door. I step to the side and hold the door open for him. He halts at the top of the stairs.

"Need help getting down?"

He shakes his head no. I stand next to him and walk slowly as he descends down the staircase. One hand over the other. One stain

on the right side, one on the left. Each one alternates per platform on the staircase. I'm worried he might fall. But to my surprise, he seems to be able to keep his balance well. I make sure that his hairs don't prick me on accident.

Eventually, he makes it towards the bottom of the stairs. I'm actually… quite proud of him. He doesn't seem to be exhausted from it. I figured he would be after being stationary for so long. But I suppose he's used to the exercise, judging from his physical figure.

"Alright, what was your idea?"

I point to the piano in the living room. He looks to be in a slight state of disbelief.

"I haven't… I haven't done this in years, you know? I'm not even sure what I remember, what notes to play. Let alone if I can play at all. Look at my hands, my fingers are all different sizes and blood, if it even is blood, stains whatever it touches. I get you're trying to be nice, but I'm not sure if this is a good idea."

"You've been cooped up in that room for days. This could give you something to keep your mind off of things. I know, you don't

like the way your arms look. In fact, I know how disgusted you are by them. But still, they function, right? And I'm also aware of the last time you played it. A small time after high school. So yes, it's been decades since you last played anything. I also know what's associated with this instrument. Those memories of yours attached to it won't go away. I'm not asking you to play a whole song or a whole performance. I'm not asking you to jog down memory lane either. But I also know that by doing this your memories will come flooding through. Just... just play, alright?"

His face looks up at me before quickly staring at the floor. He's not saying anything.

"You can crawl there or I can sit you up at the bench. I know part of you wants to do it."

He exhales heavily before saying something.

"Yeah alright whatever. Just... just sit me up there. I'm not sure if I can get up by myself."

I smirk before crouching down and picking him up. I'm careful to avoid the spikes on his hairs and from popping any scabs. Slowly, I sit him down on the bench and make sure he's stable. I move

the sheet music away from the lid and slowly pop open the top. My fingers open a page on the book before I hear something come from his mouth.

"Don't worry about it. I don't need it. Just let me try it, okay?"

I nod my head and sit down on the couch adjacent to the piano. The book is on the cushion next to me.

I hear him play a key.

I see the string vibrate as it's hit.

I'm not sure what note that is.

Then, his fingers play multiple notes at once.

He tells me that's a, "chord".

I see blood on the white key he played before.

The chord he played left the same red stain across multiple keys.

I cross my legs and listen attentively.

This is my first time listening to someone play.

My first time listening to music at all.

A familiar note rings in my head. I know what song it is. I know the structure already. I know who I lost. The tendril in my right palm pulsates and shifts beneath my skin. I do my best to avoid hitting it against the keys. My fingers press on the opening chord. Am6, then E7, followed by a D9/A and an Ab7. There's other chords that continue. This song strays from a traditional four chord repeating pattern. As I play, I move away from the original chords. I know what notes progress and transition into one another. It's not how the song is played. Yet, it still remains the same song regardless. I know this by heart, despite the decades of time passing by me.

The bridge of the song arrives. I play the rhythm, where the saxophone sings its beautiful tune. A 12 measure section. Then, my solo comes along straight after. The length of it remains the same as the last. I play the opening chord and follow the notes along in the scale. Sometimes I hasten my notes, sometimes I slow down and choose carefully. I'm not sure what the exact notes I played before, but it's close enough. And to my ears, it's still beautiful to me as it was before.

I remember it now, so clearly. In my time to shine, she would smile at me. On our last performance together, the first time I played this song in front of an audience, Claire looked at me warmly. This is the part of the song where she takes a break from singing. When our saxophone played prior, she looked at the ground and bobbed her head. When it was my turn, she gazed at me directly. She was center stage, I was off to her right. The audience saw her turned away from them and began to look at her. I'm sure they took notice of her gaze. How long is this section of mine? 30 seconds? Perhaps 45? I don't keep count. All I know is that she stared at me for that length of time. I lifted my head to her at points, still trying to play the right notes, and I'd smile right back at her. I never needed the most intense focus on my instrument anyway. It was and will always be, a sweet moment of mine. I'll cherish you forever. Goodbye, Claire.

The bridge ends as the vocals resume in this section of the song. Her beautiful voice resonates with the audience once again. A memory of mine replays once more. I'm watching the woman I love sitting across from me. Her eyes gaze into my soul and she smiles

warmly. She asks me how my day has gone and reaches out to me from across the table. I feel her soft palm caress my hand. We stand up and dance at our dining room table. Liszt's *Years of Pilgrimage* plays in the background. She looks up to me and smiles, I take notice of her oddly-perfect teeth. My hand is under her arm as she asks me if we can stay like this for a while. I nod my head. We slowly dance to the piano as my temple rests against hers. I smile and look in her eyes, she smiles and looks at me in return. Her breasts are pushed up against my chest and her arm is wrapped around me tightly. I say nothing. I simply want to take in this moment. It was an amazing time in my life. I keep recalling her face, again and again. I recall how beautiful she was with her hair splayed against the bed. I was on top of her. She had this smile. She was happy. Happy it was me. She chose me, instead of anyone else in the world. I sank my head into her chest and cried as she held me. At times recalling it makes me feel like I'm being taunted. It will never return. All of the beautiful possibilities back then are of a future that never came to pass, robbed by the vacuum of time. Eira, my beautiful wife, I'm

not sure where you are. Whether or not you're alive or dead, I'll always love you. Please remember that, regardless of whatever happens.

The song nears its end. 16 measures remain. I'm recalling these memories as I play. It feels soothing and melancholic. Yet, every part of me wants to cry. My eyes have been shut for a while now. It's not an attempt to hold back tears. This whole time, I've been forcing myself to, yet I can't. For every loss and setback I've faced, it's all hit me now. Though for some odd reason, I can't cry nor shed anything. I want to. I'm mad at myself that I can't. Part of me thinks something is wrong with myself. It's spread to me. To every inch of my body. To the core of my existence. It infects me, wherever I go. It's much more than nothing. I know what it is. This feeling of mine, this *roaming emptiness* persists.

Jane sits to my left. Her legs are crossed and her eyes are shut. She seems to be entranced by the music. My legs, my stumps, dangle over the piano bench. I don't move them as I sit still. It truly felt as if I were back to performing in front of everyone once again. An audience of mothers, fathers, children, classmates, and teachers. Now, I play for a solitary soul. A soul who remains a mystery to me. Whose aid I can

never truly thank enough. Who I've hurt already. Who I may hurt as time progresses. I'm sorry Jane... I'm sorry if I hurt you as they start to regrow.

The tempo of the song slows down. The decrescendo begins. Eventually, the song comes to a close. My final chord rings out.

"Was that *Corcovado*?"

"Yes, yes it was. I've made it obvious haven't I?"

A tear strolls down from her cheek. Nothing comes down from mine.

"It's... beautiful. I get why you hummed the song so much. To tell you the truth, this is the first time I've really, truly listened to music. You've given me a new experience. A very elegant one. Johnny... thank you. Did all of it come back to you?"

She wipes her face with her finger.

"It did. Thank you for the suggestion, Jane."

"You're welcome. I had a feeling it would come back to you. Muscle memory right?"

I chuckle a bit.

"Yes, I suppose it is."

I notice the stains on the keys. From left to right, a good majority of them have turned red. Not all of them.

"You uh... need help cleaning? I know I leave stains behind but I can still help out."

"Don't worry about it. I'll handle it."

I see her smile at me warmly.

"One of these days... you should teach me piano. I mean it."

"I'd love to."

I smile right back at her.

We're back in the room again. I'm laying down on the pillow once more as Jane sits in front of me with her hand on her chin, staring into my eyes. The stains from earlier have been cleaned up. I have to be more careful as to where my hand goes.

"I wanted to ask you. Your wife, what was she like?"

"That's a pretty broad question. To be honest, I'm not exactly sure where to begin."

"Well… I know where you two met. Was there anything else that happened you know, after?"

"After we met at the park, I exchanged contact information with her and we planned to meet at a coffee shop the following week. You ever been on a date before?"

"No, can't say I have. Romance doesn't really strike me in a world like this."

"Seriously? Never even been interested in a guy? Or a girl?"

She sighs.

"My answer is still no."

"Alright then. Well, I take it, you still want to hear about my coffee date?"

"Yes."

"I'll tell you then. At first, it was awkward. We hadn't seen each other in a week and weren't very comfortable with each other at that point. Texting and being in person are two different planes of interaction. I was comfortable with the former. The latter took a while to get used to. She had a tendency to laugh nervously and I had a tendency to be quiet. Both of us ate in between to lighten up the mood. She told me what she was busy with up until that point. Assignments, teachers, classmates, work, and all of that. I told her I was just studying

and working. Getting by as per usual. I guess I'm rather boring at first glance huh? Anyway, it was one of those situations where the ball had to get rolling. And when it did, it did. We gradually opened up more as this date of ours went on. It went from surface level conversations about school and work to our future. We had both feared how things might end up. If we chose the right career path, if we made enough money, our regrets in the past with those we met before. Like I said, I never mentioned Claire. But, I did mention old classmates of mine who I miss dearly. Ones that I never had the chance to see again. She had that as well, but her friend group was more close-knit than mine. I always saw my high school clique as acquaintances more than anything. I still cared for them though. After our coffee date, I had to walk her to the car. This is when we were really hitting off well, as well as we did in our initial encounter at the park. As we approached each other's car, she asked me to take a photo of her. Of course, I did. She posed in front of a tree as the leaves fell down and threw a small peace sign up. I kept that photograph with me when I joined the military."

I catch myself smiling like an idiot.

"After I took that photo, I remember she walked towards me and hugged me. She dug her head into my chest. Not for very long, but it was still nice all the same. She told me that I smelled nice and kissed me on the cheek. I watched as she walked to her car and waved goodbye to me. She had these dimples on her face when she smiled, she was ashamed of it but I always thought it was cute."

"That sounds very nice. You two had a good relationship huh? What was her name?"

"Eira."

"That's a beautiful name."

"Yes, yes it is. I still think about what might've happened to her though. I never saw her again after I joined the military. The world got too chaotic, and I ended up being stationed from country to country."

"I don't want this to sound too personal, but when was the last time you two saw each other?"

"Well, talking about her is personal anyway, you know? I'm not upset at you asking. But to answer your question, the last time I saw her, she was crying in my arms. We had both seen the state of the world at this point. People killing each other and abusing each other by any means. Global destruction, I'm sure you know it by now. I told her I was joining the military prior to that. She was upset then and even more upset the final day I was there. She held me tightly. Her arms wrapped against my back. She kept stalling again and again. Telling me I forgot this and that before I left. Stepped in front of me a couple times to block me, holding back tears until she couldn't. At some point, I had to go. I remember walking to my car, opening the door and seeing her for that final time. She just leaned back against the door frame and looked solemn. Didn't wave back at me when I waved at her. She just... wanted to get it over with."

My face looks down at the floor.

"To be honest with you, I'm not sure why I joined. I don't particularly care so much for the country I fought for or have a burning desire to save others. I just... did it. When I did, I had this regret that lasted with me for a long time. Particularly at the fact I had a child on the way. It was a stupid decision to join."

I sigh.

"At the time of joining, I didn't even seriously consider my own child. I guess the idea of having one didn't really click with me. I don't think it clicked with me at all until after all of this. In a way, I just feel selfish. Like a fool who only learns his lesson when the world beats him down. As if that is the only way I can learn or even feel a bit of remorse. Jesus christ... I don't even know the gender of my own kid"

Jane looks at me solemnly.

"Do you know how far she was during her pregnancy?"

"It was four months. A small bump had formed on her stomach. She would tell me that she felt the baby kicking in her stomach. I don't know what was wrong with me at the time... but I would often react with just total apathy. I could tell she was getting fed up with my disinterested response. And when I broke the news with her about me leaving... that's when everything boiled over. I regret it. I regret the way I handled it. All those years ago."

I chuckle a bit.

"This is gonna sound terrible, but when I heard she was pregnant, I felt as if part of my life was ripped away. That I could never have parts of my old life back. Sure, I had wanted this. Not as badly as she did, but I still wanted it all the same. But the day of, when I got wind of it, it was like something spat on my face. Like what I had built up until that point was going away."

My teeth grit. Something about it feels off, almost misaligned.

"We scheduled an ultrasound. But... my day to be drafted grew nearer. I didn't have a choice. I had to leave the day before the day of it arrived. I hated it. I hated the fact I had to do it. I hated the fact that I joined. I hated the fact that I didn't have a good reason at all. I hated the fact I enjoyed my time away from her. I feel guilty, I feel hateful, and I feel stupid. Every single one of those emotions eat me. Every. Single. Day. And it's all my fault. I had something good. Something special. And I'll never see that day come to pass. Maybe, maybe in another life I could've had that. A future with her, with my child. I could've had a happy ending. Something beautiful. Something akin to fantasy. But that's a fairy tale. None of this changes what happened."

I clench my fists. I feel the red gelatin like substance more than anything. It barely feels like there's bones in my fingers.

"I remember one time, when I was deployed. It was my first time seeing the world go to hell. Do you know where South America is? That's where I was. I saw people act like animals. That itself is quite the understatement. There was so much chaos. Fire had erupted within the streets. The orange haze had blinded me and blurred my vision. My nostrils couldn't get scent of smoke out of 'em. And yet, through all of this, I saw everything. A mob beating my fellow soldiers to death. Making them kneel, beating them with pipes and blunt objects, smiling as they stabbed through skin and bone. The funny part? They didn't stop at violence. No... that was all surface level. I saw a group of men tear the clothes off a female soldier in my unit. I watched as they smiled when the look of her face changed. She became so wide-eyed, so fearful. Yet, all four of them couldn't stop laughing. They were brimming with excitement at the sight of her despair. She screamed no. They didn't listen. I didn't see most of it, I saw them ripping her clothes off and one of them penetrating her against her will. My guess is, they took turns. All of this happened so fast."

Jane looks uneasy.

"But she wasn't the only one who met the same fate. There were more of them who did. Sometimes civilians, sometimes soldiers. It didn't matter who, everyone got caught in the crossfire. Murder, rape, or looting. Everything happened. There's no changing human nature, as awful as it is. I wanted to kill them. The people who did that to that poor woman. But so much was happening around me. The first person I killed was entirely an accident. He charged at me with a knife, and I shot him in the throat as a reflex. I remember him writhing and squirming on the ground so, so well. And when I did regain myself back in the moment, I ran like hell. A small group of this mob ran towards me. I was a fair distance off so I was able to lose them in a park. It was so nerve racking, watching this group of civilians hunt me down with the intent to kill me. You know, firepower means nothing when the other side has the numbers advantage. Or perhaps, we were simply taken by surprise. But as for this group of people, I didn't have it in me

to kill them. Simply because I was wounded and there was only one of me."

"Where are you going with this?"

"I'll tell you, don't worry. I got the chance to evade them by sneaking into a bathroom in the center. I locked the door quietly and watched outside the small window until they went away. Unfortunately, someone came through the door. I was cautious and got the drop on them. It turns out, it was a young woman. Probably no older than twenty. I pinned her down, made sure she didn't scream, and plunged a knife into her chest."

I blink my eyes. My body rises and falls slowly. I remember what I've done.

"There was something odd though. Her hair, the color of it, the length, the way her face looked. She looked like Eira. Her hand clutched her stomach when she died. That's when I saw it... a small ridge on her

stomach. Whoever she was, she was pregnant. I put my hand over her stomach, my glove was soaked in her blood. I felt it, a small kick. It resonated on my palm. I didn't know what to do. I just... sat there afterward, thinking about what I had done. All I wanted to do was sit there, next to the corpse of the woman I had murdered. All I could do was hold her hand and stare. Not like that made any difference, but it put my mind at ease."

Jane's voice lowers.

"Jesus Christ..."

"It wasn't my wife, but she looked like and reminded me of her. In retrospect, that could've been a civilian. Someone just trying to hide from all the chaos in the area. Her poor luck meant she ran into me. And my first instinct was to kill her. Call me a coward, but I wanted nothing but to go back after that day. Except you and I both know the world never did."

Jane looks at me with an expression of sadness. She can't mutter a word.

"Jane... I've done things. Horrible things to other people. And yeah, they deserved it. But part of me still regrets doing the things that I did. Killing, beating, inflicting violence by any means necessary. These people, if you could even call them that, were monsters. If you met them, the way I did, then I think you'd understand why I did the things I did. I beat them down with whatever I had. Sometimes I just used my hands. Do you know what the worst part of it was?"

Her breath shakes slightly.

"What?"

I grin a little.

"Part of me enjoyed it."

Chapter 17

"I can tell you're partially disgusted by me. There's no need to hide it."

"Johnny... what are you doing?"

"I'm not sure. I'm not sure what I'm going to do. I'm not sure what I'll even turn into. It's scary, but you can't stop the inevitable."

Jane's eyes widened slightly. We sit in silence for a moment. The room feels colder than before. Outside the circular window, tree branches sway in the pale moonlight. Their shadows stretch across the floorboards and crawl over my legs. Over my stumps. Over the new flesh growing from one of them. Jane opens her mouth, but nothing comes out. I laugh quietly to myself.

"It's alright. Really."

My fingers twitch against my knee. Its red liquid texture glistens across the cracks at my skin.

"I see the way you look at me sometimes. You try not to stare for too long, especially when the scabs move. The liquid inside floats around in their little bubble as I move my arms."

Her face tightens.

"That's not-"

"It is."

I lift my arms slightly. The skin along it spasms beneath the hairs. Something shifts beneath the flesh. Slowly writhing. Slowly mutating. Jane's face says everything I know already.

"Do you know how awful this world really is? The extent of humanity's cruelty? Do you?"

"Not first hand. No."

She's never looked so uncomfortable before. She looks down at my hands once again. Not for very long, but just enough. She tried to hide it afterward. Her expression doesn't change. Playing pretend as if the movement beneath my skin doesn't bug her. I know it does. I don't blame her for it.

"You look for the good in others don't you?"

She looks towards me.

"I think people can still care for each other."

I chuckle at that response.

"That's not what I asked."

The room remains silent. My fingers twitch against the stump of my left leg. Something there feels like it's moving. A hot, scorching feeling takes over in the center of the missing limb.

"You've been isolated here for far too long. I'm not sure if you've seen the extent of what I have. But I know what people become when they truly stop caring."

My eyes shift towards her.

"There was a man I encountered when scavenging. He seemed like someone I could trust. Invited me over to his house. It was in the middle of nowhere, just like this one. He saw me walking out on the porch. I was curious to see what he was like. Did I trust him? No. But in a world so lonely, I felt inclined to join. I remained alert, of course. He seemed like a kind man. Round glasses, blonde hair, square face, early 30's. He looked like he wouldn't hurt a fly."

Her face eases up, ever so slightly.

"I stepped inside and he held the door open for me. He had asked if I was a soldier, to which I said I was. I made sure my eyes were kept on him at all times. Trust is a very hard thing to come by nowadays. I waited for him to walk in front of me, and he motioned me to sit on the dining room table. The place was nice. Some old-Victorian furniture and dishes in a glass shelf. A window was above the sink, though the blinds were down. Oddly, there were two bowls on the table. One where he sat, and the other was placed where I was. My bowl was empty but his was full of what looked to be some meat on a bone. I asked him if he was expecting someone. He told me no. I asked him what the extra bowl was for and he said it was for the other person in the house. My eyes squinted at him. He put his hand out and motioned me to pick up the spoon in my bowl. He told me to take a bite. I didn't want to. This man.... something was off. Just then, I heard a loud scream coming from beneath me. It was muffled, as the floorboards dulled the noise. I put my hand over my hip, where my pistol was. He noticed and told me that it

was alright. I remember what he said. His voice was so soft, almost alluring."

"You wanna join in on the fun?"

"He had this disgusting smile on his face as he said that and grinned from ear to ear. He stood up from his chair and asked me to follow him downstairs. I'm not sure why I did, but I obliged. He opened a door leading to the basement. I took notice of the man's appearance. The kitchen itself was dim, the light bulbs seemed to have almost died out but the illumination leading downstairs were much brighter. He was frail and skinny. Didn't look like much of a threat. As we walked, I heard the stairs creak against my boots. They felt old, as if one small step meant I would fall through. The man reassured me that the stairs will hold fine, almost as if he read my mind. I nodded my head and continued to follow him towards our descent. As I did, I heard the muffled screams get louder and louder."

Jane looks at me with a serious look. Her eyes are piercing at me, staring right through my flesh.

"When I arrived at the bottom of the basement I saw nothing but an unfinished room and cracked walls. However, the screams still echoed through one of the walls. His hand pointed towards a bookshelf and he began to move the bookshelf to the right. I can tell it was heavy for him. I heard the bookshelf scrape against the concrete floor. A dim light peered through the opening as he did. When the bookshelf was fully out of the way, that's when I saw her."

Jane's head tilts. Her eyes squint and blink excessively.

"It was a little girl. Couldn't have been no older than 10 years old. Her ankle was chained to a radiator and she laid on a mattress in the room. The smell of it... I'll never forget. Urine, feces, blood, sperm, all of which contained itself in a small concrete room. I saw scratch

marks near the wall and noticed the girl's fingernails had been chipped. My hands clenched as I saw the man in front of me starting to smile."

"Do you want to take your turn?"

"I lunged at him then. Grabbed his shoulders, and pinned him against the wall. The man in front of me wasn't scared, he had this smile on his face the whole time."

"Don't you want to enjoy this? It's right there in front of you. You can do whatever you want."

"I grabbed his hair and slammed it against the brick wall. The back of his head ricocheted off and his eyes rolled backwards. His eyes had widened at this point. The smile wiped off his mug. And he was afraid. It seemed like he was about to say something, but I'm not sure if it was to beg or not. I had interrupted him, put my hand on his face, and spun him around. With as much force as I possibly could, I pushed his head into the nearby mirror. Glass shards had indebted to his face. He

started to scream. He asked me to stop. I grabbed the top of his head with one hand and pulled it downwards, his head was still encased in the mirror. On the way down, the broken glass shards made contact with his face, striking the ride side of his cheek all the way down to his jaw. He told me how much it hurt. I pulled his face down slower in return, until I eventually reached the bottom of the mirror. I pulled his head back and saw what he looked like. Pieces of glass were stuck onto it. Blood had dripped from his cheeks and mouth. He was gasping and his arms flayed weakly around me. My hand still grabbed the top of his head, pulling on his hair. I wasn't done yet."

I spread my fingers and clench them into a fist. Jane stares with a face full of intrigue and fear.

"I walked in front of him so he could face me. A sorry man was kneeling before my eyes. He had an ugly face now. With both hands, I grabbed the side of his head and struck him with my right knee, straight into the center of his face. A stream of blood followed out of his nostrils

as he slammed down onto the floor from the impact. I pounced on top of him and pulled out my flashlight from my right pocket. I swung onto the frontal part of his cranium. One strike. Two strikes. Four. Seven. At some point I no longer needed to count. A small hole had opened from his skull and a small chunk of his brain could be seen sticking out. The flesh from the top of his head made a wound. I forced my fingers in between, penetrating his brain. From here, I began to move my hands outwards. When I felt the squeamishness of his brain, I curled my fingers inside his head. I could feel the bone touch my fingertips. Blood kept oozing out from his opened wound. It trickled down to his neck and I felt a hefty resistance when I pulled. At first, it was quite difficult to spread the top of his head apart. But as I kept going, the skin began to loosen up. By that point, most of his face was covered in a sharp crimson. His left eye had partially popped out of its socket. His tongue contorted inwards. At this point he had to have been dead."

She's looking at me funny now.

"I picked up his corpse and stood it up vertically. With my right knee, I began to strike his chest. My legs had felt numb due to my long voyage earlier. However, the more I struck, I could feel the wear on my legs loosen up. It was as if the pain from before had dissipated in the heat of the moment. Perhaps the adrenaline took over. As I struck, I could feel the bones shift and crack. The costal cartilage felt as if they separated from the sternum. Popping noises came from the center of his body. At some point, a hole had ripped through the fabric of his shirt. It was the same size as my knee. A purple bruise began to take form. Then crimson. Then muscle. Then bone. I stopped and turned my attention to the girl."

Jane opens her mouth.

"What happened with her?"

I clear my throat.

"There were so many scars on her. She had only worn a dress that was tattered and torn. I had noticed urine beneath the mattress she was sitting on. There were cuts, specifically around the lower half of her dress, where her thighs were. Her legs were cut all over. Some vertical, some horizontal. Lines upon lines of red. The same was true for her arms. Underneath her pillow, a shard of broken glass stuck out. It's pointy end had blood on it. Her hair was disheveled and her right eye appeared to be bruised. I looked at her arms again. It appears something had dragged on it, leaving red marks behind. That girl... I wonder how could anyone do this? Why would anyone do this? She was crying. So, so many tears. Her arms and legs were curled together, she sat in the corner of the cell. I noticed now she was staring at me. Despite her head being buried by her legs, her eyes were visible. Through her tears, her gaze had pierced me. I looked to my right and saw the corpse of the man who had done this. I had killed the man, all in front of her. I lost myself. The man in front of me is gone, never to do such a thing again. But I've committed a sin all the same. I asked her what her name was. She shook her head. Tears still flowed down her face.

I began to laugh loudly. My throat begins to burn as I do.

"But something was off. She... didn't know. She had no idea just how awful she was being treated. It was... normal to her. Despite the abuse she took, she had no sense of how a child was meant to be treated at all. She told me how much it hurt. How she was in pain whenever she came to her room. The girl told me how nice the man was when the two of them ate in the kitchen. She was confused why he became so mean when he came to her room. I was told how much she dreaded going back in that room after, in the darkness. Her getting a bit of light was something she was ever so thankful for. The light bulb in the center of the room kept dimming, it was about to give out. I didn't know what to say. I was covered in blood and there was a child in front of me who was as confused as she was tortured. However, she was still oblivious. I picked her up with my hands and covered her eyes with it as I passed his corpse. They couldn't stop shaking. And as I climbed up the stairs and reached the top, I removed my hand from her face. She had immediately looked at the bowl of food on the table and asked if she could eat. Her

stomach growled when she asked. I obliged and let her down. She immediately sat down and started eating. Behind me, I shut the door to the basement and took a seat across from the girl. She took a spoonful of paste in her mouth, eating a big bite every time. It was almost as if nothing had happened. She had this smile as she gulped down food. And me? My hands just kept shaking, and I couldn't stop sweating. That's when I noticed something."

My throat soothes. I feel at ease.

"The living room was in view where I was sitting. I saw a picture on the table in the corner. A man holding a little girl over the top of his head. She's smiling ear to ear. I walked over and picked up the picture frame, the little girl in the photo was blonde and had hazel eyes. The same as the girl in front of me. I looked at the man in the photo, this time with greater clarity. Round glasses, blonde hair, and a square face. They were... related."

Jane's voice becomes shaky.

"The girl. What happened to her?"

"I took her to a community and filled them in on what happened. They took it from there. The last I ever saw of her was her confused face. She had asked me why she couldn't stay at home. I didn't say a word. I'm not sure what happened to her after."

Silence lingers between both of us. Jane looks pale and her hands are folded tightly together. I look at the crack in the floor.

"You know what the worst part of it was?"

She hesitates.

"What?"

"She cried more when she left the house than when she was inside of it."

Jane's expression changes.

"That girl never understood what happened to her. To her all of it was normal. The room. The chains. The abuse. Him touching her. She thought that's what life was supposed to be."

I rub my fingers against my temple. It feels slimy and slippery.

"And me? I couldn't stop thinking about it afterward. For months on end. I keep thinking about that basement. About that smell. About the way she smiled when she ate. I rack my head and wonder how many times that man sat across from her and acted normal. How many conversations they had. How many times she was tucked into bed after he hurt her."

Jane says nothing.

"I began to realize something after enough time passed."

I look straight at her.

"The world doesn't break all at once."

My fingers twitch. The stump of my left leg feels warm. Something is enveloping inside of it.

"It breaks slowly. Quietly. One person at a time."

My jaw tenses. Skin in my left leg begins to form, the surface of it looks rough. Scabs and hairs appear on my thigh. Past my knee, a jagged and twisted foot is created. My toes twist and contort. I hear the sound of bones cracking within. Jane watches in horror and apathy. She can't say anything. My mutation has expanded to another limb.

And so, I feel an inch closer to being complete.

Chapter 18

Jane is sleeping. Our conversation earlier seemed to have mentally exhausted her. As my leg regenerated, I recalled the way her face looked. Tired. Empty. Confused. Questioning everything. She didn't say a word after I told her about the girl. Just silently walked over to the other side of the room and went to bed. I've upset her, haven't I?

What a very beautiful woman she is. Pale skin. Long flowing hair. I remember when I was nothing but an amputee. She held me in her arms, like a mother holding her newborn child. Her touch felt so soft, so warm.

I crawl over to her. My hands stain the floor as I move. The wood groans beneath my weight. I feel myself become heavier. Am I back to my normal weight yet?

My face gets a little closer towards Jane. Upon a closer look, she really does look like her. The shape of her lips. The size of her breasts. The way her hair falls over to the side of her face. Even down to the way her chest slowly rises and falls as she sleeps.

Eira... she's like her.

My breathing slows down for a while. I stop as I reach her. My eyes look at her for a while. She doesn't notice me. One of my hands twitches against the floor. The skin around my fingers writhes slightly. Thin strands of green leak from beneath my scabs. I no longer pay attention to it anymore.

My eyes remain fixed on Jane. For a minute there, I imagine Eira laying there instead. My chest tightens at the thought of it. I slowly reach out my hand towards Jane's face. Then stop. My fingers hover inches away from her skin.

I want to feel her again. Another person. The touch of pale skin contacting mine. Something intimate. Something warm. Something physical. I want to pretend so badly. Pretend that none of this ever happened. That the world outside still existed. That I can still go home.

But something's wrong.

Not with her.

But with me.

I look down at my reflection in her half-opened eye.

The yellow in mine glows in the darkness.

She remains fast asleep.

My eyes open as daylight engulfs my retinas. I still feel weird. Johnny's words, what he said, what he's changing into. I'm not sure how to feel. He's turning into something. Something awful. I can tell. But... what? What do I even do? I'm not even sure what to say to him. I'm not sure where this goes between me and him. Maybe, just maybe in the slight offchance, this won't end in a horrible way. I'm hoping so. All I can do is hope. I don't want to abandon him. I can't... I can't just do that to somebody.

I look to my left and see bloodied handprints on the floor. The fingers point towards my direction. Did he do anything to me when I was sleeping? Johnny's fast asleep now. His chest rises up and down, his singular reformed legs stick out. The blanket he was sleeping on is tossed into the corner of the room.

I feel exhausted. The weird part is I don't feel it physically. Nothing on my body feels out of place. Mentally, I feel worn.

My legs stretch out. I lift myself up and walk towards the door. I feel odd. I can't shake it. I know why I feel this way, yet I also can't put a finger on it. All I want to do is figure out what to do. Or figure out a way out of this situation. Though, I also know I'm the one who brought him here.

That doesn't mean it's my fault. I'm aware of the risk I took. But I didn't know nor could I have ever known that this would've occurred. It's simply... inhuman.

My hand reaches towards the bathroom door and I stare at myself in the mirror.

There's lipstick, mascara, and a hairbrush on the sink.

I have no need to use it.

Somebody came here.

Someone I took under my care.

My hair is tangled from sleeping.

I don't have the desire to fix it.

Not even to look pretty.

My face...

I look awful.

The house is quiet.

No footsteps outside.

No voices.

No gunshots.

Only a man breathing in the other room.

I return to the bedroom again. The man greets me with a warm smile. Yet, I can't help but feel off about his appearance. Is it his grotesque body? Is it the way he's talked as of late? Is it my concern he's changing into something... else? Perhaps, it's all of it.

"Good morning, Jane."

"Good morning, Johnny."

The room goes quiet. I see the stains in the center of the room. The red handprints from the other night, leading towards me.

"Are you okay? You don't look so good."

"I'm fine. I'm gonna find something to clean up the mess here."

"Sounds good."

I grab a bucket full of water and a rag from downstairs, then head back to the room to clean up the mess. Johnny awaits me with a cold expression in his eyes. I crouch down beside the stains and soak the rag in water. I scrub the floorboards and watch as the stains fade out. Johnny watches me the entire time. Usually, when I clean the room, his eyes wander towards somewhere else. The ceiling. The window. The walls. But not today. His gaze follows every movement I make. I can feel it against my skin. I wring the rag out into a bucket. The water turns pink.

"Did you sleep alright?"

"I slept well enough."

His voice sounds calmer than usual. My attention focuses on his new leg. It hangs off the side of the blanket. The skin twitches from it every now and then. Small, incremental movements beneath flesh. His fingers tap against the floorboard. Small puddles of red are left as he does.

"You were moving around last night."

"Yes, yes I was."

He sounds calmer than usual.

"The fingerprints... they point towards me. What were you doing?"

A small grin lights up across his face.

"Getting a good look at you. You have been taking care of me after all."

"You're making me uncomfortable, you know."

My heart's not racing. My voice is as calm and stable as ever, despite the situation. He chuckles.

"Sorry about that then. I didn't mean anything by it."

Me and him both know there's something else to it.

"Your leg. I see it's back. How do you feel about it?"

I wring out the rag into the bucket. It slowly turns into a darker shade of red.

"It's almost like I'm going back to normal. But you know how it is."

I nod my head up and down. The last bit of crimson is cleaned up off of the floorboard. All that's left is a bucket of dark red water. I toss the rag in the bucket and stand up, planning to toss the liquid out. Then, he talks.

"Hey Jane... wait."

"What?"

"Yesterday, I knew I irked you. I've made you uncomfortable and feel uneasy. I can't apologize enough for that. I know you're helping and I also know you're trying your best to work with me, given my... condition. I say these horrible things, these awful stories. I'm aware I'm pushing it. But... these things, they've changed me. Turned me into the person I am. Both the good and bad."

He stops talking abruptly.

"I get it. The things you've seen. The people you've dealt with. I know how much they can hurt someone. But there's a limit to that you know? And yeah, the world is awful. I agree with you there. But still it's..."

I go quiet myself and take notice of Johnny. He's looking down at the floor. He shifts his jaw. His fingers wiggle. His left leg writhes slightly beneath the blanket. He's gone quiet for a while.

"There's something else you want to say isn't there? I can tell from the look on your face."

He clenches his jaw and inhales.

"There's someone I remember."

Chapter 19

I sit down in front of Johnny. His face has looked at the floor for the past couple minutes. Every now and then, he blinks and grunts. I'm not going to say anything. Whenever he decides to talk, he will. It's just... been quiet.

I recall his story from yesterday. The man he beat mercilessly. The girl he saved, who was blissfully unaware of the horrors surrounding her. How brutal he was, how afraid he seemed when he recalled seeing the girl, how remorseful he was when he saw her after. I saw all of those feelings wash away once his story was done. He had looked as empty as ever after the fact.

I recall the sadness on his face when he told me about the pregnant woman he had murdered. He had choked on his own words when he recalled the event. He didn't say much after. His own face did the talking. I could see it in his eyes.

I recall the remorseful look he gave me when he told me about leaving his wife for the military. How much of an idiot he felt like when he tossed what he had left. How he can never regain what he had lost. And maybe, just maybe, if he could go back in time, things would've changed between him and Eira. Perhaps he could've had a family. A child whose name he couldn't come up with. A regret he'll never live down.

I recall the man who laid in my arms as he told me the story of his first love. The girl whose life was abruptly taken away from her. From an accident. An accident that no one saw coming. An event no one had any control over. One that affected him for the rest of his life. One that chipped away at him, day by day. Sometimes small, sometimes big. Sometimes, that feeling just passes.

I remember the person, the man, the tortured soul who played piano in front of me. Who hasn't played in decades. Whose heart rings out for the people he's lost. Who lives with regret, hate, and mercy. Who still played with the talent he never lost. Who still played with the memories of those he loved. I saw him. Looking upwards, his eyes shut and feeling everything. Every little emotion searing through. A man who tries to cry. A man who's too whittled down to feel even that emotion.

And I remember... I remember the way I felt when I saw him play. For the first time in my life I heard music. Calming. Serene. It was almost as if I could forget about what the world was for just a moment. He was the man who showed me a different aspect of life I may never forget. One that I wish to cherish. I had never smiled at something so hard in a while. I'd never had the urge to bask in peace and cry all at once.

There's something. Something still in there. Even if he tries to hide it or bury it. I still see the man beneath all the horrors. I know why he slips. And despite his appearance, the ways he's worrying me, and his declining mental state.

He's still... human.

Johnny's voice rings out. It's soft and sincere.

"Jane... I... You're not the first person I've gotten close with after the world imploded. There was someone else. Someone I grew to care for. It was after I had killed that girl in the bathroom. I had... I had lost myself. Every little emotion of mine came through. Yet, I couldn't feel anything. I walked out of that bathroom, blood on my gloves, hands completely still, both nervous and calm. A little while later, another part of my unit popped up in the area. They were called in on the scene after they got word that there were little to no survivors. I was picked up in a truck and driven to a location where a plane was planning to depart. On the ride there, I was in the back of the truck with a couple soldiers who I didn't recognize. They saw me, covered in blood and shaken up. When I first saw them, one of them, a girl with brown hair, put her hand on my shoulder and looked into my eyes. She didn't say a word. I had a feeling she wanted to console me, but I suppose she had a feeling that it wouldn't mean much. She ended up just nodding her head and motioned

me to sit. I did as she asked. And next to me, a man was humming to himself. His head was laid back, humming a song I didn't recognize. He turned his head and smiled at me. The blood on my uniform and gloves didn't seem to bother him. He told me his name was Takeya."

I hear him swallow. He inhales and exhales quietly.

"Admittedly, I was surprised a Japanese man had been in the same truck as me. My prior unit consisted of mostly Americans. There was the occasional European here and there, but no one else. Having somebody whose accent was native to a different country was something I wasn't used to. I'll be honest, he bugged the shit of me. Wouldn't shut up and he kept trying to talk to me but I wouldn't budge. He kept calling me some big strong American man. To be fair to him, he was pretty built as well. Not to my extent, but certainly more bigger and fit than your average male in Japan. He spoke English pretty well though. Though, his accent made it difficult to discern what he was saying sometimes. But it was clear he had a good grasp of the English language. And even though he was talking my ear off. I still kept my

mouth shut. He, of course, noticed. So, he took off his helmet and pulled out a card of his favorite baseball player he kept in the interior of it."

"Look here! You're American right? That means you love baseball! Yankees and Dodgers or whatever. You know the teams. This guy, right here, is my favorite!"

"I told him I didn't care much for sports. Hell, I didn't even recognize the guy on the card. Next thing you know he's in my ear like an annoying gnat asking me all these questions. What America's like, if the women there really have big breasts like they say, and if we're as fat and obese as they hear on the news. I told him some of it was true. And he began to spill all the things he wanted to do in America. Sight see New York, go to the Golden Gate bridge, watch a Yankees game, and of course, motorboat the large breasts of an American woman. He told me he'd feel especially lucky if he got to have sex with one. I told him he'd have better luck in another life. He said I was just being negative and that, just like him, I've got an opportunity to travel the world. I told him that the world was reaching its breaking point. That there was no

feasible way I would be able to enjoy "traveling" because of what me and him had to do. What our jobs were. That's when I realized that idiot got me talking."

He chuckles. I watch as a smile forms on his face. He looks at me warmly.

"On the ride to the plane, he started to ask what America was really like. What state I was from, what I did before. I was just surprised at his vast knowledge of the USA. It was quite clear he really wanted to go there. I asked him if he joined just because this might be a free ticket to travel there. He had said that it was but that wasn't his primary goal. His main intention for joining was a lot more simple. He simply felt like he didn't have a purpose in life. He had done as much as he could. Takeya didn't bother finishing college or anything like that. In a twisted way, the world imploding on itself had afforded him the opportunity to be somewhat free. So, he took his chance and ended up there, with me. He told me he didn't care about making friends in Japan or anything like that. He had gotten particularly good at learning the English

language in his teenage years. Partly because it was a requirement in school. But, English turned to something he enjoyed learning. He never thought he would have any use for it until now.

That's when I started opening up to him. I told him I had a wife and kid on the way. He congratulated me and asked when I plan to return. I didn't know. Nor did I tell him about the argument me and Eira had before I left or that I had to leave the day before I was deployed. I wasn't sure if she even wanted to see me again. Actually, I wasn't sure if I could see her at that point, even if I wanted to. Takeya knew the topic was sensitive so he switched the subject to something else. He wanted to know if I had any particular hobbies. He collected baseball cards and figurines of anime girls. Plus, he did rock climbing and walked late nights on the streets of his hometown in Shinjuku. I told him I worked on cars, my car specifically. I was never much of a modification guy, but I always liked to maintain and make my car look better when I could. That, and walking around in a park or city area. Takeya laughed and put his hand on my shoulder. My uniform was still soaked in blood. His hand had stained red and he wiped his hand on his pants afterward."

His face tightens up a little bit.

"Eventually, we arrived at the plane. Takeya went out of the truck first, and I followed behind him. When we were about to board, Takeya had motioned me to sit next to him. I chuckled when he asked, but I took him up on his offer. From there he spouted more bullshit about what he wanted to do if he ever got to America and I simply told him what it was like to live there. He wouldn't shut up about wanting to meet women with double D and E cups that whole plane ride. That, and how all the women in Japan were flat-chested. He told me he was a modest man who didn't mind the chest size of a woman. But he also told me he had a burning desire to bury his face in a woman of "bigger qualities," or so he says."

His eyes peer towards the ceiling of the roof now. He stares intensely at a crack in the center of it.

"When we got back to the base, I was shocked to find I was stationed somewhere else. The old one didn't have the space required to hold more people. This place wasn't just one building, but a series of multiple structures crowded together. People from all over the world began to arrive. There were people who stood in the center, visible for everyone. A mix of politicians, military leaders, and CEOs, all from different countries. There were translators next to them. One of them spoke, this one in English. It was explained to us that countries from different continents were banding together. People were killing each other left and right, doing more and more atrocious acts. It was difficult keeping everyone in check. Funds and resources were running dry and so various governments and cultures collided. This was when the world began to collapse. We were still ordered to keep the peace. To still disperse and be sent out to countries that needed aid and support. I had lost hope to meet Eira at that point. Though, a small part of me wanted to see her again. To apologize, to go back into her arms. But the other part of me? The other part of me knew that I would never be given that opportunity.

And that's when it hit me. I was stuck there for the foreseeable future. Left to be deployed from place to place. "Keep the peace" or whatever. See how humanity implodes. Watch the violence and atrocities right before me occur every single day. I didn't have a choice. All I had to do now was accept the reality that awaited me. After the man who spoke concluded his speech. I saw the fear in his eyes. I saw the fear in the politicians and CEOs. They didn't have the guts to control it themselves. They sent us to clean up their mess. A mess they didn't want to touch. We were disposable. And Takeya knew how I felt. He didn't say a word. He was watching my reaction during that speech. All he did was put his hand on my shoulder.

Takeya said he knew some guys here and once we were free to walk around, he showed me where they were. A group of 3 guys were playing cards at a table. They were friends in his unit and one of them asked if I wanted to play cards with them. I didn't say a word, but Takeya said I would've loved to play with them. I sat down and played some blackjack. I wasn't too interested in the game itself. They were all passively talking about their lives up until that point. One talked about

how bullshit it was that they were stuck doing this. Another one talked about how he figured everyone here would be doomed to continue. That he really knew that there was no going back from all of this. That we should all just suck it up and accept where we are. The other guy just didn't seem to care. To him, it was an interesting shake up in his life. He figured he'd have some fun. Then, they asked me what I felt about the situation, what my name was, and how I got here. I fed them some bullshit about how I just joined for the hell of it. That I didn't have anything going on in my life. I said to them that I had no idea why I joined, didn't care about my country or fighting for glory or for protection. I just did it. I didn't mention Eira or my kid on the way. I didn't trust these guys.

Our game wrapped up and while Takeya knew them, I never met the other three again. He had walked with me after the game ended and followed me to the sleeping quarters. His hands were behind his head. He had this grin on his face. It was almost as if he wasn't affected by it at all. I asked him why he was sticking so close to me."

"I can see the emptiness in your eyes."

"I looked down at the floor after that. Like a robot, I began to lay my bed out in my sleeping quarters. Since the place we were staying at was packed, nobody was assigned to any specific area to sleep in. More of a first come, first serve kind of deal. Takeya noticed and helped me set up my bed. Organized some of the stuff for me and told me to take a shower. I had been covered in blood at that point anyways. He pulled out some clothes from out of his bag and said I could take them. But he was unsure if it would fit me. I thanked him anyway.

After I got out of the shower, Takeya had already made his bed. Of course, he chose the bed next to mine and asked me to sit next to him. At this point, it was early in the morning. I wanted to get some rest and nap. But, I felt compelled to sit next to him. He had asked me to take a look around the barracks. I took notice of the people there. Everyone was from various ethnicities, cultures, and countries. Men and women were of various heights, body types, and skin tones. Some are more scared than others. Some are more calm and ready. Some more foolish, some delusional, some at ease. Many people were getting their

beds ready, others were talking, some knew each other, some made new friends. A good chunk of them were sleeping, others played cards, others cleaned their weapons. Hell, some of them were flirting. I had asked Takeya why he asked me to look around. He looked at me and had this big smile on his face."

"*The world has destroyed itself. Yet, look around my friend. Everyone from all over. Regardless of cultures and any other differences they might have, they are all here. Grouped up in this one place. Talking, laughing, playing, flirting. Yet, people are still making their best efforts all the same. It's funny. Everyone here almost seems united, at the expense of the world collapsing. A girl in front of us is laughing at a joke. That soldier, who is clearly exhausted, is trying to flirt with her. Look to our right, a man is teaching someone younger how to speak and read a different language. People are sharing cigarettes and trading food for something they prefer. A woman who sat alone, staring at a photo of what I can only presume to be someone she cares for, now has another person she's talking to who understands her. Both seemed to have become friends. For people to get along, as peacefully as this, we had to destroy each other, didn't we? In a way, all of this is beautiful.*"

"He seemed... hopeful. Takeya told me to get some rest and that he'll shut up for the rest of the night. He knew I was exhausted. I

thanked him for today and he told me that it was just Japanese hospitality. Said he'd talk to me tomorrow. For the first time in a while, I had gotten a good amount of rest."

Johnny stares away from the ceiling. He turns his eyes towards me.

"From that day on, me and Takeya were deployed together. Military units themselves were no longer organized by anyone higher up. The world kept breaking as it did spinning. We got less organized in return. Resources were strained and so was manpower. What was once a mission that started off with light amounts of firepower, ended up with everyone involved being strapped to the teeth. Lethal force was no longer the last resort. It was authorized to use whenever. I could feel everybody losing hope. Morale was dwindling amongst everyone. As we got deployed on missions. The same ordeal happened. Get deployed to some country. Could be in Europe, could be in South America, could be Asia, and do some crowd control or keep people in check. We would start off peaceful. Hold our shields in front of them, help them get

resources back. But, it was pointless. A lot of people had gotten violent at this time. I don't fault them. When the world has lost its resources, people lose their homes, their families, their way of life. How could they be anything but frenzied? You can't control people, let alone a mob when they have nothing left. Nothing to bargain with or leave any room for peace. Sometimes, they will just lose themselves.

So, mission after mission, day after day it would end up the same. People got violent, we killed them in return. We got so armed with weaponry the idea of peace was no longer considered. Eventually, word got around that we were just killing people and inciting fear left and right. That we couldn't be trusted and that soldiers were killing civilians. If you ask me, peace was no longer a realistic goal. We tried that, we really did. There was no other choice except to combat violence and atrocities with itself.

I had gotten good at it. Killing people. Part of me hated that fact, part of me enjoyed it. I still tried my best to maintain some sense of disassociation from it. That what I should be doing was necessary, but also that I shouldn't enjoy it for what it is. It took a toll on me. Takeya

noticed. He'd crack jokes in the middle of our missions. Tried to keep me sane, keep my morale up. It didn't work all the time but I noticed the effort. I also noticed the way he was changing.

At first glance, I always thought his upbeat nature kept him from spiraling. But as we went to more places, we killed more and more people. I saw him. The look on his face. The way he laughed when someone begged to be spared. When he pointed a pistol to their temple and pulled the trigger. When he stabbed someone in the throat or shot a guy in the mouth. He took pleasure and often gloated about how good of a sharpshooter he had become. Granted, the people he killed were going to kill him. But... I didn't expect him to change as much as he did.

After our missions I'd always ask him how he felt. After the first one we did together, he was shaken up but still tried to keep a positive attitude. But the more we did it, the less shaken up he was. He was enjoying it. Enjoying what was happening. At some point, he stopped hanging with me after missions. I wasn't upset at this, but I took notice of him hanging with the same three guys who invited me to play cards with. Gradually, me and Takeya grew apart. We still went on

missions together and he'd talked to me then. But after, right back to those same three men. I'm not sure what they discussed.

I could tell something was up with everyone in the barracks though. We had lost plenty of people up until this point and what was once a bustling place of soldiers with slight hints of optimism turned into an emotionless, empty void of a place to live. I would hear what the soldiers talked about. Some of them miss the old ways of life. Their families, friends, and the things they used to have. But a good majority of them, they loved it. I talked about how great it felt. To be free. To be vindicated. To do whatever they want. They had no consequences for their actions. I would hear them laugh and joke about what they've done. Killing was just the tip of the iceberg. They wondered what they could get away with, if they could even do it. Of that group of people, Takeya was one of them.

I'd watch him talk with that friend group of his. I knew something was going on, but I wasn't sure what. I tried to talk to him about it. But each time I did, he just blew me off. Most of those days ended up with just me sitting on my bed staring at the ceiling. Watching

the numbers of my barracks dwindle. Old military generals, politicians, and CEOs all phased out. Some died, some went somewhere else, to places I have no idea about. To do "business" they didn't want us to be informed of. I recognized one of them later, in a warehouse. My hand was on his throat. He had raped a young woman, along with four other men. But that was years later.

At this point, we had no leaders. No reason to be sent out, no reason to stay either. We were still getting resources. Guns, weapons, food, and things like that. All just to stay afloat. But everyone knew resources were dwindling. Any reason or morale left, had dwindled. And then it happened, on a random night."

He exhales heavily. Almost as if it were a sigh of defeat. He begins to choke on his words. A tear falls down his cheek.

"I awoke to the sound of gunshots. When I jolted out of bed, I was able to discern more noises. Screaming, laughing, running, explosives. Everybody was panicking. I noticed it came from one of the other buildings. But still, I remained alert and grabbed a rifle and a

knife. I was sleeping in my uniform that night. Other people gave up wearing it since they saw no point. I was able to quickly arm myself and grabbed what I could from my bag. Other people in the same room as me had done the same. But... there weren't many of us. Only five, including me. The four of them moved out to check the commotion. I didn't join them. I moved in a different direction. There were more of the same noises there. I told them I would check it out but they said I should stick with them. I didn't listen. I stepped out of the room, walked towards the noise, and headed outside.

Fire had spread out from one part of the building in front of me. An orange haze had surrounded me once again. My vision blurred from the flames. The smell of smoke returned. I heard screaming from both men and women coming from inside. I rushed in and kicked the door down. I saw everything. It was just like South America once again. Male soldiers stabbed and shot each other. Some begged for their lives. Others had no reason to beg. The ones who pulled the trigger had a smile on their face and grinned as they killed. Others were kicked down onto the floor and beaten by a group of men. One of the bodies they

kicked down stopped moving, and they kept kicking and laughing. Then, I saw a couple people looting the bodies of the dead and stealing the memorabilia from underneath the beds. But that... that wasn't it. The fire hadn't spread to this side of the building, instead a corner far off. Yet, near that corner, I saw a group of men.

A good chunk of the female soldiers had their clothes ripped. They were fighting back as best as they could. But couldn't do anything as other men were pinning them down. One of them pried her mouth open, sticking it inside there as another man penetrated her vagina. She tried to scratch him and hit him, but all he did was hold her by the wrists. She didn't have the physical strength to get him off of her. Much of the same story happened with the other female soldiers. I averted my gaze towards something else. I saw a man, the same man who flirted with that woman whom Takeya pointed out, having his way with her. She kept screaming, saying to get off him, telling him to stop, telling him no. He didn't care. Other men kept saying to them that none of this was a part of the plan. But they did nothing to stop it, they themselves

were far too gone anyways. Their uniforms and faces were stained with blood. And that's when... that's when I saw him."

His jaw clenches. I see his face start to squirm.

"Takeya had his hands around a girl. There was a good distance between me and him. She was someone from our unit. Someone I had a passing knowledge of. I remember her. It was the same brown-haired lady who put her hand on my shoulder before I went on the truck. The one who got me here in the first place. She was being pinned down and ravaged by him, like a frog being dissected. There wasn't a hint of kindness in his eyes, only straightforward sexual pleasure. He flashed a knife and rubbed it against her thigh. Her pants had been removed. He tapped the tip of it on her a couple times. I ran towards him. I saw him slowly moving the blade across her clothes. It slowly sliced the fabric of her uniform, revealing more and more skin. She couldn't scream. One of his hands was on her throat. I saw her face getting progressively more purple as I ran. That's when he saw me. That's when I saw the last of him.

I tackled him onto the floor and removed the knife from his hand. Despite the commotion going on, the soldiers were too focused on their actions to pay any attention to me. I was a stronger man than he was and pinned him down onto the floor. He couldn't escape. I began to punch him in his face. I watched as a black eye formed around him and he began to bleed from his mouth. Eventually, I struck so hard I knocked a good bit of his teeth out. He told me to stop, but I kept continuing. That's when he tried to grab the gun from my holster. I grabbed his hand and broke his wrist. He screamed in agony. And that's when I put both of my hands around his neck. He started to flail around with his broken wrist. Trying to hit me with it. Punching me in the face with his other hand and trying to jab his thumb in my eye. I bit his thumb down when he tried that. Biting through bone is hard, but when I was able to rip it off, I spat it out next to him. The taste of his blood stained my tongue. But still, I never stopped. I didn't want to. He deserved it. My hands remained firmly around his throat. His face turned into a slight hue of purple. He tried to grab the knife from my belt. Even with a missing thumb and broken wrist, he still tried to put

up a fight. But he couldn't. At some point, the hand that reached out to my knife stopped trying to move. The loss of oxygen was clouding his head, his consciousness was gradually fading. I saw his face turn into a deeper violet. I stared into his eyes as I did. That's when I realized, a tear had fallen down my cheek. Then another. Then another one after that. I couldn't stop crying. But I still tightened my grip on him. Even though I felt his legs dangle and squirm behind me and his arms flailing, I did nothing except make sure he could never breathe again. He kept trying to say my name. Tapping my hand around his neck. But I saw his face. His eyes. The fire began to spread across the building now. Some people began to leave. Not me. I still watched him. I wanted to make sure the light faded from his eyes. And sure enough, after a few more seconds of struggling, I saw his eyes roll to the back of his head. He was gone. I removed my hands from his throat and wiped the tears from my face. I stood up and got a good look at him. A red imprint of my hand on his throat, a shattered right hand that sat upwards, a left hand with a missing thumb, and eyes that turned white. Next to him was his helmet. I looked inside of it and saw it, the same baseball card

he showed me when we first met. I took it and put it in my pocket. I'm sure I left that in my bag somewhere. I look at it from time to time. Just to remember.

I turned my gaze towards the woman. She was covering her skin with a blanket. Fire began to spread towards the building. We heard more commotion outside. I grabbed the pistol from Takeya's hip and handed it to her. Her bag was right next to her, and I said I would hold it as the both of us had to leave. When we stepped outside, we saw it. The same screaming, the same sounds, the same violence. I told her to run and to stick behind me. The exit to our living quarters wasn't too far off. So, we ran like hell to get to the outside exit. And we did. We avoided much of what was occurring near us. Part of me wanted to go back and save them, save everyone who was stuck there. Yet, the other part of me knows that was a suicide mission. She knew I wanted to go back, but told me we had to go. I knew she was right, and the both of us began to move.

When we were a safe distance away, we began to just sit on the side of the road. A wooded area had engulfed us. I tossed her bagged

over to her. She reached for a pair of pants and she told me to look away. A bit confusing, considering she was pants less the whole time and I was watching her put it on instead of off. But, I obliged all the same. She put new clothes on and we ended up just taking a rest near a tree. I remember she laid her head on my shoulder when I was sitting. I dozed off shortly after. When I woke up, I remember the back of my head hurt. The woman was wide awake and told me she had directions to a nearby base to head to. I ended up following her to that base after walking for almost 8 hours. We ended up staying there for a while until I had to move to a different community to watch over them. That's actually the last community where I lived before I was... here. I never saw that woman after that. But she did tell me she could never thank me enough for saving her that day. That was the day before I had to leave. I smiled at her."

Johnny smiles at me. His face appears warm and gentle. Yet simultaneously, his transformation is slowly overriding it. I am both comforted and unsettled by his story.

"Why did... why did you tell me this?"

"Because people are complicated Jane. Because humanity will never make sense as they are. People hurt each other in the most atrocious ways imaginable, yet there will always be those who do the opposite. There are those who love and care for one another despite everything. Despite the world breaking them, despite other people not deserving of their care, despite being used for selfish gain. Human beings contradict themselves constantly, yet it all exists at once.

I know what Takeya did was unforgivable. In fact, I despise him for it. But even so, I'll always miss him. I'll remember the fond days I had with him. The day me and him first met. The way he would crack jokes with me during our missions, or when he offered me a drink when he saw me feeling down. He would let me just rip my feelings out when it was just me and him in the barracks. On the same table, standing outside, at lunch, bullshitting about life. Saying stupid shit just to pass the time. I remember all of it.

But I will never, never forgive him for what he did. I will stand by the fact that I had to put him down. But I can't erase the good

memories either. Awful and beautiful memories can coexist inside the same person. I think it's okay to miss someone, even if they were awful."

"Why can't you just despise him? I don't understand..."

"Because people are the sum of their own sins and successes. It's contradictory, but both of those can exist at the same time. I still cared for the man that he was before, even if that version of him died long ago. To me, he was both the same person and a completely different one."

Johnny chuckles at me. The skin on his face begins to peel. But this look of his.... it's not malicious, nor is it double-sided in any way. No deception. No bitterness. Just something painfully genuine. Warmth. Kindness.

And even as his body grotesquely forms into something else, something inhuman. I can't help but notice the man in front of me is still trying to hold onto something good. To keep something alive within himself, no matter how terrible his situation becomes.

Johnny sits up. The circular window pierces daylight behind him once more. He spreads his arms out, as if to feel the bask of the sun. I hear the skin crawl and twitch from his right stump. The final

starts limb to take form. Soon, he may have it all back. Not back to the way it was before, but he'd still have something. Something to have back.

I hear him utter something. Something quiet.

"Human nature is so cruel and violent. Yet, so kind and merciful."

Chapter 20

He's had that smile on his face for a while now. Johnny's not sleeping, despite his eyes being closed. He's absentmindedly humming a tune. A song I'm not familiar with.

"What are you humming?"

"A song Takeya used to hum. He hummed it all the time. When we were deployed, when we relaxed at the barracks, when we got drunk, or when we ate lunch. I asked him what song he hummed frequently. At that point, he had hummed it repeatedly, but the thought of asking him never crossed my mind up until that point. He told me it was called *Kiss Me* by Sheena Ringo. It kept his spirits up whenever things got hectic. Sometimes I'd catch him listening to his CD player alone at night. Sitting on his bed, looking up at the ceiling, he'd smile. On that day he noticed me staring at him. He had paused his CD player and took his headphones off. His hand reached out over to me with both of those objects in hand and asked me if I wanted to listen. I took him up on his offer, as I could barely sleep as well. He restarted the track for me, and I

listened to it. It's an upbeat song. She sings in English for the very beginning and then the instruments kick in. I remember he was geeking out about it to me. How it wasn't the most popular track on the album. How the track was a little basic compared to the rest of the compositions in it. But that was alright with him. To him, even if it was basic, he enjoyed that. Simpler things were better. Takeya liked the song so much because of how romantic and lovey-dovey the lyrics were. I couldn't understand a lick of it as the rest of the song was in Japanese. Except for the ending, which was in English. To him, the song reminded him of a life he never had. About a romance that never blossomed. He knew a girl who moved away to a different city. They never spoke again. He's not sure what happened to her. After she moved, he tried to meet with different women. But he never felt anything between any of them. I remember he always told me he had always wondered what it was like to love another person. To fall in love with someone else. I never knew how to answer that. He tried to get me to listen to the rest of the album, but I declined as we had to wake up early for a mission that day. He rolled his eyes at me and wished me goodnight."

I'm reminded of something.

"You have his baseball card in your bag right?"

"Yes, I do."

I grab his back from the right side of the room and toss it in front of him.

"Which pocket is it in?"

He sticks his hand out and says something.

"I got it, don't worry."

I watch as his fingers unzip the front pocket of his backpack. He sticks his hand in the open hole and rummages around. His other hand is holding the bag. Blood stains it from where he's holding it. I wonder what the mess looks like inside of it.

After a bit of searching, he pulls out the baseball card. There's text on it, written in permanent marker. It's in some kind of foreign language that I have no idea how to read. Johnny laughs a little.

"Even after all this time I still don't know who the hell is on this card."

He zips the bag up and tosses it to the wall of the room. He's still holding the baseball card in his hand. Looking at it and inspecting all the fine details. On the card is a man in a white shirt and pants swinging a baseball bat. He's got some kind of green helmet on his head. Every time he shifts the card around in his fingers, it gets progressively more red.

Blood from it drips onto the floor. Johnny pays no mind to it. He appears to be lost in memory. He's stopped humming the song. His gaze is solely focused on the face of the man on the card. There's something I take notice of.

His fingers... something is forming over them. It's not a lot, but there appears to be some kind of skin over it. It's not smooth, it doesn't appear to match his skin tone, and it looks rough. But, it partially covers the muscle that was exposed prior. Plus, his fingers appear to have changed shape. Some of them, particularly in his right hand, seem to be the right size. His left hand still has some fingers abnormally larger than they should be.

The room remains quiet. He's still absorbed into his own memory it seems. He's rather casual about the way he handles what's happened. A lot of his memories are soaked in violence and loss. In a

way, it's admirable. Admirable that a part of him still kicks despite his losses and his transformation. And all he's doing now is smiling warmly at a baseball card,

My stomach growls. Johnny stares at me and glares into my direction. I guess that snapped him out of his trance.

"You should probably get something to eat."

I nod my head at him.

"You'd be right. You want something to eat as well?"

"I'll be good, but if you bring me something to eat, then I wouldn't mind it either. I'll leave it up to you."

I smile at him and head downstairs.

The pantry's full of sardines. Admittedly, I'm too lazy to cook up something. Stew wouldn't be terrible, but that requires me setting up a pot full of water and cutting vegetables. Something canned and quick wouldn't be half bad right about now. But what could go along with it?

There's canned tomatoes, sweet potatoes, beets, corn, chickpeas, green beans, and salmon. I guess I could toss the green beans, sardines, and sweet potatoes in the same bowl. That sounds gross when I think about it, but I'm too hungry to think properly. But I can't help but notice something. It's a feeling, I can't shake it.

This house… it's too normal for what's happened. I mean everyone's practically been wiped off the face of the planet. It's dangerous to even consider going outside. People out there are killed, dissected, and raped just because. And yet here I am. Having a place where I can grow my own crops and make my own food. I've got water all to myself. Ways to be entertained like a piano in the living room and a nice view to watch through a window. It's not much, but it's something. And sure, I can't exactly go outside safely. But this is a nice place. Taking care of someone in my house. Someone I'm preparing food to. Actually, I realized I pulled out two bowls. I had intended to make just myself food. But it'd probably be best if I gave him something to eat.

And even that… that's what gets me too. I've gotten so close to him as of late. Gotten to know someone else after what's been at least over a year of total isolation. Yet… it feels normal. I mean sure, the whole regenerating thing is far from normal. But just talking to him, getting to know him, caring for him. It's all… it's all changing me. But it's not bad. It's a good thing. All of this is good.

So why? Why can't I shake the feeling that something is off? That something should be off. If something were to confirm my

suspicions or feeling, then would I be vindicated by it? I think part of me would. I also think the other part of me wouldn't. Yet, here I am. Prepping food subconsciously for the man who I've let into my home. A home that isn't mine. A home that I took from people who I never met. Yet, this place has held memories for me I've been making recently and before. I'm not sure how to feel. All of this... it's just so...

I hear Johnny talking casually upstairs. Talking to himself I take it. I can't discern exactly what he's saying. Perhaps he's still remembering Takeya, or anyone else that came into his life. I wonder what he thinks of me. How I'll play into his life as time goes on. I know he thanks me for helping him. But outside of that, I'm curious to know what he thinks. Is it aligned with my thoughts about him?

Both bowls of food are in my hand now. They serve the same thing, mostly. My bowl contains canned salmon, carrots, and green beans. His bowl contains sardines, crushed tomatoes, and beets. I head upstairs towards him, bowls in my hand and hear his talking turn into humming. I push the door open.

His humming stops. He's sitting upright. For once, he's not laying on the floor. Something from his eye begins to squirm and pulsate. It's almost as if it wants to pop out. The baseball card lies next to him. I hear the soft noise of flesh shifting and bones cracking. I see him smiling.. He greets me.

"Hello Jane. I see you've brought me food."

His voice sounds healthier. I nod my head to him and lay his bowl down on the floor. I lay mine next to where I sleep. I reach out my hand to feed him, but he stops me.

"I can feed myself. You don't have to stress yourself out about this sort of stuff. Let me handle it."

His hand reaches out towards the spoon in the bowl. As he grabs it, blood trickles down from the opening of his fingers and drips into the food. It mixes with the tomato paste and beets. Part of it gets onto the sardines, of which he's taken a spoonful of. He doesn't seem to mind as he gulps it down with a smile still on his face.

"Part of me is happy. Real happy I get to use my hands again."

I hear his bones and fingers crack in his hand.

"I haven't been able to do this in so long. It feels like a luxury to do such a thing."

He takes a good look at me.

"What's wrong? You're not eating your food. Is something bothering you?"

I'm not irked by anything specifically. There's simply a lot on my mind. A lot I can't communicate properly, not at this moment. It's all just hit me now.

"Helloooooooooo.... Jane? Are you there?"

What happens when he grows his leg back? What will he do once it does? I don't want to accuse him of anything, because he hasn't done anything yet. It's just... a feeling. A feeling I can't describe. A feeling of unease. It'd be wrong if I accused him of anything. That wouldn't be right. I just... want answers. I want to know what's going on. Because I felt lost. Confused. Out of it. I'm thrown for a loop.

I'm not scared of him. But I am worried. Worried as to what will happen. His appearance is one thing. Having all these hairs, scabs, puss, and liquid seeping out of him is horrible. But once he grows that final limb, what action will he take? I know he's been through a lot. Hell, that itself is an understatement. I just...

I hear the floorboard creak underneath his weight. He's halfway done his bowl of food now. I haven't touched mine. He's been staring at me this whole time. Probably wondering what's going on in

my head, why I haven't been talking. I have my reasons, but he doesn't know.

"You gonna eat your food?"

I'm snapped out of it. For a brief moment. I grab my spoon and begin to eat what's in the bowl. I cut bits of the salmon with the spoon. Sometimes combining the carrots and green beans in one bite. Sometimes all three are the same. I'm not eating particularly fast nor slow. I'm simply going through the motions. Putting the spoon in the bowl. Lifting it up. Directing it towards my mouth. Opening it. Biting down. Swallowing. Rinse. Repeat. Again and again. Until there's no food left.

I notice Johnny isn't done eating. There's still food there. Blood has dripped onto the floor close to his bowl. He's still eating spoonfuls with his own blood mixed in. He's still smiling as he eats.

Something inside of me shifts. Not physically, but mentally.

"When was the last time you felt a sense of normalcy after the world ended the way it did?"

He stares up at me. Taken aback by my question.

"That's a broad question. And to be honest, I couldn't tell you. The closest thing I've ever gotten to being normal as of late was getting my limbs back. Why do you ask?"

I think for a little bit. My eyes squint at the ceiling above me.

"This whole thing. Taking you in. Nursing you back to health. Watching your limbs regrow. It's all happened so... fast. Yet I've gotten accustomed to it rather quickly. And I can't help but shake a feeling that something's off. I can't tell if it's you or if it's me. Or maybe... this was all natural. Like it was supposed to happen."

"What are you getting at?"

"I'm just saying this is all a little insane if you take a step back and look at the situation. I find you, limbless, in the middle of the woods. And through some miracle you're barely alive and I take you all the way back here. I patch up your wounds, change your clothes, feed you, and practically make you someone else who lives with me. The cherry on top is your limbs. The way they're regrowing. The way they're *mutating*. The way they're changing you. It's just not normal. Yet it didn't bother me then. So why's it bothering me now?"

"Are you saying adjusting so quickly is a bad thing? I'm lost here."

"No no... it's just an absurd situation to take in. A lot has happened, you know. It feels like I've both processed it and not processed it at all. Are you almost finished with your bowl yet?"

As if it were good timing on my end, he takes his last bite. He looks at me and tilts his head. He wipes his mouth with his arm, being aware to use the part where there's no hairs on it. We stare at each other for a while. I hear nothing but the wind blowing outside and our respective breathing. Johnny seems to be strangely peaceful, given everything that's happened. I take a good look at him. Something about him still sticks out to me. That beneath his appearance, he is still a person. Yet, I'm just not too sure. Could it be a never ending paranoia I have? Is it me? Me who doesn't trust anyone. And that now, for the first time in a while, I have someone who I can trust. Perhaps it's this that throws me for a loop. But is it really that simple? Could there be something more? Maybe there is nothing more. Perhaps it's my own mind finding things to worry about that aren't a problem. Or am I right? Would it be a good thing if I was right? What would that prove? Would that prove anything good? I'm not too sure.

Johnny breaks the silence.

"I wanted to ask you something."

His voice is as calm and collected as ever. He sounds healthy, though his appearance may say otherwise.

"How did you figure out how to take care of me so quickly? The improvised diaper, changing out my clothes when I'm laying flat on the floor, and bathing me? You know a lot about taking care of somebody. How?"

I stay quiet for a bit. My head is still scrambled.

"It's something personal isn't it?"

I begin to look at the floor.

"You don't have to answer it. It's alright, I understand."

I speak up.

"No... it's just. This situation and everything that's happened. You... remind me of someone. Someone I miss. And looking at you, doing all of this, my memories of her just seep through. I.. I don't know how to feel about all of it."

Is that it? Is that where all of this stems from? Have I already answered my internal question through the question of another?

"It's alright. You don't need to-"

I feel obliged to. Like I have to. I'm not sure why.

"No, no. I think you should know. You've told me stories of what's happened to you. It'd only be fair if I told you as well."

"Are you sure?"

"Yes. It's fine, really it is."

My head peeks up towards him. And so, an unnatural urge to spill something comes out of me.

"You were in your own community at some point. You've seen nurses and various other "jobs" within your shelter. Growing up,

in my community at least, they made everyone be some kind of worker. Especially at a young age. Children would choose what they wanted to be when they grew older. Though, this would be only after they had learned the basics of reading, writing, and the occasional bits of math. But I remember they had these little doodles of somebody from each respective job on the whiteboard. There were soldiers, medical professionals, farmers, and so on. I decided to be a nurse, get into training for that. I didn't know it at the time. But, it was rather common for women of my age to start with nursing training. When I was a teenager, that's when it all started. I practiced with other people on how to flip patients, change clothes, and all that. We had a bunch of spare dummies and clothing. Our center used to be an old college before we turned it into what it is then.

Anyway, I learned how to do all of that on mannequins. Never on an actual person. You're not the first person I've had to nurse. But, you are the first man I had to take care of this way. That's why I was shocked to see *that* for the first time when I changed your pants. I've only ever seen that on plastic dummies, never an actual one until that day. As for my first actual patient, she was a friend of mine. Me and her grew up in the same building, with the same bunk beds for children to sleep in. Of course, armed guards would watch the place when we slept. They wanted to make sure we were safe. But I had met the girl through our first math class.

I remember our first meeting so well. I had no idea how to tie my shoes and she came over to me and noticed I was crying. I was

about 7 at the time, learning to write for the first time. I struggled to hold a pencil, I could barely learn to figure out how to use my hands. Then this girl comes along, with long brown hair and a missing tooth. She had this sense of innocence to her I'd never seen in anyone before. She asked me, so kindly, if I needed help tying my shoe. I had cried so much, my tears showered my face, and it was over something so small and minute. I nodded my head yes while wiping my tears and she tied my shoes for me. She put her hand over my shoulder and asked if I wanted to learn how to tie my shoe. I said yes and she wiped my tears with her sleeve. Through her, I was able to learn how to use my hands to do something for the first time.

That was something complex. At least, complex at that age for me. She told me her name was, "Beverly."She asked me what my name was, I told her it was Jane. She then asks what my parents were like and I told her I'm not sure what happened to mine. She had simply said, "*Oh*". But, she patted me on my shoulders and asked if I wanted to be friends with her. I quickly said yes. From there, me and her stayed near each other throughout our school years. We'd help each other with math homework and reading. I wasn't very good at math, but she was. Beverly hated reading though, but I ended up getting into classic literature. I ended up helping her with any reading problems. She was just too lazy to read a chapter from any book. Actually, she'd just ask me what happened in the chapter so I recapped it for her. I don't think she ever read anything to be honest. In a way, we both covered our weaknesses.

When we were both teenagers, that's when we started to drift apart. It was the time to choose a career path. Like I said earlier, I went down the path of being a nurse. For her, she had wanted to be a soldier. In retrospect, it makes sense now as she became a lot more brash and hot-headed as we grew older. She ranted to me about how much she heard about the outside world. How much she wanted to help this community. She saw how awful it was becoming from the inside of our shelter. People were turning up missing, or found dead somewhere, or they came back with some kind of physical wound, or how some of the children here get captured, don't come back. But the children that did come back ended up talking about how their crotch area hurt. They didn't know how to describe it because they had no what happened to them. All of that just set her off. I don't blame her. But at the time, it didn't make much sense to me. I still saw her as the kind girl that helped me tie my shoe. I never thought she was the type to pick up a gun and start shooting. But it doesn't change what happened.

The school for nurses and soldiers were separate buildings. That's when I practiced with medical supplies and dummies for the first time. I made new friends, well they were more like acquaintances. She was always on my mind though. We'd talk from time to time, after our respective training hours would end. She would talk to me briefly, but she became good friends with a lot of people there. We'd make plans to meet about once a week. Then once a month. Then, we just didn't anymore. In fact, she just stopped seeing me altogether.

Slowly, she phased me out. Me and her just kind of stopped talking. There was no bad blood or ill will. I... just didn't have a place in her life at that point. Training picked up. My mind focused on that instead. I got good at it. Really, really good at the whole nursing thing. Beverly stopped being on my mind. I would think about her here and there, but I just kind of accepted what happened, you know? But I remember one day, it was shortly after I had finished my training and could join the big girls and guys who became nurses, I saw her again. Two people were carrying someone to a medical bay. They laid her flat on a bed. From afar, I got a good idea as to who it was."

I begin to cry. A tear falls down on my cheek.

"I got a little closer and took a good look at the body. My suspicions were right. It was Beverly. Her uniform had been ripped. Her pants were torn off and I could see slashes all around her chest and legs. I noticed a red hand print on her throat. There was blood coming from in between her legs. I looked down some more and I realized her left leg had been cut off. A stump remained. Then, I looked at her face. Her left eye was gone. Parts of her hair were ripped off. Blood came out of her mouth. When she clenched her teeth, I noticed her top tooth was missing. I called out to her. She was feral, erratic, like a wild animal. She was as detached from a human being as one could be. I didn't get a response from her. The two people who dragged her in told me to give them some space. I did what I was told

and walked away. The next day, I came to see her. She was sleeping and I saw new clothes were put on her. Her stump had been bandaged, as was her left eye and head. The bleeding appeared to have stopped. I didn't want to wake her so I ended up just staring blankly. There was no point in me just standing there so I decided to walk away. That's when I heard my name."

Tears fell down my face at a rapid pace. My face becomes engulfed with water. I feel my voice being caught between the bile of my throat and tears from my eyes. It mixes together as I speak. I take in more breaths. It feels like I'm hyperventilating. But still, I have the urge to speak.

"Her voice was soft, but I could tell she was tired. It was raspy too, just like yours when I heard you speak for the first time. Her voice lightens up. In a softer tone, she asks me how I've been. I tell her I've been good. And just like old times, we catch up like nothing happened. What our lives have been like since we last met. Ever since we stopped seeing each other after we went down our respective career paths, she admitted she missed me. She apologized for being an asshole and not talking to me when she could. Apologized for being dodgy when I tried to talk to her. She apologized to me that I had to see her like this. That for our first real conversation in years, I see her mutilated and turned into some kind of half-amputee. I told her there was nothing to apologize for. That I was really happy to see

here again after all this time, even if this horrible thing happened. I told her how much I wanted to help her, how much I regret not being there for her. I regretted so many things and she just told me that it was alright. What's done is done. It's happened already, she told me not to bother changing something that I can't. From that day forward, me and her would meet everyday. I'd bring her food and at lunchtime, we would talk like old times. At some point, the bandage on her stump had given out. I ended up having to put a new one on and learned how to do so. That's how I knew how to bandage your stump. Talking with her again was nice. It was peaceful. I miss those days. I miss her."

For the most part, my tears have subsided. Johnny gazes at me softly. Perhaps, coldly. I hear the sound of flesh writhe in his last stump. As if something is being squished internally.

"One of those days I did ask her what happened. I shouldn't have asked her this. It was stupid of me. To ask such a revolting question. But I did it anyway. I don't know why, maybe curiosity or something. But I don't know. I asked her what happened. I immediately regretted asking that. But she told me it was okay. She tells me that it was a raid. To get supplies for the shelter and come back here. Her and her group of four other soldiers were sent on a low-risk mission. It was at some abandoned facility holding a bunch of medical supplies and canned food. Something we needed,

desperately. In fact, we were running out of people. Out of soldiers, out of medical professionals, out of pretty much everything. As for those five soldiers, they didn't expect other people to be there. There were ten men in the same building. My shelter had no idea people occupied that spot. The five of them tried to put up a fight, but they were overwhelmed fast. These men were stronger and faster, and had better weaponry. After the firefight, the only person who was alive was her. They contemplated killing her, but decided to spare her for other means.

She was kept in a dog cage for weeks. Locked up and only taken out to be used as an object. They beat her, slashed her, choked her, and penetrated her. All ten of those men took turns on her. Some came inside. She didn't know if she was pregnant or not. Day in and day out the same process would repeat. She was fed only the same paste of food. Sometimes oatmeal, sometimes just water, sometimes nothing. She never had a change of clothes and was forced to urinate in the cage. There also wasn't a bucket given to defecate in. She had no choice but to defecate in that cage. She told me how awful it stunk. To sleep in the same place with her feces and urine in the same cramped area. Eventually, the men got so fed up with the stench of the room, they gave her a bucket to shit in. But they blamed it all on her. She continued enduring their abuse.

At that point, she just gave in. Stop trying to seek help. Stopped believing that anyone would save her. She believed she was fully abandoned. She would tell me how much it hurt. How much

pain she felt in between her legs, how hard she would gag when they used her throat, how her asshole stretched to an extreme degree to the point she figured she would pass out. She even told me that sometimes, they'd use all of her holes at once. I remember the look on her face when she said that. She had laughed and smiled, while her only eye twitched rapidly. Every day, she wanted to kill them. But she knew she couldn't. She was too weak. These men were stronger than her and she was an emaciated slave to them. At some point, they cut off her eye and leg to please someone. A friend of the men. Someone who enjoyed the taste of human flesh. I'm not sure who it was. She was awake during that whole process. They took a big knife and sliced away bit by bit, slowly moving the blade up and down through her skin, eventually cutting through her bone.

One day though, she saw an opportunity. 9 of the men had to leave, to scout for supplies. One of them stayed behind to watch her. All 10 of them wanted to go but they figured they'd leave one behind just in case. To them, they only needed one person since she was too weak to fight back anyways.

Once those 9 had left, this was her moment to strike. Hidden beneath her pillow was a small knife she had stolen from one of the guards. She had taken it while he was penetrating her. He was too distracted to notice her taking it from his pocket. She called the man over to the cage and asked if she could defecate. The man obliges and as his back is turned, she stabs him in the neck. She tells me she stabbed him as many times as she could. She had also remembered

the layout of the building and that the exit was located to the right and straight. She took notice of where the men would exit the room and head out. From where she was being held, she had an angle towards the hallway of the room leading out of it. It was only two doors and she would be led outside. She grabs the dead man's pistol and tells me she crawled out. That whole time, she was afraid the other 9 would arrive and catch her. She told me how bad her heart was racing. If she got caught, she would repeat that cycle again. But if she did, she told me she would point the gun to her head and shoot herself. But, when she was outside, she never saw them.

She remembered the route back to our shelter and when she showed she told me she remembered the look on their faces when they saw her. How horrified they were to see what had happened. They opened the gates for her and she told me it was like seeing the gates of Heaven itself. She was picked up by them and put there. She had asked them why they didn't save her when they all went missing. They didn't give her a straight answer. Later on, she got word from somebody that they figured they were already dead. If they were alive, then they have no manpower or resources to save them. So, they sent no one. I didn't know what to say after that. She ended the conversation there and said she'll see me tomorrow. I told her I would, that I'd be there at the same time as I was that day. But when I showed up tomorrow, she wasn't there. The lady who oversaw the medical bay came up to me and told me what happened. Last night, there was a gunshot near the guard's building. Beverly had snuck in

via a window with a loose lock and stole a gun from one of the guards there sleeping on the job. She snuck in... stole a gun... and then... she shot herself. They had found Beverly there shortly after they heard the noise. I was in a separate building, far off from that place during that time. I was sleeping soundly. I thanked the woman for letting me know. I saw the look in her eyes, remorseful but empty. She had done this too many times already. After I heard that, I went back to my room, packed up my stuff, and I... I just left."

I have an urge to bury my head in my legs. The sound of my own sniffling is getting on my nerves. I watch as bits of my tears hit the floor beneath me. I wrap my fingers tightly around each other. Out of the blue, my tears begin to pick up. I can't control it. More and more hit the floor. I feel my arms shake erratically, as do my legs. I want to wail but I also want to remain quiet. To hold it in. I swallow a tear.

"I'm gonna get some air. I'll be right back."

I get up from the floor and wipe my tears with my sweater. My face has most likely turned a deep red. Tears enter my throat as I sniffle. I gag on it. My hand reaches out to the door in front of me. As I leave, I see Johnny sitting upright. He's quiet. His gaze feels empty. The only thing I hear from him is the flesh moving in that stump of his.

Still, I can't seem to stop myself. It's been years since I last saw her, since all of this happened. Now, I guess all of it just resurfaces through my head huh? My foot tripped the wire on the front door already. Guess I'm not paying attention either. The sun beams my head and I shut the door behind me. I can feel my face starting to get rough from wiping my eyes and nose so much. My nose begins to hurt when I wipe the snot away. Crops surround my side and the dirt trail lays in front of me. I slump down against the front door and look up at the sky. It's bright blue and the clouds are pure white. Each of them have different shapes. Some look like animals I would see in picture books, others look like an unintelligible shape. The sun is far off, to my right. For once, the light can't get in my eye. There's no wind, but the temperature isn't too hot either. It's nice outside.

God... I miss her. I really do. We'd laugh about other people in our community. How this stupid guy named Edgar tried to impress us when we were younger by opening the door and pulling out the chair for us. We'd play along with his acts of chivalry. I liked him, but never had the chance to talk to him. Beverly found him insufferable. We were kids back then. None of us had any idea as to how the world really was. Just playing board games from the world before and playing tag outside. There was only what, like 15 of us in the same class? Haha, yeah. Beverly had just become friends with me for a week at that point. Kept talking my ear off about any little thing she could. Asking about how I didn't know how to tie my shoes yet, how smart I seemed to be because I did a good chunk of the math work for her,

and why I was always so quiet all the time. She was always so curious. Even when one of the kids tried to pick on me for not being able to tie my shoes for a while she came to my defense and reminded him of the time he pissed his pants in front of the class. I remember one day after class, she asked me if I wanted to meet her parents. At this point, she knew I didn't have any, so she invited me over to her living quarters to meet them. They were the loveliest people I've ever met. So kind, so caring. They had told me their names.

Her mother was named Rose. She had such a kind demeanor. Whenever she spoke, her voice was always soft and merciful. I remember how much of a good cook she was. Her father was named Victor. I remember my first time seeing him. So tall, so gruff, and so massive for a man. He had a voice that never matched his appearance though. But he extended the same kindness his wife did. The first thing both of them had asked me was how I became friends with Beverly, and I told them she helped me tie my shoes. I remember how both of them smiled that day, that their daughter had made a friend. Now that I'm older, I get why they smiled. Both of them asked me what I wanted to do, I remember Beverly butted in and said the two of us would just play around. They had both smiled and decided to leave us alone, only telling both of us that they'll have dinner in about an hour. Her mom wanted me to join. I didn't know what to say. Beverly had put her hand on my shoulder and said that it'll be fun. I took her word for it.

After that, me and her played around the living quarters. We started off playing board games. She had pulled out a checkers board. There were a couple pieces missing and the mat itself had tears on it. This however, was not enough for us to stop playing it. I ended up beating her in it for two games straight before she asked to play something else. I noticed another game on the table. At the time, I didn't know what it was. It had these pieces of a castle and a horse on it. Beverly's dad had tried to teach her how to play, but she could never wrap her head around it. Later on, I realized it was chess. I started to get into that game after me and Beverly went our separate ways into our respective career path. Checkers was her favorite though, along with Connect 4. Sadly, that had missing pieces as well. Beverly herself moved around quickly.

She got bored of checkers and Connect 4 after two games for each of them. I enjoyed Connect 4. That day I beat her twice in a row before she asked to play something else. As to what that was I remember she told me she was thinking. There were other games on the shelf but she wasn't in the mood for board games. Then, as if a light bulb had gone off in her head, she asked me if I wanted to race her to the other side of the room. I told her no as I didn't really like to do much physical activity. But, she grabbed me by the arm and pulled me to the end of the room. She pointed to where we were meant to stop. I told her I really didn't want to before she began to count down and ran in front of me. For some odd reason, I started to run to catch up to her, even though I was far behind. When I reached the end, she

of course, had beat me. In retrospect, I think she wanted to play a game where she could easily win. I was out of running. Out of the blue, she had said we had to run back. I remember asking her if we could do something else before she took off running to the other side. I ran off as well to catch up. Again, she won. Beverly giggled at me, boasting about her victory to my face. I remember just looking at her, exhausted, and laying down on the hard wood floor.

She had decided to lay down close to me. Together, we saw the ceiling. All the cracks in it, how run down it was. We pointed to random cracks and pondered about how random scribbles got on it. Making up stories about how they got there. She joked about aliens and kids who were super tall and could reach the ceiling. I pointed out that they could just use the bunk beds. She told me that she was joking. I hadn't caught on and she giggled once more. My eyes shifted towards the window outside. There were various stars that night. Beverly liked to stargaze. She pointed out to me the various shapes stars could form. I didn't get it at first. But as she pointed her finger around and dragged it to make an imaginary line, I began to see it. I saw the Big Dipper, Hercules, and Pegasus. She knew how much of a reader I was, at least turning into. So, she told me she would give me a book that had different star signs on it. One day, she wanted me and her to sit on the grass and stargaze at some point. I still have that book with me. It's here, somewhere. I took it with me even after I left. Her face then turned to me and said she had a question.

"Do you want to be friends forever?"

I told her I would like to. Even then, I'm not sure why I said that. I had no experience with other people and the concept of friends didn't make sense to me at the time. But, I had this feeling about Beverly. She seemed so nice to everyone. She had this warmth to her. I could trust her with just about anything. Her parents had called for both of us to eat. Beverly told me that I'd love what her mom made. We both got up off the floor and she dragged me by the arm to the dining area. Four plates were on the table and I sat next to Beverly. On the table were mashed potatoes, carrots, and meat with gravy on it. At the time, I had no idea what gravy was. To me, it was just some weird brown liquid that looked off-putting. Her dad explained to me that it tasted good and that I should try it. I took his word for it and ended up loving it.

In fact, I ended up too much of the meat at first. Something tasted different about the meat though. It wasn't chicken or beef like I was used to. When Rose had arrived at the table to put dessert, I had asked her what it was. She told me it was Turkey and that during this time of year, families would celebrate something called, "Thanksgiving." I didn't know what that was. To this day, I'm still not very familiar with the concept. According to Rose, families would gather once a year to say what they're thankful for (hence the name) and eat together as a family. Though, she tells me the meal is more important than actually saying thanks. From there, Rose sits down

and eats with all of us. There's extra turkey on a plate, along with mashed potatoes and gravy. In the center is the cranberry pie for dessert. She had cans of cranberry sauce and used those for a filling. Rose told me she preferred the taste of pumpkin pie for dessert instead, but they had no means to make it. She hadn't had one in years. Everyone began to converse.

Beverly tells me how excited she was that we got a week-long break from school. Victor tells me he currently works as a soldier for the community while Rose is a nurse. He tells me it's a hard job and that Rose struggles quite a bit to keep up with the people. But despite that, both of them try their best to make Beverly happy. Rose tells me that they named her Beverly because Victor had always wanted to go to Beverly Hills. Some place in California where his favorite actors lived. He liked sightseeing and would often nag her to go with her one day. I remember Victor told me he was so close to saving enough to go there. However, that's when Rose fell pregnant and he cast that dream aside for Beverly instead. That was also around the time the world began to collapse. He tells me that he's not upset about being unable to go. Rose had butted in and nudged him on his shoulder saying he was. Victor smiled and said he was probably just "a little upset". Rose turned her attention and asked what my parents were like. I stopped eating and didn't know how to respond. My hand clutched my pants and I turned my head downwards. Beverly took notice and her parents became concerned. She put her arm around my shoulder and told me her mom didn't mean to upset me. I knew

that, but I began to shake as tears started to form. Victor had stopped eating and looked at Rose. Rose had apologized and had a sad look on her face. I spoke up and said something.

"I d-don't h-ha-have any..."

Rose's eyes widened. Victor looked down onto the floor. Beverly grips her hand harder on my shoulder. Just then I start to cry. I scream and I wail but I try not to be so loud. Rose gets up out of her seat. I hear the chair creak against the floor as she slides back and listen to her walk in my direction as my head is tilted downwards. I don't see her at all. As I cry, I keep wiping my eyes with my arms repeatedly. She crouches down next to me, I see her through the edge of my vision. My arms are grabbed by her and gently pushed to the side. Her arms spread open, Beverly lets go of her hand, and she begins to wrap her arms around me. One of her hands moves to the back of my head and she embraces me closer. I dig my head into her chest and bawl as hard as I can.

A tear falls down my cheek. I think this one is the last. I wipe it away with my sleeve. My face hurts from all the wiping. I direct my gaze at a cloud. For a moment, it resembles something familiar.

Why... why is this world as cruel as it is?

I noticed the sky had turned red. Sunset is here and soon, it will be night. Perhaps I could watch the sky again. Take note of the constellations tonight. I think I'd like to do that.

I head upstairs and see Johnny laying down on his bed. His face appears to be melting and his right eye seems to be popping out. He tells me not to worry as he's sure he'll feel better once his limb starts to grow back. I noticed he put up the empty bowls on the desk. There's stains on the floor and the desk itself, but I'll clean it up later.

I walk forward and stare at the circular window. No Big Dipper. But there's Hercules and Pegasus. I smile. For the first time in a while, I feel a sense of warmth. A warmth of a memory I had long since buried. The warmth of a person who is no longer here with me. Who has long since perished. Who didn't deserve the fate she had. Yet in some way, I feel connected to her. That maybe, maybe somewhere, I could meet her again. Not through death, but through a way of life. I'm not exactly spiritual, but I hope where her soul ends up, it's somewhere good. She deserves that much.

I put my hand up against the window. It feels as if I could touch that constellation on my palm. I wonder if I could be that constellation. To be up in space and view the world through a different perspective. A new angle. I wonder, what does the world look like from there? I've seen pictures of Earth, but those were in textbooks. What does it look like now? Is there fire in certain parts of the world? Has some of it shattered and been torn to bits? Or, is it the way it was before? Green and bits of blue. Unharmed through the eyes

of a being up above. Come down here though, and that's an entirely different story.

And despite that juxtaposition, there's still something good, right? Something warm. Something beautiful. In the trees and ground mother nature has built. In the man-made objects that brought forth destruction and unity. In between all of that, are the bonds between other people who shape the rest of their lives. Good moments, bad moments. Memories of joy. Memories of hate. Memories of love and fear. It all blends together. So horribly and yet, so beautifully.

Wherever I go, wherever I end up, I want it to be good. I want to succeed in whatever I do. Even when days of despair eat me, I want to come out on top despite it all. I wish for a good life for myself, and for Johnny. As best and as good a life we could get, given our situation. Maybe everyone who still lives on this planet can rebuild a better civilization for the future. I hope that's not wishful thinking. I want that to be reality. I want the world to be a better place. Is that so much to ask? I hope it's not.

Goodbye, Beverly. I'll remember you for the rest of my life.

Jane appears to have fallen asleep. I saw her earlier putting her hand up against the window. She looks good from that angle. I watch as her chest rises and expands as she breathes. Her hair still covers the same side of her face just like Eira. I can't help but smile. It feels as if all the pieces are coming together. I get all my limbs back and return to the person I was before. Of course, I look like an insect. Nobody would ever view me as human.

What's my reward for getting blown into smithereens? A revolting body that oozes some kind of liquid wherever I go. I'm really starting to miss the way I was before now. But it's almost like I can't choose.

Do I want my final leg back? Yes. But also I'd hate the way it looks. I hate the sounds my own body makes. The way it writhes and squirms as I do nothing but sit still. Moving around makes the noises worse and much, much louder. It drives me mad.

And I can't help but miss the touch of Eira. The way she held me. How soft and comfortable her skin was. How close her head dug into my chest whenever we cuddled. Her hand interlocking with mine.

That will never happen again. Pure love? That feeling. It's gone. Of warmth. Of physical touch. Of being close. No. It can never be romantic again can it? Not like this. Not with the way that I am.

Perhaps, in another life, that fairy tale ending would be mine. A happy wife, a child, a stable job. Everything was just given to me. Nothing to work. Nothing to strive for. But where would the fun be in that? Even still, it's satisfying to have. And that itself has become nothing but a pipe dream. The world would still end, with or without my fairy tale ending.

And still, I can't stop it. I can't stop what I have no control over. As the red in the stump bubbles, I feel the muscles in my skin start to form. Layer by layer, I watch as they enrapture my leg. Return it to what it once was, as best as they can. I hear it squirm and writhe. That noise still irritates me. My stump twitches erratically during the whole process. My thigh is fully formed. The skin on it is smooth, unlike the rest of my limbs. Everything below my knee begins to take shape as well. Muscles build underneath skin. And on top of that layer, hairs start to form. Still spiky, still uncomfortable, still oozing some kind of green

liquid from the tip. Yet, that part is complete. Finally, my foot begins to take form. The base of it forms in an irregular shape. But one toe at a time, they are molded into different sizes. My big toe is abnormally large and my pinky toe is abnormally small. The rest of them are the way they should be. I wiggle it as it grows and festers. However, the process is not complete. A layer of fuzzy black skin forms over top of it with yellow stripes peering through it. My sole remains red with exposed muscle.

The darkness of the room settles in. Moonlight begins to give out. It's quiet. I hear the floorboards creak once again.

At last, my final limb has healed.

Section 4:

Metamorphosis

Chapter 21

There are so many human atrocities. The holocaust would be the most famous example. Mass death is often labeled as genocide. But what defines an atrocity? The scale of death? The act itself? What it leaves behind? Or does it require violence at all?

History doesn't change because we question it. Nuclear war. Love. Hatred. Sex. All of it blurs together. Different expressions of the same species.

Heroes no longer exist. There is nothing to look up to. The world has reached its peak and began to decay from within. It wasn't a single collapse, but everything accelerated to the point where nothing meaningful could grow anymore.

And so, the world consumed itself.

We consumed each other.

All that remains is a reset. Not divine. Not apocalyptic. No gods. No floods. No single catastrophe.

Just us.

Was this always where we were headed? A species advancing until it had nothing left to progress towards? Everything became dissected and analyzed. Every detail of every person laid bare and compared, until empathy itself dulled.

The power of endless information has caused people to become more detached. More numb. Perhaps, even more cruel. At some point, nothing felt new anymore. And when nothing feels new, what does the human mind even try to reach for?

Would it take one person to change everything? Some invention? A singular historical event? A disrupt in the same pattern?

Even if it happened, would anyone even care?

Everybody is too busy looking inward. Tearing at each other. Existing in their own narrow view of the world.

Maybe... maybe this is what we were.

And we stopped trying to be anything else.

Jane's awake. I watch her stretch her arms the moment she wakes up. Her head tilts towards me. She's noticed my other leg. I watch as she stares blankly at me for a while. Neither of us say anything. The sun shines brightly through the bedroom window. All I want to do is move.

I sit up by myself and put my hand on the floor. My hand print stains the wood. I twist my torso to the right and watch as the hairs near my shoulders move along with me. My leg stretches out. I feel the cold wood pressing against my sole. The texture of it is rough. I put my other leg out. I hear something wet and floppy coming from under it. Still, I push myself forward and stand up.

I almost fall head first onto the floor, but I use my hands to stop myself in time. My face almost hits the hairs on my arms. I get a close look at what my hands look like.

Dislocated.

Disproportionate.

Displaced.

The anatomy of my fingers are all wrong. My fingernails are grown on some but not every finger. The fingers are all different sizes. My right thumb is on the opposite side of where it's supposed to be. My hands feel wet.

I attempt to straighten my back and hear the sound of hairs scraping coming from behind me. The sounds of fluids shifting internally vibrate loudly from my stomach. I feel a cramp beneath my skin.

I can't straighten my back fully. It bends near the top. No matter how hard I try to straighten it out, my body simply refuses to communicate with me. I just want to move.

My leg pushes out. Then my other one. Then, almost as if my body moves by itself, I begin to walk. Still, something feels off. For every step, my body instinctively moves downward. My legs shift unnaturally when I try to move. I lose balance.

Come on Johnny. One foot forward. One step at a time.

One foot forward. One step at a time. One foot forward. One step at a time. One foot forward. One step at a time. One foot forward. One step at a time. One foot forward. One step at a time. One foot forward. One step at a time. One foot forward. One step at a time. One foot forward. One step at a time. One foot forward. One step at a time. One foot forward. One step at a time. One foot forward. One step at a time.

I slip. I pick myself back up. The process repeats. I feel my skin squelch and want to vomit. I feel myself want to vomit. My arm wants to vomit. My legs want to vomit. My stomach wants to vomit. I am a mass of soft and disgusting flesh with a sorry excuse for mobility. A repulsive blob of meat.

Hey Jane? Where's the bathroom? I want to get a good look at myself. Please tell me where it is. I wanna see what I look like. Please Jane. Please Jane. Please.

I watch as she shifts backward in her blanket. She gets up quickly and says it's the room directly across from this room. Thank you Jane. I hear her scurry towards the back of the room.

As I move forward, I realize my right arm looks a little different than my left. Are they the right size? Is this one bigger or smaller than the other? It's off. Something's off. What's off? No. Everything's off.

My balance is off.

My appearance is off.

My skin feels off.

My limbs feel off.

Off doesn't feel like a real word anymore.

Walking straight is difficult. I keep stumbling on myself. There's a small elevation on the bathroom floor. Coordinating my left leg to move slightly up has never been so tedious. At least I'm inside the bathroom. My hand touches the sink. I almost slip again. Whoops.

What's here?

Lipstick.

Mascara.

A comb.

Who are you looking pretty for?

Is it all for me?

The glass mirror stands in front of me. It's almost like it's laughing at me. I wish it had a mouth. I wish it was alive. If it were alive, I'd be able to do something about it. But no, it just spits out what I look like.

My face looks so... funny. I look like a children's drawing. Oh. I had a child once. What was the gender of my kid? I don't think it matters.

Something's off. The proportions on my arms and legs are all wrong. Why's my shoulder bigger on the left than on the right? Why's my left thigh so small compared to my right? God... my knee is swollen. It's too wide. What's wrong with my face? Why's the right side of it so deformed? My eye looks like it's gonna pop out. Why does the right one dilate differently than my other one? Were my retinas always this wide? Has it always been this yellow? My left eye looks normal. My eyes should be white. What's moving underneath my skin? It moves so subtly. I see it writhing and wiggling. I want to pull it out. I want to rip

underneath it and see it for myself. Something's pulsating. Is it my heart? It's in my chest. What if I stand still? No... that's not doing anything. Hey, that's weird. My veins are black and green. I've got scabs all over the bottom half of my face. Something small is sticking from underneath it. It looks like a hair. And it's all in clusters. But the left side of my face. It's so smooth.

I touch my face. Red covers my good side. I should fix my hair. Red covers that too when I touch it. Nothing's working. Everything I touch gets stained. I look down. My footprints leading here are red as well.

Red.

Crimson.

Scarlet.

That's the only color I see.

Mirror, I'm still looking at you. That good part of me. The part that's normal. Why couldn't the rest of me be like that?

Eira... is that you? I see you through that glass. You're touching my face? I'd like you to. I'd like you to smother me in your

arms again. I'd like for your skin to press against mine. I want to feel your body's warmth. I want to feel your hands interlock with mine. I want to feel your head press against mine. I want to feel your lips press against mine. I miss your touch. I miss the way you felt. I miss the way you felt inside. I miss the way we touched. I miss the way you touched me.

I know it's been years. I know the last time we saw each other was decades ago. You yelled at me and wanted me to stay. But like the child I was, I left without saying anything. Anything important. I abandoned you. I abandoned our child. A deadbeat, good-for-nothing, pitiful excuse of a father. Come on, that's what I am aren't I? Is that what you think? I didn't even get a chance to come up with a name for him or her. You came up with suggestions. I blew you off. What was your last thought of me? Was it hatred? Was it love? Was it something in between? When you saw me leave I knew every part of you wanted to look away. But at the same time, you still wanted to hold onto me for as long as you could. That's why you stalled right? That's why you made up words at that moment to talk to me. You wrapped your arms around me

and cried as you laid your head on my shoulder. I didn't move. I just stood there. I wanted to leave more than see you again. To get it over with. To move on. But there is no moving on from that is there? I'm guilty, Eira.

That room we decorated. The room I helped you paint and move the crib in? Even if I was too much of a robot to do anything for you, I remembered how we decorated it. A pattern. A pattern of butterflies on the wall. You painted it on the walls. You painted it on the crib. Put stickers on it there as well. You were a painter too. I remember that. You painted butterflies on those murals of yours. You wouldn't shut up about how you got this really good picture of one when you were younger. How you caught one in a jar when you were a kid. Hell, when you were in high school you had a hoodie with a giant butterfly insignia on the back. That was... you were wearing that the last day we saw each other. I saw that when you hugged me. It stuck with me on the way out. I think that's etched into my brain. Oh hey, I remembered something. When I went to your house for the first time I saw the pair of butterfly wings in your room. You were embarrassed that I found it.

Said something about an embarrassing Halloween party that you went to wearing it. But still, you kept it. God... you were obsessed with that animal huh? Something about the way their wings look or how they flap their wings. You had so much enthusiasm for this specific kind of living thing. They're beautiful creatures, aren't they? I think... I think I'd like to become one.

You know, I think I've got a name for our kid. If it was a boy, I'd like to name him Ken, after my favorite superhero growing up. And if it was a girl, I'd like to name her Rose. You like flowers, don't you? I like them too. They're beautiful, especially when they start to bloom. They're also red. You've always liked the color red.

Eira, I'm sorry about that last day we saw each other. I'll never be able to apologize enough for it. I want to see you again. Wherever we meet. You mean so much to me. I could never... I could never tell you that again huh? I miss you. I really do. But I know. I know you're not here. You'll never be. Never again. I'll always love you.

The mirror reflects my gaze. I'm smiling. My smile stretches too wide. I wipe the smile off of my face. My normal expression doesn't appear the way it should. I contort my lips to remain straight. Same with my jaw. But it just... it looks off. Is that how I look now? I can't fix it. There's no fixing it. I'd like for someone too.

Both of my eyes begin to water. My right eye's tears are a dark yellow, while my left eye's tears remain a perfect transparent color. I feel both of them make contact with the hairs on my jaw. It feels cold.

I look away from the mirror and head towards the bedroom. I see my red footprints on the floor, the doorframe, and the sink. I just... I just want a change of clothes.

I swing the door open to the bedroom. My feet make a repulsive sloshing sound as I move. Jane's in the corner. She's trying her best to keep her composure. I notice she stares here and there. She's careful to not make long eye contact. She grips her sleeve and her shoulders tense up. She says something. She's speaking softer. I pay no mind to it. I just want to put on a shirt.

My hand reaches out to my bag. Of course, I leave a red stain on the zipper and on the side where my other hand is. That's fine. So long as I'm covered up I can worry about it later. I dig my hand in my bag and feel inside for a shirt. Crimson catches on my other belongings there as I do. Eventually, I feel my shirt and pull it out.

An olive T-shirt with nothing on it. There's a stain where my hand is. I pull my shirt over my head. Liquid stains everything. The fabric snags on the top part of my arms. It feels weird around my torso, it doesn't stretch properly on it. Especially around my shoulders. The hairs have pierced through the fabric and press against my skin tightly. It feels uncomfortable. What do I... look like?

I scurry over back to the bathroom. My right shoulder is too high up for the shirt when I put it on. It's too high up. There's things poking through it. It looks absurd. Like a child wearing over-sized clothes. God I can't... I can't even wear my own clothes.

I pull the shirt over my head and remove it. The hairs catch inside of the fabric and I feel something pop out in the process. The hairs have gotten plucked out. It hurts and what's left on my shoulders

is yellow puss oozing out of the cysts where the hairs were. It feels like it burns.

My attention redirects back towards the bedroom. I want to see Jane. I'm not sure why. I move my legs towards the door. I hear footsteps moving the opposite direction as I do. Once I open that door, I see her walk backwards away from me. She puts herself in the corner.

Have I gotten taller? She's standing up straight. Even though my back remains slightly crooked, I still tower over her. I feel broader and heavier than before. Even a basic action such as moving my arm feels heavy. She's so small. Was she always this small?

I see her quiver and shake. I mean no harm. I know... I know what I look like. I'm very aware of it. But... she knows me. She saw my limbs regenerate. She's been there this whole time and now... now she's afraid? I've done nothing. Nothing at all. Yet... I can't... I can't do anything, can I?

My eyes take a good look at the wall behind her. I've gotten used to looking at this part of the room. It's that same old wall. That same faded yellow color. It's peeling. The same patterns and tears are on

that specific corner. In another part of this room, there's a piece of mold that goes downwards towards the bottom right. On the right, is a hole the size of a mouse towards the bottom. It's near where I sleep. I've subconsciously marked the same landmarks on these walls. The same thing every single day. I remember when I first came here. I couldn't move.

I would wake up.

I'd stare at the same walls again.

Notice the same crack on the corner.

I'd stay awake.

I'd try to fall asleep.

I'd see the same woman who nurses me back to health.

She spoon feeds me a paste made of meat.

Sometimes soup.

Sometimes something else.

She would exit the room.

I'd stare at the same walls again.

I would notice a different crack in the center of the room.

And yet, in front of me is the woman who I got to know. Who's gotten to know me. Who's afraid of my appearance. Afraid of something I had no control over. Shunning me. I understand why it scares her. I don't blame her. But... I'm just stuck like this.

I turn around and open the door. The doorframe scrapes against the hairs on my shoulders. I can't even walk through a door without being reminded of it. I hear my loud footsteps reverberate as I move. My foot feels heavier. Each step feels like a sledgehammer hitting the ground. This wet sloshing sound when I move. Why does it follow me? Why can't it go away? All I want to do is go downstairs. I just need a different view.

I've reached the bottom of the stairs. I look behind and see those red stains. It's irritating. In front of me is the piano. The piano I played in front of Jane. It's clean. The stains on it are gone. It's nice of her to clean it up. She's nice. She's a nice person. I like her.

I want to play the piano. I want to play those songs again. Maybe Mozart. Maybe Beethoven. Maybe *Corcovado*. Maybe something

else. Maybe I could play for fun. Yeah I think, I think that would be nice.

I played for her that day. For Jane. That was a nice moment. A nice memory of mine. I have a lot of good memories. A lot of memories I want to keep. She seemed happy when I played it. I want to make her happy. I'd like to make people happy. That itself brings me joy.

But if I do play, then those stains would appear again. They would get on the keys, on the lid, on the top of the piano. I'd just ruin it. It'd just get everywhere. Even putting on clothes is something I'm forbidden to do. They'd just irritate my skin.

It's all just... aggravating. Anything I do, there's something awful that gets left behind. Why? Why did I turn out this way? Why did I have to get something I craved for only for it to be a joke? I want answers. I want to know who did this to me.

God, am I your punching bag? Someone to take out your hate on? Has the world disgusted you so much that you felt inclined to punish me and me alone? Were you the one who put this curse on me? To turn me into some kind of insect? Some revolting life form? Or

maybe... or maybe this is your idea of evolution. That this is what the human race should be. That this is what they deserve. This is what they should look like. I was the first one to be tested on huh? The lucky original who got to experience it first. Mankind should pay for their sins, should they not? Is this your idea of repentance? Is it your idea of justice? Is this how humanity should repay for destroying themselves? For destroying your planet? Your beautiful creation has been tarnished. Yet, you watched.

Why did you watch? Why did you just watch? Why didn't you interfere? You couldn't have just done something? To stop all the murder, violence, hunger, cannibalism, death, war, rape, and any other horrible things we do to each other. And you just fucking *watched?* From where? Your throne? Your kingdom? From the sky? You just fucking watched it all go down? You didn't save anyone. You didn't try to save anyone. You didn't want to save anyone.

You doomed Claire. You doomed Takeya. You doomed Eira. Did you take them from me? Why did you take them from me? You took

away the people I loved most for what? What was the reason? Or was there no reason at all? That'd be even worse. Tell me. Please tell me.

I still don't get it. I still don't get any of it. How I turned into something so… grotesque.

Repulsive.

Unpleasant.

Vile.

Disgusting.

Hideous.

Loathsome.

Offputting.

Nauseating.

Am I your martyr?

I feel I am reaching my limit. My hatred and apathy is rising. Towards something. Towards someone. Towards anything at all. It's just unfair. It's just cruel. It's just sickening. But all I can do is suffer.

I walk over towards the kitchen table and pull the chair out. I've stained everything. From the floor I walk on to the chair I sit on. I think the chair has cracked from my uneven weight. This home. This place. All of it. I wonder what it was like without me. It seemed so peaceful. Yet here I am. I've made it feel so... hostile.

Something is writhing inside of me. Pulsating. I can't remove it. I want to. My hands shake uncontrollably. I clench my hand into a fist and slam it onto the table. My head is all over the place. I can't think straight. It's scattered. My head is scattered. Everything is scattered.

I hate me. I hate myself. I hate what I've become.

I hate. I

hate. I hate.

I can't calm down. I can't even think properly what that would be like. Any good thought of mine keeps getting poisoned. Regardless of what I try to think, what I am not will contradict that. I get my mobility back, for what?

I've lost the people I've cared about. I'll most likely never see them again. I can't return to the way I was before. There is no way I can ever be integrated into human society or ever meet anyone outside of this again. I can't be accepted whatsoever. My clothes don't even fit me.

I can't even... I can't feel that sense of love again. That sense of warmth. Being that physically close to someone, anyone, without my own body getting in the way. That's a prison. My own body is a prison. A permanent cell. A cocoon. Something I am trapped with until the day I perish. I can't get that luxury.

All that's left is for me to dream. Dreaming about old memories triggers a frequency in my brain anyway. I can relive

something, even if it was from long ago. Then from there, perhaps I can subconsciously dig up more past events. Perhaps I'll think of their belongings associated with them. A coat they used to wear, a necklace left on your desk, or a picture both of us were in. I will cling onto those memorabilia like a newborn baby clinging onto their mother.

Yet, every single trace of me physically contaminates the place I live in. I have no winning options. No realistic choices to make. The only route left is delusion. To fool myself into thinking I have a chance again.

I hear footsteps coming from above.

I think she's coming down.

I've already left a crack within the table.

I'm sitting here.

My hands clench up into a fist.

My hands shake.

My skin writes.

Something pulsates from within.

Dread and excitement fill me.

Yet an emptiness still remains.

I've come to multiple conclusions at once.

Conclusions that I will keep racking in my head.

Conclusions that will never satisfy me.

Conclusions that will never give me peace.

I want something.

That something is so far out of reach.

Yet also it feels like it's right in front of me.

But at the same time,

I have nothing left.

Chapter 22

I'm sitting across from Johnny. The table has been cracked. I can't help but notice the stains leading down here. I saw some of the stains leading towards the piano. But, the piano itself remains spotless. My nerves have calmed down from earlier. The shock has worn off. Being like that in front of him, I wonder what his mental state is like. I certainly wasn't doing any favors. And before me, is a man. A man who did not deserve any of what he went through. Yet, it happened all the same. The world gives and takes. But sometimes it takes more than what it needs. It feeds on others and destroys them. But all the same, it gives them something in return. Something to keep them going.

The room feels tighter. That's most likely due to Johnny's size. I'm not sure what he looks like normally. But he's abnormally large for a man. His limbs are proportionally wrong. I see him. He's formed one hand into a fist. The other is opening and closing repeatedly. I see his chest rise rapidly. Something is wiggling beneath his skin. I can hear it and see it. My breathing is as calm as ever. I open my mouth.

"It's hurting you, isn't it? Everything. All of it. I know why you're angry. And I can't imagine what it's like to be in your shoes. I won't talk down to you. I won't tell you to calm down. I won't tell you how to feel. I just... I just know how unfair all of this is."

His eyes fixate on the table. His hands keep opening and shutting. His leg bounces up and down. He begins to laugh.

"You *know*? You know how unfair this is? That's easy. Really easy for you to say. Tell me, were you the one who transformed into some kind of monster? Some freak of nature who can never go back to the way he was? Who can never integrate into society again? Who can't even do so much as put a shirt on? Anything I do, I'm reminded of what I no longer am. I can't even walk without something showing me what I've become."

I know he's upset. But I'm not angry at him.

"You'd be right. I have no idea how that feels. To turn into some kind of mutated human-insect. To have my arms and legs disproportionate. To lose my limbs. To be immobile. To be an

amputee. To never be a regular human being again. To never be able to wear so much as a shirt or pants without it ripping. To go through a door without hitting something. To leave a stain wherever I go. To go through decades of my life constantly losing the people I love. Watching the same horrors again and again. Breaking me. Destroying me. Day by day. Year by year. Having that build up slowly but surely. You're right Johnny. You're right. I'll never be able to understand that feeling. I'll never understand that feeling at all."

His face eases up slightly.

"Don't try to sympathize or do that fake pity shit with me. You don't... you don't know the extent of which I've lost. And how I can even remotely be close to getting any of it back. Tell me Jane, do you pity me when you look at me? At what I've become? Before, my throat had healed perfectly. A clean, smooth patch of skin had come over it. Talking didn't hurt my voice. But that, that was just bait. A false sense of hope that was given to me. My face is deformed. Blisters and rashes have formed on it. Puss oozes out of it from time to time. My right eye has a constant burn to it that never went away. It pulsates, shakes

violently. I can't control it. The only stable parts of my body are my throat and left eye. Those are the only things that remain normal about me. As for the rest, I resemble an insect don't I? Why take care of me? Why do so? I'm waste."

I want him to understand me.

"I admit I was afraid. I was scared, seeing that for the first time, seeing how much your body has changed. The way the hairs stick out on your arms. How disproportionate you look. How much you tower over me. The cysts and scabs all over. It's off-putting. I didn't know how to react when I first saw you. But that doesn't erase who you are to me. Beneath that body that you were so wrongfully given, you're still you. I still recognize your voice from when you first talked. You were the one who played piano and let me listen to music for the first time. A wonderful experience I'll never forget. The melody of that track, how peaceful it was. I understand why you find it so beautiful now. Why you hum it from time to time. You've introduced me to it. Even when you were immobile you still tried to be gentle. I knew. I knew you were suffering the whole time. I know how you so badly wanted to lash out. But you still endured it. You endured it as best as you could without harming me. Because that's you Johnny, that's who you are. Despite all the hardships life has

given you, you're not one to blame others or hurt someone despite your own suffering. You never blamed it on me. Sure, you got upset. But you never made it personal. Because deep down, you know it's nobody's fault. And you also know that I'm trying all that I can. You're sympathetic, Johnny. You give everyone a fair shake, even when it reaches a boiling point."

My eyes remained locked onto his. He begins to gaze at me. His eye twitches. I hear fluids shifting and moving inside of him. I speak anyway.

"You're someone I trust. Someone I truly, *deeply*, care for. And you matter more to me than you could ever understand. I can only imagine what it's like to be in your shoes. To experience what you've been through. And for everything that's happened to you. All those terrible events and people you've lost, all I can say is, I'm sorry. I know that won't be enough. I know it never will. I know it can't bring them back."

"Don't bring them up. You don't know how much they meant to me. Even if I were to meet them, I don't get to be a part of civilization. I don't get to see humans the way I could before. The things I used to observe and be a part of. A couple embracing each other on the river. A stressed man working on his car's faulty engine. A man trying

to put stickers on his vehicle's trunk. Or a child pointing at things and smiling, wondering what the animal was in front of them. I don't have that. I don't get to be a part of that. I've lost that."

The table dents as he screams. Fluid drips down from his arm. I exhale.

"Yeah. You'd be right. You don't get to be a part of civilization. Not anymore. Nobody does. Except that doesn't take away the fact that we can still find things beyond that. Will it surpass that? No. Will it feel the same? No. But it doesn't have to. It doesn't have to substitute it either. Being a part of the world doesn't mean you have to do the mundane things everyone else does. Nor do you need their approval. So long as you yourself are satisfied, the rest of the world can be subsided.

And about not knowing how much they mean to you, you're wrong. I lost my friend. I lost the person who meant the most to me. I lost Beverly. And I know, I know I'll never see her again. I'll never help her with her math homework again. I'll never see her tie my shoes again. I'll never play Connect 4 with her again. I'll never run around and play tag again. I'll never eat food with her family again. I'll never see her smile again. The thing that's been burned and etched into my mind about her. I miss her. Every single day. For the past

year I miss her. I miss what could've been. I miss what should've been. What should've happened between me and her. She should've been alive. Not captured by some animals who treated her like someone lesser than human. She should've never gone through that. That abuse. That torture. All of it angers me and I so badly want to redirect that anger towards something. But you know what? You and I are both aware of the fact that the world just hurts those closest to us because that's how it is. There is good and there is evil. And somewhere in between, that's where everyone is. Teetering on the line between snapping and staying sane. And you're there Johnny. You're at your breaking point. But goddammit. Goddammit I don't want to see you break. I don't want to see you lose yourself when you got so far. You're not just hurting me but you're hurting yourself. What you still have. Because Johnny... because while you lost your wife, your friend, and you first love... you gained me. And I know the world is terrible. I know just how awful it's become. It hurts those I care about. You know the feeling. But I won't... I won't let you lose what you have left because of what your physical body has become. It's not what you are. It's not what you'll ever be. Deep down, you're still that kind man I met. The man who showed me music. The man who would listen to what I had to say. Something that was burrowing in my head for over a year. The man who told me stories of how the world used to be. How hopeful and beautiful it was before. And even now, there's still some beauty in it. Even when all of it's destroyed there's still something there. Something you and I have, each other."

He stares at me blankly, but... I see his fists slowly unclench. The room becomes quiet. He's stopped bouncing his legs. What was writhing beneath his skin begins to slow down. I hear something. Something faint. A sniffle. He says something from under his breath. It's quiet.

"Why are you... why are you still here?"

A tear rolls down on his face. The left side is clear. The right side is a dark yellow.

"Because you taught me how to live. How to keep going. In a way, I've regained what I've lost. Sure, Beverly isn't coming back. And it hurts. It's a scar that I'll have to bear for the rest of my days. But you, you never held a thing against me despite your own hardships. I want to extend the same hand to you and help those closest to me. And you Johnny, you're somebody I care for. I can't hate you. And I don't think you can hate me."

Tears started rolling down his face faster this time. I watch as it makes contact with the cluster of hairs underneath. Some gets in his throat. He coughs as it enters.

"Jane, I..."

He stops himself. He doesn't say a word. He doesn't need to say anything, not to me. I understand. He tries to wipe his tears with his arms but the hairs get in the way. I put my sleeve over my hand and get close to his face. His bigger size still surprises me. I see his leg sink into the floor. My sleeve wipes away at his face. The tears don't stop coming. I keep wiping in return.

I feel how wet my sleeves are. Before me, lies a man. A man forced inside the body of an insect. Yet, is a human all the same. Despite his appearance I see the person beneath it. The loss, the grief, and the victories in between all of it. He's lost so much, hasn't he? I can only do so much to soothe the pain. But I still want to do the best I can. I think it's the right thing to do.

I wipe his final tear and pull my sleeve back. His head is turned away from me. I put my hand out and caress his cheek. He turns his head towards me as I do. The look on his eyes, part of it is still empty. But still, there's a hint of light in there. I see my face reflect off of it.

My hand rubs against his skin. His left side is soft. I feel the hair on his jaw start to regrow. It's pointy. It partially stings. He sinks his face closer to my palm. He exhales lightly. A smile forms across his face. He smiles. I move my fingers across his cheek. The chair has stopped creaking.

For a moment, the world is completely still.

I form a wry smile across my face.

Johnny's breathing has slowed down.

In fact, his whole body seems to have relaxed.

My hand feels wet from the tears he shed earlier.

It looks tiny against his face.

I see my reflection through both eyes.

But as I do...

Something inhuman tightens around my throat.

Chapter 23

I have metamorphosed into what I truly am. A caterpillar feasting on its plant. A centipede preying on a small insect. An earthworm eating decaying matter. I am more than beneath these lowly creatures. I no longer resemble a human. I've committed a sin against God, against the world, against myself. There is no forgiveness in this. Only my own filth to swim around in. My mistake, my demise, caused by my own hand. I am disgusted with who I am and hate who I can no longer be. I am cattle. I am filth. I am a sinner beyond any form of repentance. Yet, I can't stop reveling in it. Like a small creature enjoying its fruitful meal, I'm savoring every little moment of this.

It is a forbidden pleasure. The deflowering of a virgin. Taking someone's innocence away, against their will. A terrible act. No, it is beyond terrible. Unforgivable is too light of a word. However, my own physical pleasures are something I cannot deny. I recall what women are- prey to be devoured.

The look on her face screams a thousand words. Her eyes opened wide, her mouth agape. I can see tears beginning to form down her cheeks. Sometimes, she would clench her teeth. It hurts, doesn't it? I can feel her try to fight back from time to time. It won't help much anyways. I hold her down with both of my arms but make sure not to choke her. She can't escape anyways. A man's strength greatly exceeds that of a woman.

My hands reach towards my pants. I pull them down and feel my throbbing erection take over. She's trying to swat at me. Hit me and kick me to her heart's content. That won't do. It's not gonna change what will happen. I hear her panting and wheezing. Both of my hands move towards both of her thighs. I spread her legs open and stick it in.

It was difficult at first, to insert it. It wasn't very wet. Blood trickled onto it, but I paid no mind. I want to finish what I've started. After enough movement and squirming, it becomes a good fit. I feel it open sometimes, to accept me. Other times, it shuts down and clamps, to reject me. It hurts a little to move around. It feels as if she is mentally

saying no, but her body is becoming so numb to the experience that she had begun to accept it. The feeling of disgust, of hate, of helplessness. If I were her, I'd be disgusted too. Much more than disgusted. Maybe disgusted is too light of a word. Each thrust, each penetration, gives me an immense sense of gratification.

What do you think, Claire?

Not the person I once was?

The person you loved.

The person you fell in love with.

You hate me, don't you?

That's fine.

And you, Takeya.

I've joined you.

I hate that I have.

Yet, I get why you fell into it all the same.

And my dear Eira, what do you think?

Are you dead?

Are you watching from Heaven?

You are a saint after all. Or hell?

No, that wouldn't make sense.

You were nothing but good to me.

Now, look at what I've become.

Terrible, isn't it?

What are you thinking of, Jane?

"I am watching this thing, this abomination, forcefully stick itself inside of me. It hurts. I hate looking at him. Him? No, that's too generous. It's not human, not anymore. Its skin has become nothing more than a breeding ground of blisters. Each blister contains a disgusting amount of pus ready to eject at a moment's notice. A deformity. Yes, that is what, "it", is. And yet, I can't stop it. This thing has already violated me. Every part of me is torn. It has taken my innocence. It has taken my mind. It has taken my soul. No part of me is left. I am a mere meat puppet to the thing in control of my physical form."

Is this what she's thinking about right now? About how much I've deformed and ruined her? I can't tell. I'm making guesses. My mind is racing, thinking about what is going on in her head as I continue on with my act. There are tears flowing down her face. They were rather light earlier, but now they appear more heavy. I assume she's been holding it in.

In all honesty, I find her suffering rather titillating. For a common example, I'd like to imagine that a woman's mascara disappears when tears start to form. Those little black lines beneath her eyes. Her cries of help, begging me to stop. If it were any sane man, they'd stop themselves right here. But also, a man cannot deny how depraved he can truly be. It's funny. The opposite emotion, of begging for help, of crying for mercy, only does more for the attacker. It compels him, drives him to continue. It is its own form of twisted motivation.

If this were consensual, me and her would be having a riot. This would simply be rough sex, roleplay to some extent. Why do people find pleasure in their own depravity? I'm too deep into it at this point. I've become an insect. A creature to be destroyed. To be killed,

eviscerated, wiped from the face of this planet. Yes, that would bring justice to this world wouldn't it? My eradication. But even still, I doubt that would be enough to erase what's happening and its lingering effects. After all, I am one of many parasites. Really, I should feel shame and deep down I truly do. However, I can't lie to myself. I do love this. Every moment of this. The hatred, the shame, the pleasure, the regret, the sensation, the grief, the tragedy, all of it.

I put my hands around her neck. My arms are covered with blisters, scabs, and sticky latex saps. My fingers are freakishly long but maintain a wide mass. My grip remains strong on her throat. She's flailing at me with her arms. It barely hurts. She's physically weaker than me. There's not a single thing she can do to break my hold on her. Her eyes begin to water and her look widens. She begins to grit her teeth. Wincing, grimacing at me. She's gasping for air. A weak noise comes from her throat. A scream for help, I take it. It's pitiful. She is a powerless thing, savaged beyond any reason.

I penetrate deeper inside of her. I guess this is as deep as it goes. I've reached a membranous wall that pushes back against me. It

impedes further progress. I tighten my grip once more. She's using her nails to scratch at my arms. I feel it, but it doesn't sting. Red lines appear within the blisters of my skin. They barely hurt. She's moving her legs around. She's not going to die. I don't intend to kill her. I simply intend to make this a little more dangerous. This is fun.

Her face begins to turn blue. When people are in a choke hold such as this, oxygen cannot reach the lungs and brain. People panic and often do anything they can just to breathe again. Rational thinking is thrown out of the window. She could've grabbed the nearby piece of broken table and stabbed me, but I guess the thought never crossed her mind.

The brain can last about 4-6 minutes without oxygen. A couple minutes after that, severe or permanent brain damage may occur, even death. By my count, my hands have been around her neck for 90 seconds.

Her face begins to turn purple, not a deep purple, but just enough to where she's on the verge of death. I let go of my grip around her neck.

She begins to grasp her throat, relieved at the fact she can breathe again. But I'm still on top of her. I'm still moving inside. Her temporary relief is subsided by my continued assault.

Her eyes begin to stare into mine. My face is deformed anyway. My jaw slacks to the left and my right eye has begun to turn bloodshot red as yellow puss drips down below to my cheek as the optic nerve dangles loosely in the eye socket. Oddly, my left eye is in the same place as it should be, but what surrounds it is a chaotic mess. My face must be quite the sight to behold right now.

She realizes now the danger she is still in. I can tell her body temperature rising. Her brain has finally adjusted to its original senses. I continue to penetrate her. I was slower prior, when my hands were on her neck. However, I began to speed up as I realized I no longer had to pay attention as to whether or not she would die. She takes notice of the faster speed. Before, it was difficult to move around in, but now it feels loose enough for me to continue further. Her flesh has molded to fit my rigid length. I continue to defile. To drive deeper and deeper. Until the whole of me is buried inside her. She's mine.

It hurts. The pain between my legs hurts. It's a persistent pain. It stops, then worsens at a random pace. For every bit of relaxation I get, it is over taken by an immeasurable amount of suffering I can't control. I don't know why he's doing this. No, perhaps I do. Maybe, maybe I just couldn't see something. I let my guard slip, something under my nose.

I glanced down at my lower body. It's covered in blood. My entire body feels numb. It feels all tingly. He's inserted it deeper this time. My feeble screams and shouts of resistance are ignored as he moves faster. All they are, are weak gasps of air rushing through my vocal cords. His hand covers my mouth.

As he thrusts forward, I feel a burning lump searing my insides. It's swelling inside of me. The pain aches. He keeps going. He has no intention of stopping. I am just a tool to be used until he's done.

Is he finished yet? I want this to stop. Maybe I'll get pregnant. I don't care. So long as this ends I think I'll feel better.

I'm flipped over. My face makes contact with the floor. One arm is enough to keep me pinned. I can't move. Only he can. There's little incentive for me to resist.

I feel my body rock back and forth as he moves. Harder, faster, a disjointed rhythm. I'm flipped over once again. My shirt has been lifted up to expose my breasts. He put his tongue on it. His saliva is cold. Part of his hairs brushed up against it. I felt it poke me as his

head moved. My pants have been completely removed from me. He keeps changing me around in different positions. I follow and obey. I have no other choice.

My stomach is pressed against the cold wood floor. I tried to move earlier. To kick him. To punch him. To hurt him. But it didn't work. I keep feeling it. The way it moves inside of me. The fact I can't do anything. The fact I am completely helpless. I am completely at his mercy.

I've ended up as one of them huh? Another one of the victims of this world. I never thought I'd see the day. But the world just does that, doesn't it? Ha. Haha.

Gullible. Easily used. Fool. Look at me. I tried my best and look at where it got me. Pinned down by the man I thought I could trust.

Tool.

Hole.

Meat puppet.

Victim.

Idiot.

I have no soul.

I'm just an ugly pile of flesh.

That's not me. It was just an ugly pile of flesh laying there. That wasn't me. I wasn't the one laying there. That's not me. It was just an ugly pile of flesh laying there. That wasn't me. I wasn't the one laying there. That's not me. It was just an ugly pile of flesh laying there. That wasn't me. It was just an ugly pile of flesh laying there. That's not me. It was just an ugly pile of flesh laying there. That wasn't me. I wasn't the one laying there. That's not me. It was just an ugly pile of flesh laying there. That wasn't me. I wasn't the one laying there. That's not me. It was just an ugly pile of flesh laying there. That wasn't me. It was just an ugly pile of flesh laying there. That's not me. It was just an ugly pile of flesh laying there. That wasn't me. I wasn't the one laying there. That's not me. It was just an ugly pile of flesh laying there. That wasn't me. I wasn't the one laying there. That's not me. It was just an ugly pile of flesh laying there. That wasn't me. It was just an ugly pile of flesh laying there. That's not me. It was just an ugly pile of flesh laying there. That wasn't me. I wasn't the one laying there. That's not me. It was just an ugly pile of flesh laying there. That wasn't me. I wasn't the one laying there. That's not me. It was just an ugly pile of flesh laying there. That wasn't me. It was just an ugly pile of flesh laying there.

I...

I...

I am lost in the joy of unfettered violence. Her distress is helpless. Her emotions are jumbled. Fear, confusion, hate, disgust- all ignored. I simply obey an impulse I can't deny. I've taken. I've taken so much. My filth stains her.

Her head tilts back at the pain. The sound screams woman. The sound screams meat. The sound screams flesh. The sound screams pleasure. She knows I claimed her. She's powerless against me.

It's a shame. My fun is almost over. I feel myself about to finish. And I've done so many positions with her. She's not very receptive to me. My wanton cannot be satiated.

It's difficult. Very difficult to get my fingers in there. I would've liked to rub it around while it was in there. But, my body won't allow that. Doesn't help that my fingers leave a lot of red wherever they go. My hand glides over her smooth, pale legs. I've stained those as well. My fingers dig into her flesh. My grip tightens. My sadistic impulse has found the perfect target.

She's got this dead look in her eyes. It's like glass. She's like a doll. The doll keeps staring at the staircase. At the crack on one of the

staircases. Specifically, the bottom step. That has my red footprint on it. Her body shakes. Her breasts quiver. My grotesque rod strains in an agony of lust. Her insides still stifle. My pleasure drives higher. I grab her cheek and tilt her head towards me.

His lips are over mine. I feel his eyeball dangling against my cheek. He tastes gross. Like bile. Like vomit. His tongue is seizing mine. Winding around it. Holding it tight. Tasting its flesh. The feeling of it fills my skull. Every part of him is gross. His body is revolting. From looks to smell. He smells terrible. I watch as his cysts burst. Some of it splashes on me. Green and red are now on my skin. He removes his lips and puts it onto my breasts. I feel his tongue roll around on it. It's revolting. Every part of this is revolting.

Everything is hazy. Everything feels hazy. This world is hazy. This world is disgusting. People are disgusting. All I wanted to do was help someone. This is my reward. This is my reward for being a good Samaritan.

There is no escape from this. Squirm as I might, his grip holds me in place. My only choice is to lie here, helpless, as disgust broils to the core of my brain. My tormentor pays no mind to my distress. The sound of squelching reverberates in my head.

My insides swell.

My taste buds have a rancid aftertaste.

My hands and legs used to shake uncontrollably.

But they've ceased.

The pain has subsided.

But there is no pleasure to be found.

I feel him stop moving.

He holds me in his arms.

I can't move.

I'm trapped within his embrace.

A revolting amount of liquid is released inside of me.

Chapter 24

I release her from my arms. My deed is finished. My desire is satiated. My filth is complete. She lays on the floor breathing silently. Her eyes are closed. I'm not sure when she passed out. It doesn't matter though. I've done what I want. My hunger has receded by a fraction. I have been awarded a window to catch my breath.

I stand up and look at her body. White fluid, mixed with red, oozes from the space from which it evacuated. I know what I've done. I've fallen into the same plague that contaminated everyone else. It's a sickness. A sickness I've embraced with open arms.

The room reeks of musk and sweat. She's covered in green and red liquid. Some of it from my exposed cysts, others from touching her with my hand. There's an imprint on her throat. It's beneath all the blood that came from my hand.

My back feels slimy. My arms begin to hurt. So do my legs. I slip and fall. My head almost hits the floor. I'm barely able to catch myself. I try to stand up again. I cannot maintain my balance. I trip once more. My joints feel loose. Every single part of my body feels inflamed. My right leg starts to ache.

I take a look at it. My foot begins to sink into the stump of my ankle. My toes begin to burn away. I feel the heat from it. One by one, I watch as they dissipate.

I begin to crawl. I have no reason as to why. I have no direction as to where I'm headed. I simply want to move. The heat from my toes sink into my foot, then my ankle. It hurts. It burns. I attempt to move it up and down. It's no use, I have no control of that limb anymore. The pain sinks into my knee. I know what happened. I refuse to look.

I move my left hand forward and drag myself on the floor. My hand slips on the wood. It's difficult to get a grip. My hand feels so slippery. The hairs near my shoulders get near my face. It irritates me. But I can do nothing to move it out of my way. All I can do is crawl forward.

To my right, I see Jane's body. Her hair covers one side of her face. The back of her head lays flat on the floor. Her fingers are twitching. Her eyes are shut. Her face has residue from her dried up tears. Next to her are red and green puddles of liquid. I get a good whiff of what she smells like. It reeks. Every single fluid I've poured on top of her has mixed into an unsavory scent. One that I cannot ignore as my nose inches closer towards her direction.

My eyes catch the sunlight through the cracks of the front door. The outside. My escape. My sanctuary. If I reach there, it's outside. I can reach salvation. I want to feel the warmth of the sun. To feel the elements of mother nature. To bask in the glow of the outside world. Please... please.

The cysts on my other leg begin to burst. I hear the sound of liquid trickling against the wood. One bubble at a time, it pours out. I feel something sharp press inside of my leg. Clusters. Clusters of tiny little pricks pierce me. I recognize it. It's where the hairs of my legs were.

Soon enough, that part of my leg gives out. The stump from before takes its place. The burning sensation has been replaced with something acidic. I feel something from my stomach. My abdomen is spasm violently. Something inside of it writhes and shakes. I feel it flying around in my stomach. I clench my jaw from the pain. My heart rate increases. I breathe faster now. I can't help it.

My left hand reaches the knob of the door. My eyes have never been so close to the bottom crack of it. I can almost taste the sun. As I grasp the knob, I feel my hand shake and writhe. I can feel my strength and control of my hand start to dissipate. I try my best to turn the knob. It keeps slipping. I fumble around and repeatedly grasp it again and again. Finally, I got a good grip.

I put my other hand on the center of the door and push. A door has never felt so heavy. I can feel my left arm shake and give out.

Eventually, I'm able to crack the door wide open. My body falls and hits a wire. A loud bell plays in my ears. It irritates me further. The noise is loud and disorienting. My brain starts to hurt from the inside.

I drop from the small elevation from the door. It wasn't too big of a height, yet it hurts my body all the same. As if a bat had struck the core of my chest. As I lift myself off, I see my skin peel away from the ground. The muscle from my chest is exposed underneath. I feel the wind breeze against it. It feels cold. The writhing from before begins to intensify.

My skin feels so soft in the sun. The light greets me. It feels warm. It feels comforting. I keep crawling forward as the crops to my left and right blow in the wind.

I see the pathway from before in the center. That's where I was dragged, wasn't I? Perhaps I can go a little further. Perhaps I can make it towards somewhere. Maybe I can reach the woods. Maybe I can see nature. I'd like to see the world. I'd like to see how it is now. I can still move.

I can do it. I can do it.

Fluids pour out from the blisters of my left arm. I touch it with my hand. My skin feels so soft. The outer skin of it begins to loosen. The seams begin to split. Transparent layers of flesh start to life. The old flesh from before hangs empty. They feel dry from the sunlight. Shell-like fragments drop from the returned stump. I touch what's left with my other hand. It's wet, like it was before. The shell fragments scrape against my shoulder. I don't want it to go away. I just got my limb back. That's so cruel. That's so mean. Why couldn't I keep it? I don't care if it was ugly or revolting looking. I want my arm back. I want my legs back. I want my limbs back. I want everything back. I want it back to the way it was before.

But no, I don't get that do I? I'm too far gone. I want to beg, but I know begging won't do anything. I've already destroyed the closest thing I have left. I know what this is. This is punishment.

The world has eaten me, hasn't it? Taken me as a victim. Spread its misery to me. I spread that misery onto someone else. That cycle repeats. It spreads onto others, like an infection. To repeat a cycle of despair and destruction. It's inescapable. It's constant. It's a way of life. Something that cannot be avoided. An inevitable consequence. Something always lingering. Burrowing in the background.

I suppose it's just how people are. Cruelty is a cycle that will never cease to exist. It's widespread. Sometimes out in the open. Sometimes operating in the shadows. People would hear about them if they popped up through the news, the internet, or word of mouth. And even if a horrible event like this happened, a good majority of people will not care. At some point, people become desensitized to it. The violence, the wanton depravity, the extreme horrid acts. All of it turns into child's play after enough exposure. People will acknowledge how horrible it was, but it wasn't affecting their day-to-day life. They don't

really care. People are selfish. People are cruel. But that's the way the world is. That's how everything operates. Nobody can do a thing about it on an individual level.

Perhaps, they can succumb to my level and sink with me.

I begin to laugh.

My jaw begins to dissolve as I do.

The burn from my throat returns once more.

I feel my hair falling out in clumps.

I feel the membranes from the root boil.

I see a large group of them fall onto the floor below me.

My right eye begins to burn.

Eventually, the loose nerve pops out.

I watch with my left eye as it rolls onto the dirt.

I feel my chest starting to rupture.

The outer flesh feels dry.

Yet, the interior feels soft.

My final limb remains.

It's peeling.

It's melting.

It's going away.

The stains begin to stop.

There is nothing left to leak.

Music begins to play in my head.

I close my only eye.

My last concert with her.

My last conversation with him.

My last embrace from her.

A butterfly on the back of her hoodie.

And a butterfly in the bedroom for our child.

I open my eye slightly.

I put my hand out to the sun.

I watch as my fingers dissipate, one at a time.

A feeling of warmth envelops me.

I accept it with a singular open arm.

The sun feels warm against my skin.

Epilogue:

A Brand New Day

I felt a chill as I opened my eyes. I stare at the ceiling. There's a crack above me. I take a look around the room.

A chair.

A broken table.

My pants.

A floor stained with liquids of various colors.

There's a pungent taste in the back of my throat. It's not going away. The disgusting scent on my skin stings my nostrils. I smell awful. I'm covered in a wide array of fluids. I can't help by stare at my body.

My hand moves away from my chest. Something wet hits it. It's red. There's a trail of hand prints across my body. The trail leads towards the front door that's cracked wide open.

A breeze of wind brushes against my skin. My hair blows from it. My limbs feel still. My legs feel jittery. The pain from between them still hurts. It burns. It really burns. Something red and white drips down onto the floor below me. Yet, I have a desire to stand up and move.

My arm pushes of against the kitchen counter. My sense of balance returns slowly. My breathing feels jagged. I touch my throat. Blood coats my fingers and I wipe it away with my shirt. The floor is a mess. Broken furniture. Torn clothing. Puddles of different colors.

I pull my shirt down and focus on the door in front of me. Sunlight pierces through the house. The red hand prints lead outside. I walk towards it. One step at a time. I do my best to ignore the pain coming from inside of me. The floor is cold beneath my feet. The wood is uneven and cracked. I think this is the first time I've walked through the house like this.

I trip over the puddle of crimson on the ground. Green's mixed into it as well. The trail of red follows it. I catch myself from falling. My head feels shaky. I look to my right.

The piano sits in the living room. It's clean. Only footprints lead towards it. I guess you'll never be able to teach me piano.

My foot inches towards the front door. The sun gets in my eyes. I put my hand out to block it. My eyes haven't adjusted yet.

I step down the slight elevation and avoid the wire on the door. My feet touch the dirt. It feels hot. Something on my sole feels sticky. I lift my foot up. Red flesh clings to it before tearing off of my sole. I keep walking.

The trail doesn't go very far. As I inch closer, a blurry mass becomes ever so clearer to my eyes. The smell is repugnant and gets stronger as I walk. My movement is slow. My feet dig into the dirt with each step. I am dragging my legs and forcing them to obey me.

I see him.

Between the crops his body lies still. A dark pool of fluid spreads beneath him, bubbling and boiling in the sunlight. He doesn't breathe. His chest doesn't move up and down. His head lays back flat on the dirt. His gaze appears to be angled at the sun. His limbs have returned back to stumps. There's a small opening in the center of his chest. Shell fragments are near where his left arm used to be. His hair has completely shed from his scalp. His jaw is gone. His right eye lies in the dirt. His left eye is still open, staring at nothing. It's rolled to the back of his head. Everything about him is completely still. A husk of a man lies before me. I'm not sure how to feel. But at the same time, every emotion strikes me at once.

Johnny...

I'm sorry.

I'm sorry for everything you've been through. I know my apology is worthless. I know it doesn't change anything. I know it can't fix anything. But I'm sorry. You lost people. Claire, Takeya, and most importantly, Eira. Losing the love of your life is something I can't imagine or fathom the pain it leaves behind. And I know none of this was simple for you. I know there were things you held onto even after everything else was taken away. It all just hurts. What you lose. What comes left behind after that. And I can't pretend I understand it. I can't. But I can see what it did to you. I saw what you became.

And still, I'm conflicted. I wish I wasn't. I wish I had a clear answer for how I feel. Something concrete. But I know people are complex. They can be vile. They can be righteous. Sometimes, they can be both.

The memories I've had with you will always remain one way or another. You've hurt me. But there's a part of you, a part of you that I liked. I want to remember that part about you. But I still remember... I still remember what you've done. How much it's affected me. How much it will continue to stick with me. And as the days go on, maybe those memories of you begin to fade or hurt even more. Regardless, I'll never see you again. I never want to see you again.

I don't forgive you. I don't forgive you for what you've done. What you've done to me. Just like how some people are in this world. You sunk to their level. You're nothing more now than a corpse rotting in the sun. Another body left to dry up in the world. You've disgraced yourself and done the unforgivable. What you've done to me...It's revolting. It's disgusting. It's abhorrent. It's cruel. And it stays with me.

Forever.

But you'll never hear my words. You'll never know how I feel. I'll live with what you've done for the rest of my life. Every part of me is disgusted by you. Because everything about it hurts. Because I remember you before this. I remember the music you played. I remember you listening when I spoke. I remember you tried, even when you fell apart. And I hate that I remember that too.

I'm not sure how you died. I'm now sure how you regenerated. I don't care for how any of it happened. I don't care as to why it happened at all.

I'm just glad you're gone so you can never hurt someone again.

I stare at the corpse below me.

I'm not sure why.

But I crouch down and reach towards his face.

My finger reaches his eye.

I close it.

I hear wind moving the crops next to me.

The sound of something reaches my left ear.

It's something.

Something flying.

The wings of it have an abstract pattern.

It's nonsensical.

There's lines and circles all over.

It's not remotely close to symmetrical.

Yet, it looks beautiful all the same.

The butterfly lands on top of his head.

It perches there, seemingly unbothered by its surroundings.

I stand back up.

My body burns.

Blood trickles down my leg.

I don't think the smell will ever leave me.

No matter how hard I scrub.

But I'll live with it.

I have to.

The sun beats down on my face.

It shines as bright as ever.

Inside, there's a mess I have to clean up.

And an unstained piano in the living room.

Perhaps I'll play it sometime.

I'll play a note.

I'll play a chord.

Maybe I'll learn a song.

I turn around.

My feet begin to sink into the ground below me.

I'll return back to my house.

I'll move forward with my life.

And I'll miss those who I've lost.

But that's just life.

That's just the way the world is.

Cruel and beautiful.

One foot at a time.

One step at a time.

I begin to walk.

Afterword

Thank you for reading! Hopefully the book wasn't too much or excessive. But if it was, then I kind of got my point across all the same. Regardless, I hope you enjoyed the book. Did you like the slow character scenes? The small bit of intimacy between the two protagonists? The fucked up situations I'm even surprised I came up with? What'd you think of the ending? Or was it all a clusterfuck?

This is my big debut novel! My first ever book! Entirely self-published and funded by me. I'm not too sure if people will like it, especially with the content involved. But I hope whoever reads it finds some merit here. And of course, for you dear reader, I hope the book gave you something to remember.

I don't have much to say beyond thank you! I'll leave my Instagram handle here if you ever find it so curious as to check out whatever projects I do in my future: @s0ulhound

Cheers! And thank you for reading!

www.ingramcontent.com/pod-product-compliance
Lightning Source LLC
Chambersburg PA
CBHW021443140726
48132CB00027BA/104

* 9 7 9 8 9 9 6 0 8 6 6 2 7 *